# CONCRETE GIRL

By

**David C. Brown**

# Concrete Girl

ISBN No: 9780983190714
Library of Congress Control Number: 2011900953
BISAC code:

Cover design: Eric Fritzius (www.misterherman.com)
Editor: Molly S. Brown
Published Works:

    The Thrashman's Daughter

    Serendipity Hollow

    Gap Hollow

    Sandlick Hollow

    Donnelly's War

    Boilermaker

    Caroom Raid

    Nitro Wild

 ♠ Scott Depot, WV ♠

# Chapter 1

Mike Owen had his fingers crossed. He wanted the win. It would allow him a chance to show his father he could manage a large project. The dozen other contractors in the Crawford County Annex conference room had similar hopes. They, along with him, were there for the opening of bids on this year's largest construction project in northwest Pennsylvania. So far, of the bids open, his bid was the low one, but the Global Utility Contractors bid remained to be open and they were tough serious competition.

The consultant for the French Creek Sanitary Board finally opened the last proposal, the Global bid. Mike nearly embarrassed himself by yelling "All right," as he realized the RBO's bid, his bid, remained the low one. He looked back at the Woodbrier brothers setting in the rear of room. Their Pine Tree Construction was his most important subcontractor. He expected they would share his joy at winning the contract. Instead, the brothers' exchanged what appeared to be a brief look of disgust. That made no sense they ought to be please, but Sam was the sarcastic glass half-empty sort and he had probably misread the dour man's expression.

"Great news, Dad, our eighty-five and a half million dollar bid won."

"Congratulations, what was the next low bid?" his father asked.

"A consortium of contractors from the Pittsburgh area, Global Utility Contractors had the next lowest bid. They bid just shy of eighty-six million dollars."

"Good thing you found that last-minute saving."

Mike agreed with his father: had they not reduced RBO's bid price this morning, the consortium would have won.

"Find out who is behind that mysterious Global outfit. Their webpage doesn't say. And get back to Columbus, we need to move fast."

After finishing with his father's call, Mike headed back into the Annex, pausing on the top step to watch a young person help an old man struggling to get into an F-250 Ford pickup parked by the Annex handicap ramp. The helper had glanced back at the entrance and Mike realized the helper was very attractive. His curiosity aroused, he wondered whether that androgynous person helping the old man was a male or female. The short haircut was no help, and the heavy olive Carhartt jacket effectively concealed the characteristics he normally used to determine gender. Still he'd bet the person helping the old man was a she. The two were together as the helper jumped in the pickup driver's seat and drove off.

He was in the mood to celebrate, but that would wait, and instead reentered the building to find Sam. The subcontractor was waiting near the Annex's rear exit and he motioned for him to enter the small meeting room next to the rear door. It was empty.

"Have a seat," Sam said after closing the room's door for privacy. "And congratulations on the bid. It'll be a challenge. Sure your company can handle it?"

"We'll be fine unless Pine Tree drops the ball. Should I be worried?" Mike said, not exactly caring for Sam's remarks. "Or find another sub?"

"No, of course not, there's no need to worry. Pine Tree could do the whole project itself. Who's your father going to put in charge? He'll need to be experienced. It'll be a complicated project."

"He hasn't decided." Mike intended to be the project manager, but his father hadn't yet agreed to that. Besides, it was a family matter and nothing an outsider needed involved in. To change the subject, he asked, "Who's behind the consortium?"

"It's a group of contractors. Who is in charge, I don't know. I've heard the Gambones are involved, but I've never had dealings with them."

Remembering the brothers' odd reaction when RBO won, Mike wondered about the veracity of the man's claim.

"You do appreciate a dependable concrete supplier is critical. I'm surprised you didn't lock in our price before the bid." Sam said as he offered a cigar to Mike who declined it. "

"I thought $120 kind of pricey. Shaffer has ready-mix concrete. They're just a few miles from the site."

Sam lit up a foul-smelling cigar.

"This is a no smoking area."

"You're a regular boy scout. A little smoke won't bother anyone." No, Mike thought, it probably won't, but a person who ignores such requests is an asshole.

"Rather than screwing with Shaffer," Sam added, "You'd be better off buying bags of Quikrete and hiring winos to make your concrete in a wheelbarrow."

"You may be right, but I need to check prices."

"Knock yourself out. On a good day, the old fart might have three trucks that run. No way can he supply the volumes of concrete

7

you're going to need." Shaking his head, the grouch added, "Would you believe he has a girl running the place?"

"I'm only interested in good concrete at a reasonable price." Mike said, ignoring the gender remark. "Grove City is a fair size operation. They can handle a hundred cubic yards an hour."

Sam pulled a small metal flask from his coat pocket and offered him a drink. Mike waved off the offer.

"I've got a long drive," he explained, but curious what the man drank, asked. "What's in the flask?"

"Good stuff, Dickel," he answered before returning to despairing his competitors. "Grove City's stuff's runny. They're too far away. The drivers are always adding water to keep the concrete from getting hard. It'll never pass specifications and trucking costs will kill them. We'll treat you right. I'll work up a better bid this week for your concrete."

Mike reflected on that meeting while speeding south on Interstate 79 to reach I-80 west. He had a date with Charlene in Columbus, Ohio, that evening. The meetings, with the French Creek Sanitary Board's consultant, after his meeting with Sam, had taken longer than planned. He would be late for her party.

Sam was the older of the two Woodbrier brothers. He was a stout, middle-aged successful businessman who reminded Mike of the old John Bull caricature of an Englishman. He had found Sam's demeanor amiable while working with him on the preparation of RBO's bid package, but his attitude during their meeting after the bid opening had left a sour taste. And he had known what RBO planned to bid before Mike's last-minute change this morning.

Sam might well prove to be correct about the abilities of the local concrete suppliers. However, the way to discover their ability was to ask them, not their competitor. Mike called their office manager, Steve, who had helped prepare the bid, and told him they had won the project.

"I need to lock in a ready mix supplier. Fax or email requests for proposals to supply the project concrete to all the ready-mix concrete companies located within thirty miles of Meadville."

"I thought all the local outfits were too small and Woodbrier was supplying the concrete."

"Maybe, but let's see what else is available."

Based on their response, he would decide for himself on their capabilities. He did agree with Steve that a steady and dependable supply of quality concrete would be critical to their success in building the project. That dependence on subcontractors, such as the concrete supplier, exposed RBO to third-party liabilities. One missed subcontractor mistake, such as a load of bad concrete or a box of defective steel bolts, could wreck the project's schedule, kill workers, and destroy their reputation, turning a potential ten percent profit into lawsuits and endless expenses.

Cement dust lightly coated the desk, floor, and walls of the Shaffer Concrete lab equipment room. A large white rat was perched on the edge of the trash barrel by the door, examining the empty donut box. The other occupant in the lab was a young civil engineer, Ann Lane, who was sitting at the desk studying a bid proposal faxed in earlier that day. She reflected on the benefits that an order for fifteen thousand cubic yards of concrete would bring to their business. The company that had won the contract to build the new sewage treatment plant for the French Creek Sanitary Board was seeking quotes from local ready-mix concrete companies to supply concrete for the project.

Only one other company, their much larger competitor Ace Concrete, had a batch plant close enough to the construction site to bid the project's concrete. Ann wanted to bid for the work and needed to convince Mr. Shaffer to allow her to submit a proposal. Supplying the project's concrete was an opportunity to accomplish her other ambition. Perhaps she could structure the RBO concrete bid to make sufficient profit for her boss finally to retire, and maybe then, she could persuade him to sell the company to her. The Woodbrier brothers, who owned Ace, were greedy bastards and thought Shaffer Concrete was a joke. Perhaps she could use their hubris to accomplish that goal.

Over a year of hard work, that was Ann's investment toward her entrepreneurial aspiration. Two years earlier, Mr. Shaffer had lost his only son, who also had functioned as the concrete plant manager. The son killed or murdered, depending on which version one believed, in a hit and run car accident. She had driven to Meadville for an interview with Ace Concrete and hadn't cared for the Woodbrier brothers. The chauvinistic brothers had no use for women in management, and she had wondered at the time why they'd bothered with the interview. On a whim, she had stopped to visit with Mr. Shaffer after learning during the interview that he was Ace's local competitor.

Mr. Shaffer had hired her on the spot to run the crucial quality control lab-batching plant and to assist him with management of the company. He had started the company thirty-five years earlier with a used Hagan concrete batching plant and two ready-mix trucks. Over the years, his company had grown to six trucks and upgraded the batch plant, but it was still a relatively small operation. Ace was a multi-location company with fifty ready mix trucks.

Ann's office was located in the metal building that served as the lab for the batch plant. One of her responsibilities required using the lab equipment to design concrete mixes, which she enjoyed doing. She viewed concrete mix design rather like baking, except the ingredients weren't tasty chocolate chips and sugar, but thousands of pounds of concrete-sand, gravel, Portland cement, and water along with various admixtures for air-entrainment, plasticizers, accelerators or retarders, and pozzolans. By varying the ingredients, she could make a concrete that matched the particular specifications required by a customer. That talent also allowed her to make the required concrete at the least cost.

Her grandmother would view the comparison of concrete making to baking as another example of her parents' failure to raise her granddaughter as a proper young lady and explained the lack of a husband. Ann figured any man frightened by her profession and vivacious conduct wasn't worth a second thought. Besides, she liked being her own boss and that preference in no way prevented her from liking and being comfortable in the company of men who treated her as an equal. That she refused to play the role of a cute accessory was probably the chief cause of her grandmother's angst. The thoughts reminded her that she had a message from that creep Jerry Woodbrier. That he would ever call her, after the way she had left him that night last summer, made her nervous.

Jerry Woodbrier and Paul Taylor were at the Goat Barn, a nightclub near Conneaut Lake that featured large mugs of draft beer, local and loud bands, and hefty gatherings of the college students interested in action. The building was an actual barn that someone had made into a bar. Jerry often wondered if he could do the same thing with Uncle Lou's old barn by Sugar Lake, running a nightclub would be more fun than teaching history to a bunch of dumb kids.

"Kind of slow tonight, even for a Tuesday night," Paul said. Only half dozen couples were in the place. No one was dancing. Even the music, normally blaring, played quietly.

"I need to find the Mexican."

Their usual aim was teaming up with girls who liked to party. Jerry considered himself rather handsome, which helped them accomplish that goal. His friend and trusted partner, Paul, was the

11

same age as him, twenty-five years old, which was still young enough to allow them effortlessly to fit in with the college-age crowd. Unfortunately, his friend, unattractive in appearance, had a hostile manner that caused most girls to shy away.

"Get us a couple of Miller Lites while I find a table and check the back room."

"Okay, I'll ask that brunette at the bar to join us."

The dealer wasn't in the backroom. Jerry found a table where he could watch his cousin hit on his prey and see the backdoor. Paul reminded him of a sinister toad with his bulging dark eyes, broad shoulders, and no neck. Apparently, the brunette at the bar agreed with that assessment of his friend's appearance, for she made a quick worried glance toward the cash register at the end of the pine plank bar. To verify the bartender was handy, he reckoned as he heard her tell Paul that she was waiting on a friend.

Instead of being sensible and parting gracefully, Paul had whispered in the slightly overweight but pretty woman's ear. Whatever he had said, it sent her scrambling to the restroom in tears. His conduct earned a blunt warning from the bartender to quit bothering customers.

Jerry shook his head at his cousin's behavior and thought that was Paul's real social handicap, not his looks, but that sarcastic meanness. It inevitably drove normal people, especially girls, to avoid him and that often interfered with their plans. Still his partner had his pluses; he was very strong and eagerly participated in all of their depraved schemes.

"That bartender got nerve telling me that. She is a fat bitch. What's wrong with telling how it is?"

"For one thing it turns the woman off. The idea is to pick them up, not piss them off."

"Don't you start. Let's go. The place's dead. I've got to work tomorrow."

That was fine with Jerry, since his new job started early. His father had threatened to stop the weekly allowance if he didn't work this summer for Pine Tree Construction as a laborer on the sewer plant project. That allowance threat was irritating enough, but this morning he had to listen to his father go on about the cost of his six years of classes at Allegheny College, and still no degree. Jerry knew his father was looking for a reason to cut off his funds. Not showing up for work tomorrow would give him a reason.

"He just came in. Try to stay out of trouble while I get the roofies."

"So that's why you wanted to see the Mexican. I thought you were after some crank," Paul said. "Having a few roofies might be handy Friday night."

The reason they had picked Tuesday to visit the Goat Barn was to meet the dealer who was usually available on the second Tuesday night of each month. He sold several popular drugs, including the good roofies, two-milligram flunitrazepam tablets that didn't contain that rotten green dye. His pills weren't cheap. Jerry had earlier stopped in the parking lot to verify he had enough money to make a purchase in case the dealer did show. He had a hundred and forty dollars. Jerry bought five roofies and a vial of crank.

The ostentatiousness of the evening's social event and his conversation with Sam Woodbrier had Mike in a contemplative mood regarding values. Most people believed that greed was bad and the cause of much human misery, but was ambition. In the morning the long postponed confrontation with his father would occur. Charlene interrupted his ruminations.

"Isn't it wonderful there're still people who are concerned enough to protest?"

"Who—what protestors?"

"Where have you been? The ones incensed at large toy-stores that have gender-specific toy sections. Young girls have rights."

"Is someone alleging they don't?" Mike said.

Then he realized that Charlene and her sanctimonious friends had been expounding on the wonderful service the Gender Neutral Organization protestors had provided. His date and her friends were thrilled over the protesters' effort to combat the promotion of gender-specific roles in children's toy displays in Columbus area retail stores. In their opinion, the protest could only enlighten and benefit the entire country.

"Yes, Mike. Imagine the damage to a young girl's self-esteem when her choices for acting out her dreams are limited to playthings like dishes or dolls with pink accessories!" Charlene said.

"How on earth could anyone imagine that rational store display sections damage a girl's self-esteem? Or limit a kid's toy choices? You're teasing me."

Her annoyed look suggested his date wasn't joking.

"There's more to life than business. You need to get involved, support these people. Children are the future. They need protected from corporate greed."

"Your concern is based on nonsense. Parents, at least normal ones, would just let the kid play with or buy whatever toy he or she preferred."

"Well it's not nonsense. You're just burden with outdated gender prejudices."

Whatever had attracted him to Charlene, a slender beautiful woman in her mid-twenties, her looks? For sure, she was an impressive-looking date, but as he listened to her opinions, he couldn't help wonder what lurked under that elegant veneer. Or why she cared. She'd made no secret that she considered children a burden and never intended to have one.

Then again why should he care what Charlene and her friends thought? He had zero tolerance for the atmosphere of contemptuous opinions swirling around the hotel conference room. He did enjoy the Mozart playing in the background and the delicious petite sandwiches served by waiters in tuxedos, having missed dinner.

Mike stole another glance at his watch and figured they'd be able to leave in about a half hour. The day had been long, starting with that early trip to Meadville and the bid opening. He needed rest. The RBO Construction Company ownership meeting was tomorrow. The evening wasn't a total waste; he now realized that he could never be comfortable with Charlene's sophistry. Were there attractive single women in Meadville?

Mr. Shaffer's health was not good. Sixty-five years old, he suffered from bad knees, heart problems, and diabetes, all conditions aggravated by cigars and his enormous gut. His wife had nagged him for years to quit smoking and go on a diet, sensible advice that he had cheerfully ignored for years.

Ann found her boss in his plywood-walled office located in an enclosed back corner of the old garage building reading her latest *Engineering News* magazine in a cloud of cigar smoke.

"She's right about smoking. Those rotten cigars are going to kill you."

"Don't you start, young lady. Remember I'm your boss."

"I'm just doing my good deed for the day. Have you read the RBO request for a proposal?"

"Fifteen thousand cubic yards of concrete is a lot of production to guarantee. I'm not sure submitting a bid is a good idea."

Well, at least her boss had read the request. She feared he would view the proposal as more an aggravation than an opportunity. Ann made her pitch.

"Ace won't be expecting our bid. They'll figure the amount of concrete is too large for us, and, as a consequence, Ace will bid high."

"It isn't too large?" He asked, stubbing out the nasty cigar.

"No, you know our plant can crank out a hundred plus cubic yards of concrete an hour. I'll bet you they'll bid over a hundred dollars a cubic yard."

"You're serious, a hundred a cubic yard?" He asked, pushing the empty coffee mug across the desk for a refill.

"At least that amount, probably more," she said, walking over to the mechanic's coffee pot located just outside the office door in the main part of the garage. While filling the cup, she added through the open office door, "Even better, the specifications require several special concretes that'll make RBO hesitate to set up their own batch plant. Ace doesn't know how to make two of those special concretes. Besides, they're utility contractors, not concrete people. We can bid eighty or ninety dollars a cubic yard, make a good profit. You want sugar or Splenda?"

"Sugar. You have a valid argument, but I'm worried about the financial risk from the million-dollar performance bond required. I'd be finished if we defaulted on such a bond. Fail to meet the daily concrete production of hundreds of cubic yards and you'll discover those big construction companies are heartless. It's all about the bottom line. RBO could bankrupt the company."

"It's about performance, doing what you promise. We have to deliver for them to complete their commitments. I can make and deliver the concrete, so please--spare me the lame excuses. You can get a million-dollar performance bond with a phone call."

"Maybe so, but what about serving our current customers on those days we're supplying the project's needs?"

"We'll manage. It's too good of an opportunity to pass up. Let me submit a bid. I'll make you a half-million dollar profit. And think of the bonus--you'll irritate Ace in the process."

"You're right about the Woodbrier boys. They're expecting to supply the project's concrete. You really think we can clear a half-million?"

"Sure, and you can even use some of RBO profits to give your underpaid engineer a raise."

Mr. Shaffer laughed at her pay remark before adding. "Did I read the proposal right, there's a large amount of that treacherous self-consolidating concrete. Are you absolutely sure the plant can handle that mix?"

"Sure, we can make the self-consolidating concrete. Ace can't. It is tricky and expensive."

"I'll say. Personally, I think it looks like a sloppy mess, and those new plasticizers cost a fortune."

"Doesn't matter, I'll have the cost in the price. We've been selling a couple of self-consolidating concrete loads each month without problems." Ann paused. "Also I need to go to RBO's prebid-conference tomorrow. It's in Columbus. Then I'll do the proposal and spreadsheet. Should I tell Tim to look after the operation, or will you be here?"

"I'll be here, but tell Tim and please be careful going to Columbus. Those Columbus drivers were crazy."

*He should meet Chicago drivers*, Ann thought. Also he had added, with a smile, that the Board Engineer had told him the RBO owner's son was a nice-looking young guy, in case that was of any interest to her. Now that, she thought was useful information. She wondered if he was the attractive guy outside the Annex yesterday talking on a cell phone.

Mr. Shaffer's decision to consider a bid made her happy and she headed to her dusty office to drop off the proposal package. Her banging open the lab door, startled the white rat. It scurried out of the trash barrel and fled to its nest under the pallet of five-gallon pails full of plasticizer liquid.

Tim was a fifty-year-old mechanic who definitely fit her father's opinion of how a first-class mechanic should look: no butt and a pot belly hanging over a severely strained belt. Ann liked Tim. He treated her like a favorite daughter, worrying over her safety, and constantly after her to wear a hardhat when around the batch plant and screening operation.

The crew's acceptance of her as the boss had required a few months. Initially, Tim had checked with Mr. Shaffer for his approval before carrying out her orders. He never overruled one of her orders, and Tim had quickly realized that even Mr. Shaffer pretty much did whatever Ann wanted done.

The white rat had arrived in the new two-drawer file cabinet Ann had requested that first week. A rat jumping out was the last thing on her mind when she opened the file cabinet. A loud and involuntary "Christ!" had escaped her. Men laughing outside the door told her where the rat had come from.

The terrified rat had bounded across her arm, onto the desk, and then leaped to the floor and under a pallet by the rear wall. She had grabbed the machete used in surveying and kept by her desk. Being a farm girl, she knew how to deal with rats.

The rat couldn't climb the metal walls; only two pallets and the desk in the otherwise empty lab offered hiding places. Ann flushed the animal several times out from under the pallets with a broom and chased it around the office. The rat realized it was doomed and finally laid down in the corner trembling. Suddenly, Ann felt sorry for it, put up the machete, and opened the door. The next morning the rat was still there, behind the trash barrel. Ann got in the habit of throwing her lunch scraps in the barrel, and the rat was now a pet.

The fuel delivery driver has teased her about Tim's explanation to him and the other employees as to why he put up with a young female boss. Tim's stance had been that Ann was the best-looking boss he'd ever worked for, knew the concrete business, and was pleasant to boot, so what's not to like about the situation? She sensed the other employees had come to agree with his assessment of her, even Mrs. Shaffer who ran the office. A number of customers had told her Shaffer Concrete had reverted from a fading operation to a newly invigorated business since hiring her. They gave her management style the credit for the improvements.

She found Tim by the large-size aggregate pile and waited for him to finish telling the loader operator to be more careful about getting mud mixed in the clean aggregate. The loader operator, who after receiving the caution and promising to be more careful, had remained and unabashedly listened in.

"We're considering a bid on the sewer plant," Ann said.

"Good, Ace doesn't need the business. We do," Tim said. The inquisitive loader operator nodded in agreement.

"Well, boys, we have one advantage over Ace, our onsite gravel mine. I want to maximize that advantage. Think of a simple way or method to develop two sand gradations and two gravel gradations. The extra gradations of aggregate will allow more flexibility in the concrete mix design."

Ann's goal was to reduce the amount of cement required in the concrete. Cement costs twenty times as much as aggregate. Therefore, any mix design that substituted aggregate for cement was bound to cost less. The trick was obtaining the strength required. Tim promised the new gradation plans would be available when she returned.

"Keep your plans simple and cheap. Make do with whatever old equipment is laying around the site. I don't want to spend a penny on new equipment."

Both men wished her luck in Columbus tomorrow. The loader operator also cautioned her to be careful in Columbus. She was in a reflective mood on the walk back to her office to wrap up the day and organize the trip to Columbus, Ohio. Her hopes for setting Mr. Shaffer up to retire and buying his business depended on a RBO Construction manager who was receptive to allowing a small company to bid and supply their concrete.

## Chapter 2

Mike met his father at RBO Construction's main office and equipment yard located in northeast Columbus, Ohio. The meeting was to discuss their future relationship. Continuing as his father's lackey held no appeal. Having developed and implemented the computer program that allowed their office to automate cost calculations for bid preparation, he was ready for more challenging tasks. Did his father even know who had designed the system allowing RBO to win bids with a high confidence for a profitable project? Mike wasn't sure. Regardless, he wanted the authority and position within management to reflect that and other accomplishments. So far, his father had been unwilling to consider relinquishing any authority, and he feared this meeting would just be a rehash of past requests, if he didn't change the game.

"I won the Meadville project. Now I'm going to start my own company. You can hire someone else to do this running from project to project."

"Ah son, you needn't do that. I have a better offer--the project manager job on our new project. I'll give you full authority to make all decisions, if in turn you agree to take full responsibility for the contract. Show me you can run a business. Capture that ten percent net profit your bid projects and I'll sell RBO to you."

His father's proposition astounded Mike.

"You're serious? After all the arguments that I wasn't mature enough?"

"Yes. This is your chance. Interested?"

"Yes -- thank you. Just so I understand, why finally now?"

"I was diagnosed with prostate cancer last week."

Mike's combative demeanor changed to one of concern as his father related the doctor's information that the cancer was very treatable.

"Hopefully, it should cause little trouble for years. However, retirement now looks attractive and with you wanting your own business, selling RBO appeared to be a practical solution for both our needs. Meadville is a chance for you to demonstrate that you have the drive and ambition to run a company."

How suddenly circumstances change: Mike told his father they had a deal.

They spent the rest of the meeting focused on the various details needing resolution to achieve the transfer. His father wanted the sale value based on the appraised value of equipment and real estate, along with a small percent of the company's gross receipts for a period of years. Determination of the sale price and the most advantageous method of transfer from the tax perspective would require several months. They decided that, initially, his father would simply sign and approve accounts and checks as instructed by Mike. They would finalized the transfer after the Meadville project was completed.

Mike had always preferred the business side of engineering to the design side. His talent was the ability to determine the most cost-effective sequence for the project's construction phases. He then used that information to control expenses by scheduling when each subcontractor was required, along with arranging for delivery of material, supplies, and machinery in the most cost effective manner.

Asked by friends to explain his job, he used building a privy as an example of doing a project in proper sequence. One should begin by digging the hole in the ground, then build the house, and finally install the toilet seat, not the other way around. Imagine how difficult digging the hole would be if a person had built the outhouse first and had to reach through the toilet seat. His job figuratively speaking was determining the hole in the ground from the outhouse seat in complex projects.

The knowledge Mike and Steve had acquired during the meticulously prepared Meadville bid made him confident of meeting his father's sale conditions. He thoroughly understood the potential bottlenecks that could develop and stretch out the project's time of completion and their impact on construction costs.

For example, concrete was not a big dollar item in the Meadville project cost, but timely delivery and proper concrete quality would control several critical phases of the project. The large aeration basins' walls required thousands of cubic yards of concrete and when completed, the basins acted as retaining walls for the equipment containment building. As a result, the installation of aeration equipment, electrical conduits, and piping had to wait until the concrete developed proper strength.

Irregular delivery and poor quality of the concrete would create unnecessary expenses and scheduling problems for the project. The crew pouring a large wall section required payment whether they were pouring concrete or waiting for the next truck. Mike didn't wish to think about the cost of replacing a wall section should the concrete fail the twenty-eight day strength test.

Because of this concern, the company that supplied their concrete would have to assure him they were capable of producing and delivering the required amount of cubic yards per hour. The Friday prebid-conference session when ready mix concrete companies made their pitch for his business would have his full attention. Hopefully one of the local outfits could provide the concrete and he wouldn't have to depend on Ace for the project's concrete. Woodbrier's Pine Tree Construction already had more of the project work than Mike preferred.

Contrary to the warnings, the Columbus drivers behaved fine. Ann had left Meadville at 3:30 A.M. and arrived without mishap at RBO's Columbus office and equipment yard at 8:30 A.M. She was impressed with the property. The entire lot was paved with asphalt, except for a wide strip of gravel along the back of the property. The gravel strip served as the storage area for bulldozers and other track equipment that would damage asphalt pavement with their cleats. The RBO office building was a large split block single-story structure. The office was tan and blended well with the other industrial buildings on neighboring properties.

The chain link fence enclosing the property lacked the usual bent and tipped sections from vehicle damage. The security fence ran neat and straight, except toward the lot's back section where two nice-looking Paulownia trees had grown inside the fence. The only jarring disconnect for Ann was the razor concertina wire. She was used to the typical three strands of barbwire on top of a chain link fence.

Neatly arranged by type, the excavators, backhoes, dozers, cranes, trucks, compactors, and paving equipment all appeared well maintained. Even the bone yard looked organized, with water hoses rolled up, concrete steel forms stacked by type and size, odd items like left over rebar and dowels neatly placed on wood pallets, and the small water pumps set upright with drain plugs open. Her first impression of RBO Construction Company was of a serious and well-managed operation.

She had debated what to wear and decided to stick with her work outfit of steel toe boots, the Shaffer work uniform of khaki pants and shirt, Carhartt work jacket and a white hardhat. She thought her appearance satisfactory, except for her hands, which were hopeless from working with the cement. Her hands were chapped and rough, the nails broken. She needed to get in the habit of using rubber gloves--do guys look at hands. She applied a touch of makeup after parking; after all, there was a rumor that a cute guy might be present. She left her Sierra four-wheel-drive pickup in one of the visitor parking spaces, debated wearing the hardhat, decided not to, and tossed it back into the cab. She ran her fingers through her short hair to fluff it into some resemblance of order and entered the office.

The room smelled clean and the elderly receptionist was a friendly black woman who told Ann the prebid meeting was in the back conference room and for her to go on back. She paused to read the awards and plaques commemorating various projects RBO had successfully completed as she made her way along the hallway to the conference room. About a dozen men were sitting around a large rectangular conference table in the center of the room and talking, which ebbed to silence as she entered. Ann recognized the two Woodbrier brothers, large men with the ruby complexion of quart-of-bourbon-a-day social drinkers. They politely acknowledged her wave. Everyone else in the room was a stranger.

A gray-haired man in a dark suit, white shirt, and striped tie sat at the head of the conference table. He glanced at a sheet of paper, and then asked if she was the Ann Lane representing Shaffer Concrete. She was. He then introduced himself as Robert Owen, the owner of RBO Construction. Then he asked everyone around the table to state their name and company. After the men seated around the table had done as instructed, he introduced his son, Mike, who had entered from a side office. He would be the project manager on the Meadville project. His son was casually dressed in a Navy sport coat and an open collar shirt, a physically imposing strong-limbed man. The good-looking rumor was correct. He was the man she'd seen outside the Annex the day of the bid opening.

The owner's son was a very attractive young man in a tan blue-eyed blond-hair kind of way. He was tall, maybe six feet plus a few inches. He had a large head with the eyes set well apart in a face with a high forehead and a straight Greek nose. His demeanor hinted at an energetic personality. She bet herself he wasn't the passive type and that thought reminded her of the critical issue. Her hopes for the concrete contract depended on Mike Owen being a real manager, willing to make unpopular decisions and not a handsome rich boy playing at managing his daddy's business. Alas, Ann knew appearances can and do deceive. Still, by the end of the meeting, she would have a feel for whether he was a reasonable businessman, a dilettante, or God forbid a misogynist.

Ann examined the other people at the meeting. Besides the Woodbrier brothers, there were steel-rebar suppliers and the consultants for the French Creek POTW agency, Norton and James out of Pittsburgh, and a plate of donuts. The older rebar representative must have read her mind and kindly slid the plate with donuts across the table to her. *I shouldn't eat this donut,* she thought while she helped herself to a chocolate frosted cream-filled donut, and whispered, "Thanks."

Mike looked over the room's occupants before starting his presentation. They consisted of the predictable collection of robust construction workers and professionals with one exception. *Ann Lane,* his father had addressed her. A lovely and solid-looking woman, so different from the Charlene types he'd been dating whose looks were manikin perfect and whose warmth was similarly lifelike. Ann had to be that androgynous person he had watched at the bid opening helping the old man. Her broad shoulders, muscular build and narrow hips with that short brown hair had contributed to his confusion, but her bust ended any possible gender confusion. She was a fine-looking woman with a complexion that was tan and flawless except for a few freckles on an elfin nose. Her alert brown eyes examined him in return as her lips hinted at a smile. His curiosity was aroused as to her background, but he figured an attractive woman like her was married, or at least had a special guy, or maybe a female partner. Regardless, that was her business and his today was concrete. Mike got on with the meeting's agenda.

The meeting proceeded in the typical fashion of most prebid meetings, a discussion of the contractor's concerns regarding the performance of the suppliers and subcontractors. Mike explained the paramount importance of quality control and timely delivery of the concrete. Next, he addressed similar worries regarding the cutting and bending of the steel reinforcement and the need for proper labels on the bundles of rebar. He closed his remarks by emphasizing the ability to meet RBO's performance expectations would be as important as the price in determining the successful bidder. Mike then suggested people planning on bidding to supply the concrete take advantage of the Norton and James consultant's presence by addressing any questions they might have on the concrete quality control and inspection procedures.

The room seemed impressed or at least paying attention to his discussion of the issues regarding the concrete and reinforcement. He had endeavored for a pleasant tone to promote a sense of unity. Mike hoped his congenial behavior suggested a man who was confident in his knowledge, and in control of the project, not his true state of being nervous over flubbing his first big project.

Time for questions and the older Woodbrier brother, Sam, started.

"What'll be the maximum delivery rate for the concrete?"

"One hundred cubic yards per hour," Mike said. He noticed that number caused a momentary concerned look from that concrete girl, Ann.

Sam then wanted to know if the consultant would supply mix designs for the different concrete. Sam's question caused an audible snicker from the woman, which caused all eyes in the room momentarily to turn on her.

No mix designs, the consultant responded that was the supplier's responsibility. Specifications for the concrete were performance based on the 28-day compressive strength and air content of the concrete. The use of accelerators or retarders would be weather based and decided by RBO and the consultant as necessary.

"Will the concrete bid be split between suppliers?" Sam asked.

"I might consider a split if there was a good reason, like lower prices," Mike said.

"Not just to allow small, second-rate local producers like, for example, Shaffer Concrete to be part of the business, for public relation reasons. You do know you'll get the best price by awarding the entire amount to one supplier?"

"Perhaps, depends on the prices and conditions the bidders submit," Mike said.

Sam's sneer regarding Shaffer had incensed Ann. A flash of color had crossed her face. How she responded to Sam's disparaging remark on Shaffer Concrete would give Mike insight to her resolve and fortitude. He and the room did not have long to wait.

"To avoid any wrong impressions from Sam's unwise comment, you folks should know that the Ace boys calling Shaffer second rate is equivalent to Goliath of Gath calling Israel's David second rate," Ann said.

The lady clearly was not in the mood to abide any nonsense regarding Shaffer's capabilities. The older rebar representative laughed aloud, several of the other men smiled, and a couple of the younger men had blank expressions. His father had looked startled by her comment. Mike wondered if he had nodded off.

Lou Woodbrier, angry, had started to respond to Ann's remark, but Sam shaking his head, grabbed Lou's arm and whispered, "Quiet."

Mike had trouble not gawking at the pretty girl. Her comeback to Sam's dig had triggered the thought; *those Woodbrier brothers do not intimidate her*. He gave the room a moment to settle down and then answered Sam's question.

"Absent a very compelling reason to do otherwise, I intend to issue the entire concrete order to one supplier."

"Good," Ann said.

The lady had responded to his answer before Sam could, while giving Lou an *up yours* glare. Her right fist had even come up but apparently, she had remembered the audience, and stopped the salute. The feisty woman fascinated Mike. She then turned, ignoring him and the Woodbrier brothers, and focused her attention on the consultants across the table. She asked if non-specification aggregate gradations in the special self-consolidating concrete were acceptable.

Mike watched the older consultant check with his partner. Neither consultant had a clue. They spent several long minutes huddled with the specifications. The senior consultant hesitantly answering yes, with the qualification that the concrete meets the other specifications and the aggregate did not separate out of the mix during the pour. Sam and Ann then rapidly alternated with several more questions for him and the consultant on the testing methods, criteria to determine the number of test cylinders per pour, use of a 7-day break instead of the 28-day test, and method of payment.

Finally, Ann and Sam exhausted their question duel, which concluded the concrete part of the prebid. Mike reminded the two of them that RBO Construction expected their proposals for supplying the concrete by next Friday along with a bid bond.

That concluded the concrete portion of the prebid and Ann was gathering her papers preparing to leave when Mike suddenly told the consultants to take a five-minute break before they started the electrical part of the prebid. He wanted to know more about that woman and hurried over to intercept her at the door.

"Hi, I wanted to thank you for attending the prebid meeting. What's your position with Shaffer Concrete?"

He asked while extending his hand in greeting. She seemed to hesitate, but managed to flash him a smile and then shook hands.

"I'm Shaffer's concrete technician."

That smile, those brown eyes alive with intelligence. . . *Where had this woman been all his life?* Then he realized his silent stare had made her uncomfortable as she broke the lengthening silence by commenting on being impressed with how nice their equipment yard looked. Mike recovered from her smile--*What an intriguing woman*, he thought—and switched back to business.

"Why, thank you, though the organization is more my father's doing than mine. Is Shaffer Concrete large enough to handle the hundred cubic yards per hour concrete production?"

That, Mike quickly discovered was a sensitive topic.

"Those worthless Woodbriers are always spreading that nonsense. You think I'd waste my time coming to this meeting if I didn't believe we could handle a hundred cubic yards of concrete per hour. Shaffer can easily handle your production."

The steel rebar gentleman glanced their way. Sam Woodbrier was watching her.

"I didn't realize the maximum hourly production rate for concrete delivery was in the request for proposals."

It was her turn to stare. She appeared to realize he was right, that her snippy remark was unjustified. Mike realized he had unintentionally made Ann defensive over her imprudent response to his question. He helped defuse her embarrassment.

"That's great. The more companies we have competing to supply the concrete, the better. Do you have time for lunch?"

A delightful smile flashed as she explained that unfortunately she did not have time for lunch. She had promised to visit her mom before going back to Meadville.

"Are you from Columbus?"

Ann cheerfully informed him she was not. She was a farm girl from Indiana. Her family lives near Kilmore and they were third-generation hog and corn farmers. Anyway, she needed to leave to get there by dinner. Maybe when he was in Meadville they could do lunch, she told him and bid him goodbye. He admired Ann's striking figure as she left the room with a goodbye wave to the Woodbrier brothers. He saw the Woodbrier brothers begrudgingly acknowledge her wave and wondered if she was married.

Jerry worried for a moment that he had killed the girl; she was utterly limp as he helped his cousin carefully undress her. Then he saw her take a breath and felt the rush of anticipation at the pleasure he was about to have. He cautioned Paul to be gentle with her. Their protection from the police depended on leaving no evidence, and that started with assuring she suffered no bruises or cuts. Their prey was a neat looking blond, Betty Deere, a small lissome girl who had drank the wrong thing. A freshman in education from Edinboro she had informed Jerry earlier on the back balcony of the party house. Shame she's not conscious. She was missing a real education as he started snapping pictures of Paul violating her flopped over the chair back. He had difficulty focusing on the photographing as he lusted for his turn with her.

Their main buyer wanted graphic pictures of a rape and Paul was providing excellent poses. Jerry wondered again whether the risks would outweigh the profit if they were to sell sessions with her after they finished. She wouldn't remember any of this in the morning, and the horny gang downstairs would pay big bucks for a go with that girl. *Forget the idea* he told himself. There was always the possibility of some do-gooder in every crowd that might call the police. He didn't need that hassle and he never wanted another Jenny Lowell.

The trip to Kilmore, Indiana, through Columbus and back to Meadville, Pennsylvania, was nearly a thousand miles of driving over three days; Ann was tired of driving and glad to be back to work Monday. Tim had prepared a workable plan using Shaffer's current equipment to create the four aggregate and sand gradations she had requested. She liked his plan and told him to rearrange the conveyors and screen decks and start making the new aggregate gradations. The different aggregate gradations would provide plenty of options in formulating her test mixes for the three concrete types required for the RBO project.

Before Ann settled into a long spell of making test mixes, she went to the garage office to explain her proposal. The proposed bid price per cubic yard she based on current cement content and cost. If her new mix designs worked, the actual cement cost would be ten percent lower than the costs she had used to calculate the bid proposal, a nice cushion to cover unexpected costs.

"Good, you're both here," Ann said. "I proposed we bid ninety dollars on the two standard mixes, and a hundred and five dollars on the self-consolidating mix."

"That high," Mrs. Shaffer asked.

"Yes. Sam and RBO both made an issue of the hundred cubic hour delivery requirement. I believe he really is convinced we can't handle that high production rate and won't expect our bid, or if we do, RBO won't accept it."

"What assurances are there that our plant can meet that high production rate? After all I'll have a million-dollar performance bond at risk." Mr. Shaffer said.

Ann explained how Tim's modifications to the plant and gravel operation will increase the through put of the current plant by twenty five percent, more than enough to meet the hundred cubic yard maximum required.

"I figured RBO won't consider a captive concrete batch plant unless the price exceeded a hundred and thirty dollars per cubic yard. And if our price is twenty or thirty dollars less than Ace's bid, we'll get the business."

"We're talking serious money at those prices," Mr. Shaffer said. "Are you sure we can handle the production?"

"Yes, I'm sure. You will need to replace our three oldest trucks with new or at least newer trucks. I figure nine dependable trucks can deliver hourly a hundred cubic yards to the project. Call your friend at Grove City. Find out if he will rent out some of his ready mix trucks on the busy days." Ann said.

The Shaffers liked that idea and promised to find out about the extra trucks. Other than the truck issue, if they approved her prices, she was ready to submit the proposal. After a brief private discussion between the Shaffers, she received their blessing to go for the RBO business.

"Is Owen's son good looking?" Mr. Shaffer asked.

"He's okay." She answered and walked out the office.

The only negative to an otherwise pleasant weekend was that Jerry Woodbrier had called her again over the weekend and left a message on her apartment phone. He knew her opinion of him--talk about a date from hell! She'd often wondered what her fate might have been if she hadn't awakened. In fact, the jerk's calling somewhat concerned her, Ann had a momentary preposterous thought that maybe the moron planned to sue her. She should return the bastard's call and find out what he wanted.

David C. Brown

## Chapter 3

The concrete proposals had delighted Mike. Shaffer had bid an average price of ninety-two dollars verses Ace's hundred and seventeen dollars average price per cubic yard for supplying the RBO project concrete. The cost difference between the two bids for the fifteen thousand cubic yards of concrete amounted to three hundred seventy five thousand dollars. The low bid would help meet his goal to clear ten percent on the Meadville project. Another bonus was Shaffer's concrete technician looked a whole lot better than the Woodbrier brothers did. He needed to go to Meadville and check out the operation before making a final determination.

The following Monday morning reality tempered Mike's enthusiasm. He sat in his vehicle looking at the Shaffer operation and reflected that on first sight, the operation didn't look promising. Their batch plant was an ancient Hagan unit that was older than he was. The main office was a walled-in corner in the back of the truck garage, an old single-story block building with a wood and tarpaper roof. The newest thing on Shaffer's site was a metal building beside the batch plant, probably Ann's lab.

Mike needed to be honest and admit he'd been hoping Shaffer would beat Ace because of Ann, an interesting woman, a good-looking woman. If nothing else today, maybe he could learn if she was married. He parked and as he exited the vehicle, cautioned himself for the umpteenth time not to let interest in a woman cause a foolish decision on concrete suppliers.

A fat black and white hound waddled out of the far dark corner to check him out. The arthritic mutt gave him a careful sniff, and he petted the dog's head, which seemed to satisfy it. The garage was clean and appeared organized as Mike and the mutt made their way to the tandem Volvo truck that a mechanic was servicing. The mechanic told him Mr. Shaffer wasn't in, but his wife was. He pointed toward an enclosed corner with a wood door with an OFFICE sign attached.

The old dog waited by the door. Mike could see a grandmother working at a computer through a dirty window. The dog slipped into the office as he opened the door.

"You know you're not allowed in here," the lady said.

Not certain who she was addressing, him or the mutt, he said, "I'm Mike Owen and looking for Mr. Shaffer."

"I'll be, Ann's bid must have beat Ace. My husband is not in. Can I help?"

"I wanted to inspect the operation. Be sure the operation could supply our needs before deciding on a supplier. Is there someone who could show me the setup? Answer a few questions?"

"You need Ann."

Mike thought. *She's right about that and not just for answering questions about concrete.*

"The girl is the real boss. She'll show you around the plant and answer your questions. Follow me."

They went out a side door while the mutt, taking advantage of the distraction, curled up on the office floor rug. They walked over to the newer metal building, which was the lab as he had guessed.

Ann was hard at work weighing out containers of sand and gravel when they entered the lab. Seeing her again in person reminded him of her allure that even the dusty work clothes, respirator, ugly rubber gloves, and knee boots couldn't obscure. The straps from the respirator had her brown hair jammed every direction, which she whipped off on seeing him.

"Why, hi, Mike. What brings you out among the plebeians?" she asked after a marvelous smile.

Ann appeared to be happy and in a friendly frame of mind. Her cheerfulness was infectious. He laughed at her greeting and thought *I'll rile her*.

"I'm here to check on suppliers. The local captains of industry, the Woodbrier brothers, told me Shaffer was a Quikrete and hand-mixing operation."

The smile vanished, Ann looked mad and started to say something, then apparently realizing he wasn't serious, and instead laughed.

"Well, I suppose that is better than having the Ace boys say I'm spreading my legs for the business."

"Ann! I can't believe you said that!" Mrs. Shaffer exclaimed.

Her response caught him completely off balance. His face flushed not sure what to say, knowing Sam had insinuated that very point to him after the prebid meeting. In an effort to regain control of the meeting, he said.

"I need a tour of the facility and equipment so RBO could be confident Shaffer was equipped to handle the production for the project." It sounded asinine even to him and compounded his embarrassment. What must this lively female be thinking?

Fortunately, for him, Ann looked amused that her sassy remark had so seriously disturbed and embarrassed them. That she had no desire to embarrass him was clear as she ignored his idiotic remarks and showed mercy by readily agreeing to a tour. She told Mrs. Shaffer to quit acting like a prude, that the Woodbrier brothers would be saying that or worse behind their back as soon as they found out they had lost the contract.

Ann's remark about winning the contract Mike thought was a bit presumptuous on her part. That thought apparently caused his chagrin from his earlier responses to morph into an argumentative guise.

"Stop looking argumentative. We know you wouldn't be wasting your time visiting unless there is a twenty to thirty dollar price difference between the bids," Ann said.

Mike realized she had read his changing mood perfectly and thought. *What the hell. She was right, quick, and no nonsense.* He lightened up and even managed a smile in response to her comment.

"She's right. Am I to understand she's the boss?"

Mrs. Shaffer, still recovering her composure from the racy remark, nodded in the affirmative as Ann gave him a friendly who-did-you-think look while pulling off her heavy black rubber gloves. She threw the gloves on the workbench causing a small cloud of dust to puff up. She then headed for the exit door, before stopping and returning for her hardhat.

"You'll need a hardhat."

They walked over to his new black Grand Cherokee to get his hardhat. It was the reddish-brown full rim hardhat of the type favored by ironworkers.

The tour started with Ann admitting the obvious: Shaffer's equipment was old. For example, the conveyors and bins were older than she was by a decade, but all the components subject to wear were new or in excellent shape. She explained that Shaffer had replaced all the conveyor rubber belts this spring with new heavy-duty belting.

"Our equipment is the equivalent of new as a result of this constant upgrading and maintenance. That batch plant will mix 150 cubic yards an hour, day after day, regardless of the fact that it was thirty-five years old."

"Well I'll agree the equipment looks well maintained," he said to respond while looking around.

There were several different manufactures' rollers in use on the same conveyor, but conveyor rollers were supposed to be built to the same specifications for a given load range and size. Mike figured the different-colored rollers indicated which manufacture had the best deal the year a replacement unit was required. Graphic proof Shaffer was an efficiently run operation. Still, he doubted her 150 cubic yard claim on that ancient Hagan batching unit productivity. He'd be surprised if it could do much more than hundred cubic yards an hour.

"Show me the gravel operation."

He followed Ann along a footpath worn between the frames supporting the conveyor belts overhead. The footpath ended at a ramp into an excavated pit several acres in size and perhaps twenty feet deep in which a rubber tire end loader was digging against a bank of sandy gravel. She stopped at the top of the ramp and waited for him to arrive.

"Did you hear on the news about the guy who lost his left side?"

"No! How'd that happen? Did he die?" Mike asked. Her concerned voice had startled him.

"No, he's all right now."

Mike required several seconds looking into that wonderful set of brown eyes to realize it was a joke. She'd be thinking he was dense.

"That was good, Ms. Lane. You had me going for a moment."

They both laughed, and then she described the gravel operation. They ended down by several ponds that provided water for the operation and served as basins to catch the sediments from the site. One pond looked like a giant mud hole. Ann explained the pond design was to trap the sediment washed out of the gravel and sand aggregates used to make concrete.

The other two ponds looked clean and had dense sections of cattails and watercress around their edges, and several muskrat houses made from cattail stalks sat out in the last pond. The last pond in the series had water lilies, several with buds that in another month promised attractive yellow blooms, along with the usual cattail clusters and beds of watercress. Mike could see submerged light flashes from the sunlight reflecting off fish swimming in the last pond and asked what kind of fish were in their ponds.

"Tough ones primarily carp, bullheads and bluegills," she answered.

Ann then described the previous summer's drought that caused a number of the local ponds to dry up. The ponds shrank to small puddles and to save the fish, much to her boss's distress over his electric bill, she ran a garden hose for two weeks to keep water in the pond.

"The four-foot carp survived, but hawks and raccoons eat a lot of the smaller fish and bull frogs. The snakes disappeared and the snapping turtles, ugly brutes, crawled over to Smith's pond."

She pointed toward a large pond about a quarter mile away across a newly planted oat field.

"Do the muskrat's tunnels cause any leaks in the pond's embankment?" he asked as he thought. *She really likes this wildlife business with the ponds.*

"Not so far. I think they're cute swimming around in the pond with a mouthful of watercress or a cattail stalk. They remind me of miniature beavers. I had to intervene on their behalf this past winter."

"You mean the muskrats?"

"Yes, two young neighborhood boys, the Smith brothers, they ignored the No Trespassing signs I had put up around the site and started setting leg traps for the muskrats."

40

"How old were they?"

"I would guess twelve and fifteen-years of age."

She explained that one day last November, footprints in the snow on the pond embankment caught her attention. She investigated and found ten traps; none of the traps had the owner nametag attached to the anchor chain as required by state law. So she tripped the traps, then watched the pond area and finally spotted two boys the following morning resetting the traps. She confronted them, and they ran like deer.

"I recognized them, the Smith boys, and yelled if they wanted their traps back, see me at the office. I then gathered their traps and stored them in the lab building. I involved Tim. Told him about the Smith boys and asked him to help me keep an eye on the ponds."

"Did the boys get their traps back?"

"The following Saturday two polite boys show up and asked about the traps. I told them their traps didn't have nametags and they had been trespassing. Maybe I should call the game-warden." Ann waved to the fuel truck driver as he drove by.

"What'd the boys have to say?"

"The younger one claimed he didn't think the No Trespassing signs applied to trappers. The little hoodlum's statement was so galling I couldn't help asking why anyone would think that. The older one then explained they were just trying to be helpful, neighborly."

"Trapping your rats was neighborly?" Mike asked. He wasn't sure exactly what a muskrat was. Was that white rat he saw in the lab a muskrat?

"They claimed it was. Trapping would protect our pollution control device from leaks caused by the muskrat tunnels that accidently bored through the pond embankment. I told them that I didn't buy their explanation. The nine dollars for each muskrat was their reason."

"A rat's worth nine dollars?"

"Muskrats, Mike. They have valuable fur. Anyway the younger brother wore an angelic expression, as if such crass financial concerns would never have motivated him, while his older brother allowed the pelt was another consideration."

"Altruism wasn't their only motivation. Imagine that," Mike said.

"Long story short, they promised not to trap any place on Shaffer's property for any kind of animal. I gave them back the ten traps. In the spirit of neighborly compromise, I even gave them permission to hunt on the property outside of the mine area."

"Did the young hoodlums honor the deal?" He asked while marveling at Ann's inconsistent logic that shooting an animal was okay, but not trapping one.

"As far as I can tell they have, I've seen a number of muskrats this spring. The boys even stopped after deer season to show me a picture of a six-point buck their sister shot on our property."

"Their sister?"

"Helen Smith, she's a sophomore in Allegheny College in their science program. Does RBO have any wildlife and ponds on their property?"

"No ponds, but we have pigeons, alley cats and sewer rats."

"Well, you always have the Columbus zoo."

Ann refocused on business, showing him the by-products from the sand and gravel operation as they walked back toward the screen. They stopped by a large stockpile of round rocks and another of topsoil. The stockpile of topsoil was actually the mud from the first pond, Ann informed him, which when dried makes a decent top soil substitute. Mike had thought the large stockpile was topsoil.

That was the other by-product of the sand and gravel operation she added, pointing toward a large pile of football-size and larger stones.

"Oversize gravel that requires crushing before it can be used as concrete aggregates. So far, we haven't need them. I heard people around Pittsburgh like to buy them for landscaping uses. If I owned the company, I would sure try to sell them, but at the moment, Mr. Shaffer didn't want the bother."

After a pause while they both examined the huge pile of stones, Ann laughed and added.

"Well one good thing about the rocks, they won't spoil. The other surprise is the gas well drillers are buying sand for their wells."

The tour went fine; in fact, Mike could have spent the entire day in Ann's company. Never had he enjoyed a woman's lively repartee more. She definitely had charisma. Her explanation of the planned flow sequence of material and her conservative production estimates for each operation seemed reasonable. Every operation, except the batch unit that loaded the mixer truck, was capable of two hundred cubic yards per hour. The Hagan batch unit was the bottleneck. An hourly production rate hundred and twenty five cubic yards would require everything work perfect.

Ann conceded she could have been a bit optimistic asserting the Hagan unit could hand one hundred and fifty.

Mike also began to appreciate the onsite gravel mine gave Shafer a real cost advantage over Ace. The tour ended back at the lab where he noticed the dust-covered degree from Purdue hanging on the wall. He learned she was an engineer, along with being a licensed professional civil engineer in several states.

Ann was proving to be an accomplished person. Mike was impressed. He had recently received his engineering license and remembered how tough a time he had passing the engineering test. Then he remembered that a minimum of four years' experience in your chosen engineering field was required after receiving your degree, before a person could take the test.

"How old are you?" he rather inelegantly asked an amused Ann.

"I'm twenty-four. I graduated from Purdue when I was nineteen and high school at age fifteen. Since you brought age up, what's yours?"

"I just turned twenty-seven. You're way beyond a technician. No wonder Shaffer's confident they can handle the special concrete."

Though he didn't want to leave Ann's company, he had covered everything and needed to get back to Columbus.

"I'll send a confirming letter and the schedule on our current estimate for delivery dates and amounts of concrete." He thanked her for the tour.

Ann remembered the lunch offer from the prebid meeting, as she watched him walk back to his vehicle.

"Mike, want to have lunch before you leave?" she yelled.

He was for any excuse to stay in her company and agreed by asking what she had in mind.

"A late breakfast at the Market where they serve real vessel cloggers--bacon, fried potatoes, fried eggs, all the good stuff."

Ann added she came from a long line of hog farmers and had to support them; besides he looked like a few extra calories wouldn't hurt, she added on seeing his hesitation.

"Okay, I'll follow you. I can always run some extra miles." He accepted her invitation.

Parking at the Market in downtown Meadville was usually scarce, but she thought they might get lucky by arriving in the interlude between breakfast and lunch. They were, and found two parking spaces side by side. Several of the customers and the older lady running the restaurant warmly greeted Ann and looked Mike over.

The delicious aroma of frying bacon and fresh bread awoke Mike's appetite. He told the grill lady he would have the same as

Ann's order. Looking about the Market's interior with the wood beam construction, he realized this was an old building built to serve as an enclosed farmers' market. At the opposite end of the enclosed interior space was an interesting butcher counter that was tempting him to examine. The central area had little open counter shops selling flowers, fabric, fresh produce, and home-canned goods. All and all a delightful example of how farmers' markets were seventy-five to a hundred years ago.

"What was your specialty at Purdue?" Mike asked. "Look at that cook; can you open an egg with one hand? I never had any luck."

"No, I've tried, but always break the yolk or get shell fragments in the pan."

He watched the grill-cook expertly open more eggs with one hand as he listened to Ann's answer. She had focused on structural design with a lot of emphasis on concrete members, both prestressed and post-stressed, and the cast-in-place type of structures. Ann liked working with timber structures and especially admired the craftsmanship used in old wood structures such as this market. She pointed to a mortise and tenon joint in the wall column behind the grill as an example of workmanship rarely seen today.

The food arrived and they concentrated on eating for several minutes. He complimented Ann on her choice of restaurants. The food was good. He picked up and examined the bill lying on the counter; the food was not only good, but he realized the price was very reasonable. In Columbus, a similar meal would have cost twice as much. Ann asked what his college major had been.

"Project management, Ohio State offers it in their civil engineering program."

"Are you going to use that jelly?"

"No, take it. Want the toast? My major focus was on items like critical path analysis. Our company has evolved more into project management than actual construction. We use a lot of subcontractors, which requires synchronization to avoid delays and control cost."

Munching on the last piece of toast, Ann asked when the project was going to get rolling.

"Soon, I hope in the next couple of weeks with a formal groundbreaking. I'll finish the construction flow path diagram this week, and then give each subcontractor their schedule."

"Here, I'll pay. I invited you. You can get the next one."

Ann reached for the bill after laying down a tip. Mike hesitated for a moment and then handed over the bill and thanked her. Ann paid and they walked out to the vehicles and went their separate ways.


The Woodbrier brothers were meeting at the Ace Concrete office located between Meadville and Saegertown, a one-story austere cinder block building that housed Lou's office, the scale office, and the accounting-payroll group. The layout was basic with nothing fancy: cheap metal furniture, hanging florescent light fixtures, baseboard heat, and a painted concrete floor. No rugs graced the office floor; plumbing and wires, attached to the interior block walls, were exposed. The setup was convenient for an occasional hosing out of the accumulated mud carried in by the employees.

Lou's cigar was glowing red as he listened to his brother's side of the call from Mike Owen. Sam was telling the kid that Shaffer Concrete couldn't supply 3500-psi concrete at that price. After a pause, he added RBO should consider the added expense when Shaffer's old plant breaks down and they can't provide the concrete. Another pause, apparently, his brother had sensed that Owen was not going to change his decision on awarding the contract to Shaffer, and had decided to end the call on a friendly note. Sam had offered that he did understand Mike choosing the low bid, but if RBO changed their mind, Ace was ready to supply their concrete. Sam thanked him for the opportunity to bid.

"Shaffer undercut our bid by twenty-five dollars. You have any suggestions on how to get the business?" Sam said.

"You know it's that damn girl engineer. She's the one who pushed the old fart to bid, probably after the Owen boy."

"I'm surprised. I thought for sure Shaffer was too old and sick to want the hassle of supplying the concrete."

"The best way to clip her wings is for her first concrete to fail the compression strength test. Owen can't afford to take a chance on bad concrete. He'll have to use us," Lou said.

"I doubt Owen will give up Shaffer's lower price that easy. How can we ensure a failed test?"

"There's a fair chance she'll screw up on her own. After all, who ever heard of a woman that could make concrete? But we need to help her."

Sam cautioned Lou that whatever method of discrediting Shaffer he tried, they could not afford discovery. No great intelligence was required on Owen's part to figure Ace Concrete was the only logical one to benefit from the Shaffer's sabotage.

"Remember the recycled glass fiasco?" Sam asked. "You said no one would care or know if we used it in place of sand and gravel in the concrete."

"Well I did get rid of the recycled glass without having to pay for disposal. I never thought it would weaken the concrete."

"That Penn Dot engineer wanted to have you arrested."

"The guy was an asshole. He was mad over my offer of a thousand dollars to forget the failed test. I still laugh about our lawyer telling his boss that I was just an overzealous environmentalist wanting to promote recycling."

47

"The point is," Sam said, "If the lab found that our recycled glass had created the siliceous gel that weakened that concrete, why couldn't a lab discover whatever you added to Shaffer's concrete?"

Sam knew his brother had never been inclined to waste much time worrying over the consequence of his actions and he wasn't the least bit surprised to hear him dismiss any concerned over a lab finding the material.

"Yeah, yeah," Lou said, "But determining the cause of a concrete failure takes time. My point is RBO can't afford to take the time or chance that a big concrete wall section won't meet specifications. One way to ensure that is to put fifty to a hundred pounds of sugar in a couple of the truck drums the night before the first concrete order. The sugar would get mixed in the load of concrete and cause low strength."

"Sugar, does that really work?" Sam said.

"I've always heard sugar works and we have the perfect person to do the deed in John."

"I don't know seems like a lot of risk for something that might not work."

"What the hell is your problem, brother? Do you want me to check with the girl on how much sugar I need to add to her concrete to weaken it? Everyone knows sugar ruins fresh concrete."

"Okay, try it, ask John. He might do it. After all, we sure helped him in that zoning variance hearing."

"He will," Lou said. "He knows he owes us. Hell, his truck picks up their trash around 4 A.M. The trash container is right beside the area where Shaffer parks their ready-mix trucks. His man could dump the sugar in a couple of trucks with no one giving his presence on the site a second thought."

"Maybe the better option is having the inspector mess up the concrete test cylinder. Mix a small amount of amorphous silica in the concrete sample pulled to make the test cylinders."

"I say do both. You're golfing buddies with Norton. Find out if any of his inspectors are hungry, and would like to earn some money on the side. Wait, even better--assign Paulie to the Meadville project."

"Yes--that's the answer. He's a good man and would help us." Sam said and agreed to check on Norton and James's staffing plans.

"Good, I'll get with John on adding the sugar. The other item we still needed to think about is the girl. I thought for sure the old man would have sold after his son's accident, but then she showed up. Don't know how, but they're doing better since he hired the bitch. She's a real pest."

"You're right, that property is the real prize, but first things first. Ace needs the concrete business, so lean on John. I'll get Paulie on board."

Sam had other concerns. He needed to check on the status of the approval to substitute their air duct material for the Type-316 stainless steel called for in the treatment plant plans. Pine Tree Construction had a contract with RBO to supply and install the project's air ducts. He had a deal with Dennis Norton, the project consultant engineer, to approve Pine Tree's request for an "equal to" determination.

Such an approval would allow substitution of much cheaper air duct material and avoid the cost of the stainless steel air duct material specified in the bid. Normal procedure, when substituting a cheaper and otherwise equal-in-performance material, required the consultant to negotiate a price reduction for the project owner. With Dennis's help, Sam's plan was to pocket most of the savings in material cost.

Their deal with Dennis would be the easiest million dollars they had made in a while, if RBO didn't object. Global not winning the bid had knocked Woodbrier Construction out of being the project manager and in charge. Now RBO was, and Mike Owen might discover the deception and turn the air duct material switch into a million dollar loss.

Lou found John busy making a tire inventory check at the tire storage rack beside the Gambone Collection truck garage. The company collected trash in Crawford-Erie-Mercer Counties of northwestern Pennsylvania. Walking over to meet John reminded him how massive the trash man was. Lou considered himself a large man at six feet three inches and two hundred thirty pounds, but John with his thigh-size arms and twenty-two-inch neck made him feel a bit intimidated.

Neither man cared for the other, but certain business interests required they assist each other from time to time. Lou got right to the issue of needing a favor. John's assistance was required to help sabotage a couple of loads of Shaffer Concrete. The concrete needed to fail a strength test. John wasn't in a helpful mood.

"I don't know anything about concrete other than to add water and mix. How can I help?"

Lou, though irritated over John's lack of enthusiasm, held his temper and explained knowledge of concrete wasn't required. All that was required was on Tuesday morning, when John's crew picked up the Shaffer roll-off trash container, one of his men needed to put sugar in two of Shaffer's concrete mix trucks. He would supply the sugar and truck numbers.

"Will this cause any danger to the construction workers or attract the police?"

"No," Lou answered and, with his patience slipping away, elaborated. "I want two hundred pounds in each truck, which is enough sugar to keep the concrete from passing specifications. That will get them kicked off the project. The weak concrete won't hurt anyone. Hell, no one will even know why it failed."

Lou's temper was stirring after John didn't responded. He asked if he was going soft and had forgotten who helped him with that zoning issue.

"No, but I find it irritating to be reminded about that damn zoning issue every time you assholes need a favor."

The man had a point, Lou realized and added, "Dump sugar in the Shaffer's trucks and we're even on the zoning help."

That John liked and he agreed to handle the sabotage with that understanding. With the issue settled, Lou needed to talk to John's brother Sal on the other matter.

"You have a number for Sal?"

"Sure, it's in the office. Use a burner phone to call it."

Lou nodded and John asked, "How did Sam's son make out with the police?"

"Okay, the girl changed her story, said she was mistaken and dropped her complaint."

Ann was pleased with the outcome of Mike's inspection and confident Shaffer would get the RBO business. She was proud of her accomplishment, but in moments of second thoughts and doubts, worried she had allowed her ambition to endanger the Shaffers' retirement savings. Her ambition had put their company in a precarious financial position with that million-dollar performance bond. Her self-respect would not survive failure to deliver the results promised.

Since returning from Indiana, she had focused on her new concrete mix designs and making test cylinders. She wouldn't know if her new mixes would lower concrete cost by ten percent until she broke the test cylinders. She sure hoped so, as on just the RBO business, her new mix design would reduce their cost by one hundred fifty thousand dollars. That cost saving would provide an additional safety cushion for unanticipated screw-ups and costs that could occur on a large contract.

Project specifications regarding concrete take into account the period required for the chemical reaction that is responsible for the concrete's strength to occur. Standard practice is specifying a 28-day period before testing the concrete's compressive strength: also known as the 28-day strength. Ann knew concrete that after seven days had obtained seventy percent of the specified twenty-eight day strength, with rare exceptions, always exceeded the required 28-day compressive strength, so there was no need for Ann to wait four weeks to find out if her new designs worked. The seven-day curing period for her new concrete mix test cylinders had ended. Ann got busy breaking the test cylinders to learn if her new mixes worked.

Her satisfaction with the performance of her new low cement content mixes increased as each of the concrete test cylinders broke with a bang. The white rat, who had been begging for a piece of her muffin, had disappeared after the first bang. By the end of the afternoon, Ann had to get another laborer to help remove all the broken concrete test cylinder fragments on the floor around the 135-ton press.

She was a grimy mess as she leaned on her shovel to give her back a rest, but happy. Test results had clearly demonstrated the new low cost concrete mixes were a success. Every test cylinder had broken above the required strength at seven days. Her earlier concerns had vanished; Shaffer Concrete was ready.

Mrs. Lane called that evening to check on her daughter. Ann excitingly told about the successful new concrete mixes for the big RBO project. Her mother made the proper supportive remarks on her daughter's talent in concrete mix design. Then after filling Ann in on family news and neighborhood events, talked about her worry that she would never be a grandmother if her daughter didn't start trying to meet nice young men, instead of working all the time. Ann didn't really have an argument with her mother. She wanted children when the time was right, and who doesn't want to find a nice young man? However, being Ann, she told her mother to get after her brother--he was already married--if she wanted grandkids.

Her mother's call got Ann to thinking about Mike Owen. Was he a nice man? He was a rich man's son and they are often cynical and apathetic to accomplishment, though he was pleasant the other morning during the site visit. His embarrassment from her sassy remark was adorable and suggested a sensitivity she found attractive. She reckoned Mike would prove to be a worthy man. Ah, what's a farm girl like her thinking about a guy like him? A handsome and rich man like that would have loads of beautiful women chasing after him. Ann's thoughts turned to getting her apartment cleaned and feeding her cat.

Mike was busy reviewing list of steps required to mobilize RBO's project management team and subcontractors and start the French Creek POTW construction. Prior to submitting the bid, he had completed the critical path analysis using Primavera management software to determine the optimum sequence of construction for the minimum period required to complete the project. He had also noted possible bottlenecks that might lengthen that period.

The analysis had determined a number of items that needed ordered immediately to ensure the timely completion of the project. The electrical and motor control panels had the longest lead-time for manufacturing. For that reason, the panels were among the first items ordered, even though the panel installation occurred near the end of the project. On the other hand, steel rebar for the concrete structures was readily available, but since it was required to start the foundation work, Mike also ordered the rebar.

His office manager, Steve, had been working twelve hour days the past several days to double-check they had ordered every item and permit needed to start the Meadville plant. Next, they wrote up a schedule for ordering the remaining items to ensure delivery was in time not to delay the project. Larry, RBO's senior engineer and surveyor, would leave for Meadville the next day to set up the construction office and meet with the fence contractor to start enclosing the work site. Steve's assignment was to handle the construction office utilities, phone, and electric service. Mike's assignment was to obtain the Ohio and Pennsylvania permits for moving the heavy excavation and lifting equipment from RBO's Columbus yard to the site.

Just as they were getting ready to wrap up and head home for the night, before driving to Meadville in the morning, Steve had asked how the Shaffer visit went. Did that cute girl know anything? Mike told him and Larry who was listening that the Shaffer engineer knew her business and would supply the project's concrete. He caught the look they gave each other.

"Don't get any crazy ideas. She was the low bid."

## Chapter 4

The site of the future Meadville wastewater treatment plant was located south of the town in a cornfield along the west bank of French Creek. When Mike arrived, Larry's crew was working on the initial stake out survey for the construction project. Steve was showing the trailer people where to set the storage and office trailers. A fencing crew had already completed the chain link fence that enclosed the construction site and the various utility crews were busy hooking up the temporary electric power, phones, and a water line.

The progress his men were making in organizing the construction site pleased Mike. Proof he had assembled a good crew. His plan to start the construction of the main reactor tank footings by the beginning of May looked feasible. The goal was to have the three large concrete reactor tanks and two circular clarifiers built before winter.

Lou Woodbrier arrived at the site a few minutes after Mike with the Pine Tree Construction's foreman, Jake Cooke. Lou was a younger and larger version of his brother Sam, though his weight was muscle, not fat like his older brother. He had gray eyes set close together in a face laced with red veins and dominated by a bent hooked nose. Not a friendly face, Mike thought as Lou explained their visit's purpose was to check on RBO's mobilization progress and find out when they could start their part of the project.

"Plan on starting next week," Mike said even though he was having second thoughts about using the Woodbrier brothers as his major subcontractor.

The steel rebar salesman had told him the consortium had intended to use Pine Tree if they had won the bid. Sam's knowledge of RBO's proposed bid probably explained why Global would have won if he hadn't found that last minute savings. The scoundrel had used that knowledge to try and under bid RBO.

"Okay, we'll mobilize Monday," Lou said while looking about. "I wasn't sure what to expect after hearing you gave supplying the concrete to that looser, Shaffer. Was she a delight in bed?" Jake smirked as Lou added, "We figured that was the only reason they got the concrete. My nephew said she was the willing sort and, hell, you can't blame a woman from using what she has to get ahead."

Those arrogant assholes, a series of emotions flew through his mind: amazement, anger, and finally, a determination to give them no satisfaction.

"You're pathetic. Does your brother know you're more worried about your competitor's sex life than his business? No wonder your concrete bid was so high. You need to focus on being ready to start moving earth next week."

Mike left an irritated Lou standing in the parking lot and headed to the office trailer while wondering whom the nephew was. He must be another jerk like the rest of the Woodbriers. He appreciated that one can never truly know a person from a brief business acquaintance, but he would bet Ann was not a promiscuous lady. She radiated wholesomeness, unlike Lou, who oozed sleaze and violence.

Their office trailer was brand new, but stocked with old miss-matched furniture from past projects. To lighten his mood after Lou's disparaging remarks on Ann, he teased Steve on his interior design capabilities.

"It surely wasn't easy to pick out this much office furniture and have nothing match."

"Now don't be displaying the typical engineer's pathetic knowledge of interior decor. Personally I find that scratched gray desk of yours goes rather well with your orange chair and tan-colored file cabinet." Steve responded while sorting out the computer monitors for the different workstations.

Steve took a break from setting up the office to go with Mike to the consultant's trailer located across the gravel parking area behind their office trailer. Mike introduced his crew to Norton and James project engineer Terry Westfield. The meeting's purpose was to review the quality control and quality assurance procedures a final time, before the actual construction started.

Norton and James was the design firm for the facility and represented the project owner, the French Creek Board. Each stage of the project construction required Norton and James approval before RBO could submit an invoice for payment. That made Terry Westfield, as the Board's representative, a very important man.

Mike wanted to establish a proper professional working relationship with the consultant's project engineer who was a middle age man about six-foot tall and flabby. He had long dull gray hair in a queue and a faint sour odor. The man needed better personal hygiene or he was ill.

Westfield didn't waste time on pleasantries or introducing the man standing beside him, instead he launched into his requirements for approving project construction items.

"I expect each item of the project to be built exactly as shown. If the concrete wall drawing calls for a thickness of twelve inches, don't expect approval of eleven and three quarter inches."

"What about the average of several measurements?" Steve asked.

"If rebar drawings calls for four-inch-centers, I don't want some of the rebar at five-inch centers and other's at three-inch spacing with you guys whining that the average rebar spacing is four inches. I'm not approving equivalent nonsense, only the exact measurements shown on the plans. Are you clowns clear that the field measurements have to be the same as the plan dimensions?"

"Yes." Mike answered, speaking for the three of them, while wondering about the reason for the clown remark.

"I'm concerned about concrete quality. I can't believe the concrete supplier on a project this size will be some local mom-and-pop operation. Well, that's your business, but I intend to require extra test cylinders to verify the concrete meets specifications. Paulie Pelosi is the concrete inspector. He decides on test samples."

Terry then turned to point at the thin man standing beside him, who Mike assumed must be Paulie.

The project engineer's antagonistic demeanor and voice, and now the concrete inspector's, were increasingly difficult to tolerate, but Mike resisted expressing his annoyance with their behavior in an effort to avoid starting the project in conflict with the consultant. He assured them that RBO's concrete foreman would be informed the inspector decided where and when to test concrete.

"I wanted to pour a series of the small pipe rack footings next week and then start the footings for the north reactor tank. Who will check the rebar prior to pouring?" Mike asked.

Instead of answering him, Terry turned back to Paulie and ordered him to check all rebar placements. The engineer's unsocial behavior had him puzzled and worried. A psychotic project engineer could wreck their goal of delivering the project on budget and time.

The project consultant's judgment had concerned Mike from the beginning when he read the project specifications and learned Norton had specified costly material for the plant's air ducts. The use of 316 stainless steel seemed excessive and unjustified. Now the consultant had employed a scruffy unfriendly person for their project engineer. He hoped Westfield at least proved to be a competent engineer, but the more the project engineer explained his method of oversight, the greater Mike's misgivings on the man's technical competence.

Mike had just started back on setting up his workstation when the local trash man stopped by. His name was John, six foot plus several inches, all muscle, and with swept-back black hair, early forties; he looked like an extra from the *Sopranos*. Mike's hand felt lost in the thrashman's as they shook hands. He asked him the purpose for his visit.

Gambone Collection had won RBO's disposal contract for the Meadville project and John wanted to meet the project manager. He then proceeded enthusiastically to describe the trash service they would provide: five roll-off boxes around the site that he'd empty every Friday. The weekly service should cover their disposal needs, however, if not, just call. Mike hadn't realized the magnitude of the effort required to remove trash from a project of this size, and told John he thought the service arrangement sounded fine.

After John had left, Steve came back to Mike's office.

"If there are any trash problems, you handle them. That trashman is one scary-looking dude. I thought that Westfield guy was an unpleasant jerk. Hell, he even smells bad."

"Maybe he's sick. Just remember that bum has to sign off on our invoices. As for John, let's keep him friendly. I'll see you tomorrow."

A monstrous man in dirty green coveralls, black work boots and a build that would give pause to a wrestler from World Wrestling Entertainment, walked into the Shaffer lab. Ann has seen man around town and she knew his name.

"Mr. Gambone, come in."

He had stopped in the doorway and looked carefully around, as if checking for competitors lying in ambush in the corners, before nodding to her. She stood up at her desk, while hoping he wasn't as violent as he looked. Though he had a deep menacing voice, he surprised her with polite thanks for seeing him.

"Miss Lane, I wanted to check that you're satisfied with my service."

"Please call me Ann, and yes we're very satisfied with Gambone's disposal service. In fact, I recently told Waste Management that Shaffer had no interest in changing waste haulers."

"Good. If you're ever not satisfied, please call me direct. Just ask for John."

He looked around the lab. *What was he looking for?* Ann wondered, as he bent over and picked up one of the thirty-pound concrete test cylinders stacked on the floor with his left hand. The same cylinder that Ann had used both hands to move earlier, John was nonchalantly holding in his left hand, as if the cylinder had suddenly morphed into a feather.

While scrutinizing the cylinder, John asked, "Do you do the engineering and quality control for Mr. Shaffer?"

"Yes, I'm responsible for the quality of the concrete. Why do you ask?"

John gave her an intense look, as if weighing her character, Ann hoped, not trying to decide how big of a hole he would need to dig to dispose of her body. After a pause, he set the concrete cylinder carefully back on the floor.

"Just curious, my daughter was telling me about Mr. Shaffer hiring a woman to run his operation."

"I don't believe I know your daughter. What's her name?"

"Kathy. She's a junior at Alleghany, going to be a doctor."

"Good for her."

"Yes, I'm very proud of Kathy. . . Back to business, I heard all kinds of rumors and nonsense. I know Shaffer won the bid for the big concrete job. You might want to watch your equipment very carefully. Check things before making concrete for RBO."

His comments alarmed Ann. How did their conversation veer from his daughter to that? Was he forewarning or threatening her?

"Why are you telling me this, Mr. Gambone?" Ann knew a loaded 45 automatic was in her purse in the lower desk drawer. The machete would be useless: he'd probably use it for a toothpick.

"That's not important. If you have any problems with my service, please call. Oh, I noticed there's a rat hiding in those rags. Want me to kill it?"

"No, I'll deal with it." Ann wasn't about to try explaining the prank and her feeling sorry for the rat to this ogre.

Ann sat at her desk after John had left and decided that was obviously a warning. Threats usually say, you had better do such and such, or else this may happen. But a warning about what, sabotage? Then she wondered if Ace could or had done something to the plant. She went looking for Tim after taking a moment to verify the concrete cylinder still weighed thirty pounds.

Mike and Terry worked together to check the twenty-five pipe rack footing forms, rebar and anchor bolts for correct placement prior to ordering the concrete. The concrete crew had done a fine job and to his surprise, Terry expressed satisfaction with the crew's workmanship. He gave approval to pour the footing concrete in the morning and promised to instruct Paulie to be ready at 7 A.M. to check the concrete quality and make the necessary test cylinders. On returning to the office, Mike told Steve to call Shaffer and order fifty cubic yards of footing concrete for morning. Have the first ten cubic yards at the site by 7 A.M., followed by ten cubic yards each hour, until the fifty-cubic-yard order was completed.

RBO's first order put Ann on alert. Earlier Mr. Shaffer, Tim, and she had discussed John's warning and checked the plant carefully. All appeared to be in order and they had agreed to meet at 5 A.M. for a final check before preparing and loading the RBO concrete.

"How juvenile," Ann said.

Tim and she had discovered some jerk had flattened the front tires on two of Shaffer's concrete mixer trucks during the night. She had planned to use those trucks, their newest to deliver today's concrete as part of her effort to create a favorable first impression with the site's concrete crews.

"Tim, get the mechanic to check the engine oil and fuel in each truck before anyone tries to start one. We'll use the air compressor on the mechanic's truck to air the front tires. Thankfully, the tires don't appear to have been cut."

Were the flat tires the prank Gambone warned her to be on guard against? Or was it a distraction to cover something more serious? Ann left Tim and one of the mechanics airing the tires. She wanted to check something.

The east horizon was just starting to lighten and the stars fade. The clear sky promised a beautiful day. A light frost was on the equipment as Ann got her light and started climbing the drum hopper ladder on one of the new mixer-trucks for a look into the drum. The metal of the ladder ring was freezing and Ann dropped to the ground and walked back to her pickup for her gloves. Finally properly dressed she was up the ladder in a few seconds and looked in the drum. A white granular power was visible at the bottom of the mixer drum.

Rats, Ann would have to climb into the mixer drum to investigate. She noticed a small amount of powder had caught on the bottom edge of the mixer drum inlet and was close enough for her to reach without having to unbolt the guard plate.

She pinched up a sample with her fingers, climbed down from the drum, and smelled the powder. Sugar! Someone had poured fifty to a hundred pounds of sugar into the mixer drum. A quick check of the other new truck also showed sugar lying in its drum. Ann deliberated the best response as she stood by the mixer truck waiting to for Tim to finishing airing the tires, which fortunately were undamaged.

"Sugar, it had to be the trash guy."

"I don't want anyone to know about this, okay."

"Okay, but why?"

She explained her plan to Tim and had just finished as the two drivers arrived.

The early clear morning was too beautiful to sit in his office. Mike decided to check the site. He left his office and walked over to the pipe rack footings to watch the project's first concrete pour. An angry discussion between Ann and Paulie, at the footing pour, attracted his attention. Westfield had also noticed the spat, so Mike jumped across the row of footings and hurried over to join them. The inspector was furious. Ann looked perplexed.

"What are you two arguing over?" he asked, beating the project engineer there.

"This girl is questioning my test cylinder procedures."

"I don't know what his problem is. I asked him if he was using the ASTM C-31 protocol to make the test cylinders. After all, I'm responsible for the concrete quality, and I want to know the testing is correct. Why is this yahoo suddenly so defensive?"

Ann tuned directly to inspector. "You are familiar with C-31?"

"I don't know who you are, but I'm not allowing my inspector to be harassed, so get off this site!" Westfield declared before Paulie could respond.

Ann was incensed over the dismissive response to her question. Mike was already familiar with the man's rude behavior and sick of it. To avoid a needless confrontation, he stepped between them.

"Ann is Shaffer Concrete's engineer. She has every right to ask about test procedures." Ignoring Westfield, he asked Paulie, "Are you using C-31?"

"Yeah, what else would anyone use?"

"That was her question wasn't it, bud? So next time just answer her question without the BS."

"Where are you planning on setting the filled test cylinders," she asked. Paulie looked confused and she added, "They have to be protect them from being disturbed for eight hours to allow the initial concrete set."

"Paulie will put them where he damn well pleases," Terry said and added, "Now get this first truck sampled. And you—Ann, is it--quit bothering my inspector and stay out of his way. He's the expert here."

Ann was aggravated, but she held her tongue as Mike motioned for Terry to follow him. After a short and silent walk toward the office, Mike stopped.

"You need to reel in your shitty attitude. Contractors are entitled to respect. They have responsibilities, and they were within their rights to question the consultant's procedures. Her questioning the inspector's handling of concrete test cylinders was perfectly proper. Paulie had no business being an asshole."

Terry looked surprised for a moment, and then smiling, told Mike he had a lot to learn and walked off as Ann walked up.

"I'm not putting up with that jerk. Something reeks about that inspector. No one should act like that. I'm making my own test cylinders."

Mike watched her march over to her pickup, grab two empty test cylinders, a small shovel, and a half inch diameter steel rod about two foot long. The inspector looked alarmed on seeing her return with that rod.

If their argument deteriorated into a fistfight, he'd put his money on Ann. She was beautiful, but also strongly built with well-defined muscles in her arms and maybe an inch taller than Paulie at five-foot eight or nine-inches. Mike couldn't hear what she said, because of the equipment noise, but it made the inspector scoot out of her way.

She slammed down the test cylinders and shovel beside the pile of fresh concrete being used to fill RBO's test cylinders. The Shaffer truck driver was an alert older man who eased over beside Ann. Paulie would know she wasn't alone. The driver helped her between spurts of unloading concrete into the footings as the concrete foreman instructed.

Mike was tempted to help her, but knew if he showed much interest in her the gossip would start. Besides any woman as pretty as Ann would have a boyfriend or even possibly a fiancé, so he best not get involved. Westfield stopped later in the morning to tell him the inspector thought the Shaffer concrete had a funny feel, sticky like. Mike had seen a lot of concrete over the last four years, and thought the concrete looked fine. He wondered if Paulie was a fraud.

"The concrete looked fine to me. Are you sure the guy knows what he's doing?"

"Paulie's the best concrete technician in western Pennsylvania. If he said the concrete is not right, a smart person would wait for the seven-day test results before setting the pipe racks. Save yourself the cost of removing the pipe racks in order to tear out the defective footings."

"You plan to let us use the seven-day test?" Mike asked. "What percent of the twenty-eight day strength will you consider passing?"

Seventy percent was fine with him, which meant footing concrete needed a compressive strength of 2450 psi at seven days to pass. Mike knew that was very reasonable. He agreed they would use that number on future concrete testing. Maybe Westfield wasn't the dud he had first feared.

Mike decided to play safe and wait on the results from the seven-day break of a test cylinder to verify Shaffer's concrete did meet the strength specified before ordering more concrete. Mike had RBO's crews concentrate on Basin No. 1 footing excavation and setting concrete forms and rebar for the footings during the week required for the first concrete cylinders to be ready to test. The week passed quickly. International Testing would call the results on the first set of test cylinders in the morning.

*What a miserable day,* thought Paulie as he hung-up the phone after Lou's call The seven-day break of the Shaffer concrete test cylinders had averaged 2600 psi, way over the required strength. The results confused him. He had even hit the cylinders about half way through the eight-hour period allowed for the initial set in order to break the initial cement gel set and weaken the test cylinder. Maybe Lou's claim that sugar weakens concrete was wrong. Regardless, the next set of test cylinders had better fail or he would have to return the thousand-dollars. That would be difficult, since it was gone. He needed amorphous silica.

Lou was having a McDonald breakfast with his brother at Ace's Erie office trailer when Paulie had called.

"Something didn't work. The concrete passed with flying colors. You think Gambone's men didn't place the sugar?"

"I visited John last week to satisfy that very concern. He assured me the sugar went in the drum."

Lou shrugged, "What else would the dago say?"

"Yeah there is that, but later I ran into Jimmie, who knows the Gambone roll-off driver. He told me the driver was bitching in the bar about the difficulty of carrying fifty-pound bags of sugar up the side of the truck using the drum hopper-ladder. The driver told him to tell his genius uncle, next time, buy ten or twenty pound bags. So I'm confident the sugar was placed."

"Genius uncle--the asshole's lippy, but right. I'll bet carrying a fifty-pound bag up that ladder was a bitch. I never gave it thought," Lou said.

Sam called John and told him the sugar never made it to the concrete. Did he have any ideas why? They talked for several minutes. After completing the call, he summarized the conversation for his brother.

"John figured the drivers rinsed their truck's mixer drum before loading the concrete."

"Why would they do that?" Lou said. He got up and walked over to the small refrigerator for the ketchup bottle. "You need anything?" Sam shook his head no.

"His advice was to leave Shaffer alone. That girl engineer is smart enough to catch on and cause them all trouble. John thinks she'll soon get bored with a small outfit like Shaffer and move on."

They sat in thought while they finished breakfast. The brothers realized John was probably right. She would find a better job in another year or two, but that was no help to their current goal of having Shaffer tossed off the project. Ace needed the RBO concrete business. That would be a nice win, but their current approach of using Paulie to sabotage Shaffer Concrete didn't address their main goal of forcing Shaffer to sell at a distressed price. They both knew the Lane girl needed to go. If she weren't there, the problems of management would fall squarely on the old man, along with all the hazards of making the special mixes required by RBO and protecting his million-dollar performance bond. The brothers' consensus was after several weeks of those headaches, convincing the old man to sell the business shouldn't be difficult.

"You have any suggestions on how to run that girl off?"

Lou was surprised at his brother's last comment, since he thought they already had decided.

"I trust you agree she's not the timid type. Or be easily run off."

"No. Her disrespect at the Columbus meeting removed any hope I harbored that she'd be sensible."

"Jerry claims she's a nympho." Lou laughed and added, "That prissy Owen is in for a surprise."

"Don't remind me of my sorry excuse for a son. You're lucky not to have children. Also I put him with Jake's crew to start earning his keep."

"Our choices for getting rid of her are either a car wreck or a disappearance. Which one do you think is better?"

"I didn't like either choice. Two Shaffer managers dying in car wrecks might get the wrong thoughts stirring, and a disappearance of a young lady had the potential to attract a lot of news interest and questions after that college girl disappeared. We don't need Fox and CNN on it."

"What about a rape-murder? It the most easily explained mishap. There would be nothing to lead the police to suspect a business connection. After all she is a beautiful lady living alone,"

Lou said. "If you're okay with that idea, I'll check around and talk to Sal." Sam nodded.

Lou drove to his Saegertown office and found one of the prepaid cell phones. He went to Alleghany College soccer field to watch the practice and call Sal who answered on the second ring.

"I need some nasty work done quickly here in Meadville. You have a crew available?"

"No, but I have a contact in Brooklyn that works with some Russians who might be able to help."

"How about contacting them for a meeting at one of your places in Pittsburgh, so I can talk without worrying he's some FBI agent? I'll cover your expenses," Lou said.

"I'm not sure I want involved with another one of your deals, after that baby," Sal said.

"What are you talking about? That whore you shredded?" Lou asked.

"Me? You're the one that killed her. I'm talking about her baby, the one you didn't know about. The one you abandoned to freeze to death. That deal put a curse on my life. I'm talking about your impulsive deals that have blowback. That tempts fate. Understand?"

What had made Sal mention that ancient history? That murderous dago acted like Lou had done something wrong. It was seventeen years-ago. He'd hate to think the man was going soft, be bad for business if they stopped helping each other eliminate problems.

"Yeah, that was bad business, but it worked out," Lou said. "I'll keep you out of this, just setup the meeting. It's easy money."

"I'll set up the meeting with that understanding," Sal said. "Take about a week to arrange. He'll want cash. How much I'll try and find out."

*Sal's baby comment brought it all back. Lou's thoughts returned to that winter night in Pittsburgh when Sal had bailed him out of a mess. Seventeen years ago, how time flies. He had handled a small heroin delivery for Crazy Sims, a local drug dealer in Pittsburgh. Part of his payment was a cute Thai prostitute for a night at the Holiday Inn near Robinson Town Center. He had caught her trying to steal his wallet. In the ensuing scuffle, her neck was accidentally broken. The motel room was on his credit card. He couldn't just leave the body.*

*Lou knew the Gambone family had connections to the Dalporto car shredder operation in the area, and Sal, the oldest son, owed him a favor for an alibi he had provided in a murder case. The prostitute's car, an old Dodge, parked in front of his motel room, offered a solution. He would put her body in the trunk and have Sal arrange for the car and body to be shredded. Sal hadn't liked the idea, but finally agreed to help with the understanding that going forward, they were even.*

*Lou found her car keys but was disappointed to find only three dollars in her purse. She had weighed less than a hundred pounds, and her body left a lot of room in the Dodge's large trunk. Snow had started falling by the time Sal arrived with another man to drive her car to the shredder. Lou and Sal were in the motel room having a beer when the driver came back in the room and told them there was a problem. There was a live baby in the car.*

*"Damn Lou, you said nothing about a baby," Sal said. "No way am I shredding a live baby. I'd end up in hell for something like that. What is it, boy, girl?"*

*Sal's driver, holding the bundle wrap in a pink towel answered, "A girl."*

"I didn't know," Lou said. "Who'd leave a baby in a freezing car? What an irresponsible bitch. Give it to me. I'll break its neck."

"You're sick. Get out of my way," Sal's driver said. He shouldered Lou out of the motel room doorway and carried the baby into the motel room where he deposited her on the unmade bed.

Only the need to avoid unwanted attention prevented Lou from grabbing the baby and using it as a club to beat the driver. And he needed Sal's cooperation to dispose of the dead mother. Lou held his temper. The driver, sensing his hostility, hurried past and drove off in the whore's car.

"Do what you want, but I'm out of here," Sal said. "Give me her wallet, shoes and coat. I'll get rid of them."

Lou decided the cleanest thing would be break the kid's neck and throw her in the I-79 rest area trashcan on his way back to Meadville. A perfectly formed, dark-eyed and dark-haired baby stared back at Lou. The smell meant she needed a change; no wonder, left untended in a freezing car for hours. She hadn't made a sound. He reached for her neck; her sudden smile immobilized his hand.

Hell with it, he'd drop her off alive at the rest area. Let that God that Sal's so worried about decide her fate. He stole a large towel from the room to bundle her in and then stuffed her and the towel in the empty cardboard box that had contained quart cans of motor oil. She had sufficient sense not to let out a peep.

The snow was accumulating on the road by the time they arrived at the Grove City rest area on I-79 north. Snow was no concern to Lou with his 4x4 F-250 Ford pickup. The baby had whimpered several times, but otherwise remained quiet. He needed to get rid of it. A stop by some curious state cop would be his end. How would he explain who she was? The rest area was full of trucks. Lou stopped by the entrance to the rest room and decided he would make a quick search of the area, before he set the kid on the sidewalk.

*Damn good thing he did, too, because a state cop sat in an unmarked cruiser across from the entrance watching him.*

*Lou drove out the rest area with the kid. The state trooper pulled out and followed. At the intersection of I-80 and I-79, Lou went west on I-80 toward Ohio, figuring the trooper would say on I-79. He didn't, the trooper followed several car lengths back. The snow had worsened. The trooper exited at the last Pennsylvania exit. Lou crossed into Ohio for several miles and pulled over.*

*Irritated at being force to drive out of his way, he ran around to the passenger side and opened the pickup door. The baby started crying. Lou grabbed the cardboard box with the squalling baby and sat it on the road shoulder. Snow had already coated the box top by the time he pulled back onto I-80.*

*Her death wasn't his fault. He'd tried to do right and he would have if it weren't for that damn nosy state cop. Lou exited at the SR-7 and looped back through Greenville to I-79 and home.*

*Sal had called him a few days later and told Lou about a snowplow crew finding a live baby girl along I-80. He had wondered if there was a connection to the motel problem. Lou told Sal about the state trooper. Sal had sounded relieved and offered that God works in mysterious ways. Lou figured the road crew had been checking the box for something to steal.*

Mike liked what he was reading and thought, *Way to go, Ann Twenty-six hundred psi* as he reviewed the lab report on the six concrete test cylinders. Terry had handed him the reports earlier without comment. Now that he knew Shaffer's concrete was good, it was time to push the basin footings construction. He called Terry.

"That first pour's concrete looks good, so I plan to pour the first reactor basin footing tomorrow."

"Yeah, I'm surprised how good the concrete turned out. Paulie told me the forms checked out and if your crew finishes the rebar placement today, fine with us if you pour. What's the pour size, one hundred cubic yards?"

"Yes." And Mike told Steve to order the concrete.

Ann was sitting in Mr. Shaffer's office when the RBO call for a hundred cubic yards of concrete came in.

"What will the Sugar Gang try with this order?" he asked.

She didn't see them trying the same trick again. Her concern was that weasel concrete inspector, but along as she made duplicate cylinders, she didn't see how he could hurt them. Tim will check everything again in the morning, and she would be at the pour site.

The project engineer, Terry, walked over to Ann as she exited the pickup. He had a number of questions about her background, family, and education. She was anxious to check the concrete, but decided taking a few minutes to develop a more friendly relation with the man made sense. As a result, she missed the morning's first two loads of concrete and had to sample the third load, which Paulie didn't sample. Instead of sampling the rest of the loads, he left. Therefore, she was not able to duplicate a Paulie's test cylinder for that pour.

Ann was busy making a test cylinder and whistling some unrecognizable tune when he ambled over to check the concrete pour. She gave him a friendly wave and inquired as to how his project was going and if he was on schedule.

"It's too early to tell. If I can start the reactor wall forms next week off this section of footings being poured today, then the schedule will be starting right."

"There's not much steel rebar sticking out of the footing, only enough to hold the water stop gasket that seals the wall stem from the basin floor. Is this some new design?" She asked.

"I'm not a structural engineer. All I can tell you is that is the amount of rebar the plans call for. Is there a problem?"

"Aren't the basin walls twenty-five feet high?"

"Yes, they are large aeration basins, twenty-five foot deep, forty foot wide and two hundred feet long. The walls are two foot thick. A lot of concrete, you should be happy."

Ann appeared to be in a good mood, but Mike sensed something was bothering her.

"I am. Shaffer Concrete appreciated that Norton and James decided on using massive concrete walls, but I'm curious about the design they used. Long walls of this type behave like modified cantilevers that required the transfer of a large tipping moment into the footing and floor. You know the typical L-shaped retaining wall."

She sensed he wasn't following her explanation and added, "The design always requires a lot of steel rebar between the wall stem and the footing. As you can see, there's no heavy rebar in this footing. Do you care if I checked the aeration basin design?"

"Not at all, I'll get you a clean copy of the plans from the office, while you finished the test cylinders."

She thanked him, went back to whistling and making another set of test cylinders from the concrete a Shaffer truck had unloaded into the massive footings.

The RBO's form crews had worked a week to finish the erection of the massive twenty-five foot wall section forms on the first footing. Mike planned to pour the wall section, four-hundred cubic-yards of concrete, on Monday. The big pour would ensure his schedule stayed on track. He had just finished a conference call between the aerator equipment manufacturer and the electrical contractor on who was responsible for installing the aeration equipment, when a smirking Terry barged into his office.

The project engineer tossed several sheets of paper on Mike's desk with the comment that his inspector was right. Shaffer's concrete was no good. The footing concrete had failed to meet the required strength.

"You'll have to tear out the footings and construct new ones. Use proper concrete this time. Shame you already have the wall forms built," Terry said. "They'll have to be removed."

Mike thought goodbye schedule, nothing good is going to come out of this, and to better grasp the extent of the concrete problem, asked Terry what strength Shaffer's duplicate cylinders had showed for the seven-day compressive strength.

"I didn't ask. Their cylinders don't count. Only cylinders made by an approved technician like Paulie count."

"Be nice to know if their cylinders failed," Mike said.

Terry clearly enjoyed delivering the bad news and jerking Mike's chain added.

"Things like this happen when a manager lets pussy mess up his mind. Call Ace and find out if they're willing to supply concrete. You need to keep the footing work going. No need to delay the project."

"Thanks for the insight. Now if you don't mind, I have work to do. Close the door on your way out."

Mike called his forming crew foreman, stopped the wall form construction on the first footing, and switched the crew to the next footing form. Next, he called Shaffer Concrete and asked for Ann.

"The footing concrete test cylinders broke at 1650 psi and will fail the twenty-eight day test. What did your test cylinders break at?"

"That can't be right. Paulie is messing up his test cylinders. Mine broke at 2600 psi. There is nothing wrong with that concrete."

Mike was irritated with Ann's angry response. "Do you understand how devastating a bad batch of concrete is? Removal of a previously poured footing and the erected wall forms will wreck my schedule. Not to mention the extra cost."

"I do understand. That's why I'm so careful with our concrete quality. That concrete is fine. You're a damn fool if you tear out the concrete footing because of that weasel's so-called test cylinders."

Though his future goal of buying RBO depended on the success of this project, he tried not to get mad.

"Wild accusations are no help," Mark said. "If the problem cannot be resolved, and RBO has to remove that footing because of substandard concrete, then the contract will go to Ace. I hope you understand that I can't afford to wonder about the quality of each concrete pour. Stopping the forming crews to wait on concrete test results would ruin my schedule. Unfortunately, that is exactly what has occurred."

"That concrete is not bad."

"Then prove it. The problem needs resolved, so instead of getting angry, figure out what went wrong. You're the expert."

Ann's temper threatened to explode. Couldn't Mike see that those bastard Woodbriers had managed to sabotage the concrete? She knew her concrete was good. Mike's harsh remarks had released the uncharitable thought that he was just taking the easy path. What was a third of a million dollars in savings to RBO and a rich guy like Owen? She struggled to control her anger and disappointment. What she said next would define their relationship going forward, and Ann paused to collect her thoughts. Her hope for buying Shaffer depended on the RBO business. Somewhere, she found a calm voice to explain the first step toward resolving the problem.

"I need, or better, the *lab* needs to examine the failed Paulie test cylinders. Are they available and where are they?"

"I assume at Pittsburgh, but I'll find out," Mike said. He abruptly ended the call. Ann sat at her desk and wondered what exactly had the inspector done--slip in large dose of sugar?

Mike walked over to Terry's office, thinking so much for Ann and his relationship going anywhere good. He found Paulie in Terry's office.

"I want one of your test cylinders that failed," Mike said.

They laughed at his request and allowed they didn't think the lab kept the failed cylinders. First, a pissed-off Ann and now these jokers giving him sass. Mike was getting seriously irritated and felt his temper awaken.

"Standard procedure is for the lab to keep failed specimens for a period. Are you telling me that International Testing doesn't?"

"Beats me, who would want broken cylinders?" Terry said. Paulie looked happy.

"Aren't there cylinders for the twenty-eight day tests at the lab?" Mike asked.

Terry looked to the inspector who nodded, before saying, "Yeah, there are cylinders for the twenty-eight day test. Are you proposing to waste three weeks waiting to see if those cylinders pass?"

"I'm going to discuss the problem with International Testing and ask their opinion on the reason the concrete was weak."

"Suit yourself. We get paid setting or inspecting," was Terry's indifferent response and propped his feet on the desk while lighting a cigarette. Paulie, unlike his boss, suddenly didn't appear so smug.

Mike thought *what a worthless bunch.* As he turned to leave their office, he realized the inspector's trailer was turning into a pigsty. The waste cans and ashtrays overflowed. Tracked-in dry mud coated the trailer floor. The contract required RBO provide Norton and James an office as part of the contract requirements. Still, RBO owned the trailer.

"Clean this mess, instead of setting on your butts. It'll be a damn health hazard in another week," Mike said.

"We're not janitors. You want it clean, get a broom," Terry said.

"You need to read the contract. Norton and James are responsible for maintaining the office in clean condition and to RBO's satisfaction. You don't want to clean up your mess, fine. I'll ask Mr. Norton for his suggestions. I'd be happy to clean it and bill you." Mike had the satisfaction of annoying the two lazy pricks.

The person he spoke to at International Testing told him the Norton and James inspector had given them permission to dispose of cylinders after the test, so they didn't have the failed cylinders. They would be glad to break one of the other cylinders and save the pieces, if Norton and James gave their permission.

Sitting at his desk, he considered his options for resolving the matter. Clearly, Terry would be no help. Ann was the only one on the project that was actually knowledgeable about concrete. He suspected Paulie and that jerk Terry knew even less than he did about concrete mixes. Ann, even factoring in her conflict of interest, was the person who could best resolve the cause of the failed test cylinders, and mad or not, it was in her interest to resolve the problem quickly. He called her back, brought her up to date, and asked what she suggested.

Ann's business like-tenor pleasantly surprised Mike. She suggested the lab break one of those test cylinders waiting for the twenty-eight day test and then perform a petrographic examination of the cylinder fragments. That microscopic exam would help identify the minerals in the cylinder's concrete. If the lab thought something looked suspicious, tell them to supplement the petrographic examination with a chemical analysis. Those steps would determine why the test cylinder was weak.

As for determining if the concrete footing meets specification, have the lab obtain a concrete core sample from the actual footing. She knew that International Testing normally had a crew available that could drill and test a concrete core in one day. Ann would also give the lab one of Shaffer's cylinders for comparison.

"What kind of money are we talking about?"

"I figure with the core work, total cost will be around two thousand dollars. I'll pay if the concrete is at fault. You pay if Fearless Paulie messed up. Okay?"

"Sure, only it will be Norton and James who pays, not me. I assume I have to make the call to International Testing to request these tests?"

"Actually the project engineer should, that worthless bum Terry."

"Okay, I'll keep you posted."

Mike went in search of Westfield while marveling at the difference in the attitude between Ann and the project engineer toward resolving the problem. He found him smoking by the footing with the questionable concrete. Mike relayed her information on the tests that Terry needed to request from the lab in order to resolve the cause of the weak concrete. He then asked him to call the lab and instruct them to perform the tests.

Mike's request annoyed Terry, and he turned uncooperative, refusing to authorize the tests or make any calls. The first excuse was Norton and James project inspection budget wouldn't cover the cost.

"Why bother making test cylinders," Terry said, "if every time something doesn't turn out as expected, RBO wants me to spend more money to prove the test cylinder results were wrong."

"Listen, pal, tearing out that footing will cost a fortune. I'm not willing to do that without some additional proof the concrete is bad. I don't share your faith in Paulie's expertise."

"He has been testing concrete for years," Terry said. "You caused the problem with your choice of an inexperienced outfit."

"I've had enough of your dismissive attitude and convoluted reasoning. I have a plant to build, and I'm not waiting three weeks to resolve the matter when it can be resolved this week. Call the lab, or I'm calling Dennis Norton and telling him I want a project engineer interested in getting the project built, not in who supplies the concrete."

Mike knew from Terry's concerned and alarmed look, he had finally connected with that threat.

"Wait a minute, I meant I don't have money for the tests. If I did I'd do them."

"Shaffer Concrete batched bad concrete or Paulie messed up, so who ever made the mistake pays for the extra test cost. Time is wasting. Make that call."

Terry made the call and International Testing promised preliminary results by the end of the next day. A crew to take the core sample would be on site by 10 A.M. Paulie had vanished. Mike later called Ann to advise her about the scheduled 10 A.M. footing core. She was welcome to watch. He then told her the lab had requested one of her duplicate cylinders. Sounding relieved, she told him she'd have the cylinder at the lab in Pittsburgh before they closed today.

After his son's call that evening on the possible bad concrete in the footing, Mr. Owen decided to make a quick visit to the site in the morning. He was aware Shaffer's concrete tech was very pretty from meeting her during the prebid conference and that his son wasn't blind. Now with concrete failing test strengths, he needed to talk to the parties in person and form his own opinions.

He was on the road at 3:30 A.M. and in Shaffer's parking lot at 7:45 A.M. in his black Cadillac Escalade, feeling stiff and old as he got out. He went looking for Mr. Shaffer and found him in his office with Ann Lane, his concrete tech, and an old hound.

She was quick to recover from her surprise at seeing him and jumped up to shake his hand while introducing him to Mr. Shaffer. Everyone exchanged greetings.

"Are you here concerning the failed compression strength test yesterday?" Mr. Shaffer asked.

"Yes and several other items I wish to clear up on this trip. My interest here is the story on the concrete. Why did it fail?"

Ann thought. *Don't disappoint this man with excuses.* Mr. Owen declined the offered seat, and remained standing. Ann also remained standing and proceeded with her formal explanation. The cause of the Norton and James test cylinder failure has not been determined, but should be by early afternoon. The confusion regarding the quality of the footing concrete was from their test cylinders passing the seven-day compression strength test, and the Norton and James test cylinders failing. If both sets of cylinders had failed, clearly bad concrete was the cause.

She explained how the matter would be resolved and concluded her explanation by telling Mr. Owen the core drilling would start, 10 a.m., if he wanted to watch.

"How much will all this extra testing cost?"

"Two thousand dollars. The deal with your son is I pay if Shaffer is at fault, and Norton and James pays if their inspector messed up. Mr. Norton may not yet be aware he's paying if Paulie messed up."

Mr. Owen recognized that the young lady had set forth a concise summary of the issue that had the solid ring of nothing but facts. He was impressed.

81

"Thank you, Ms. Lane, for the explanation. I hope the problem is the inspector, and the concrete proves to be fine. I need to head to the site now. Nice meeting both of you. Good morning."

Steve was surprised when the owner walked into the office trailer and asked for his son. Mike was surprised and pleased when his father walked up to him at the Basin No.1 footing. He was watching the forming crew from the high wall-form construction get started back on building more footing forms while they awaited a decision on the footing concrete.

"What brings the big boss out to our muddy site at 9 A.M.? You must have gotten an early start," Mike said.

"I was worried that bad concrete might wreck your schedule. I see you are switching the crew, which is better than just standing around. Is International Testing's crew on site?"

"Man, you're well informed for just arriving on the site. How did you know about International Testing sending a crew? Did Mr. Norton call you?"

"No, I stopped by Shaffer Concrete first to hear his side of the problem. Only it was a she that explained the bad concrete issue and your deal with her."

"You did get an early start. How did Ann do explaining the issue?"

"I was impressed. I wish my four hundred dollar an hour lawyer was equally capable at explaining problems and issues. It's a shame she's so homely."

Mike had to laugh.

"Right, I have a hard time not staring at her. I'll be very surprised if Shaffer's concrete proves to be bad, but we'll know by the end of the day. There's the testing crew and Ann's behind them."

International Testing's well-organized crew had a neat four-inch diameter by eight-inch-long cylinder of the footing concrete by noon and on their way to the Pittsburgh office. Paulie was looking morose as he watched the drilling of the core.

Ann on the other hand seemed very satisfied with the core. She had charmed his father for the half hour they watched the footing core drilled. She was full of humorous stories about the adjustments required by a country girl raised on a hog farm going to live on Purdue's large campus. She cracked a few jokes about Ohio State engineers for Mike's benefit.

Mike's father asked him for a quick tour of the rest of the site before he left for Columbus. During the site tour, Mike made a point of introducing his father to Terry Westfield, Paulie, and Pine Tree's foreman, Jake. He figured his father would notice Terry and Paulie's sleazy demeanor and be better able to judge future conflicting opinions that always arose during large construction projects. Mike also realized Ann had done a brilliant job of selling herself to his father. What that effort might portend for their future relation, if anything, he didn't know.

After seeing his father off, Mike had gone to the project engineer's trailer to find out if the lab had called. He arrived with the lab's call to Terry, who put the call on the speaker so both could listen. The lab technician told them the next Norton and James test cylinder broke at 1600 psi; more or less consistent with the earlier breaks and the Shaffer cylinder broke at 2850 psi. The core sample broke at the equivalent of 2800 psi, which indicated the footing concrete would easily obtain a 3500 psi twenty-eight day strength. The lab technician went on to say the Norton and James cylinder had unusual amounts of siliceous gel present that would explain the low compressive strength. Normally, this condition occurred in concrete mixtures using large amounts of recycled glass, but no glass was present. His best guess was amorphous silica had somehow gotten in the test cylinder, perhaps through improper storage. A full written report would follow.

Terry said, "Apparently, Paulie didn't use clean test cylinders."

"Or he sabotaged the test cylinder on purpose by adding some type of silica material. You need to replace him. I'm willing to allow the issue to drop if you pay for the extra tests and replace Paulie."

Terry looked stricken, and holding his head, he leaned forward against his desktop and explained his problem complying with that request.

"Paulie's my boss's son-in-law. I can't just fire him."

"I don't care whose son-in-law the jerk is. He has to go. If nothing else, put him some place where he is not involved with sampling or testing. And you two need to think about for whom he's really working. It sure isn't Norton and James."

Mike was just starting to call his father when Steve told him the consultant was on the other line. Mr. Norton was not happy.

"I don't appreciate contractors telling us how and who can inspect their work. Clients hire consultants to assure substandard workmanship doesn't occur. That construction is according to plan. I can't do a proper job if my inspectors are harassed and run off every time a contractor disagrees with the test results. Paulie's staying as the concrete inspector."

"No, Mr. Norton, he is not. I have to assume you have been ill informed about the reason for Paulie's removal from inspecting anything on the project."

"You don't remove an experienced concrete inspector because he accidentally used some dirty test cylinders."

Mike did not understand their resistance and said.

"International Testing was just being polite. Someone added amorphous silica to that test cylinder. Whoever added it had to do it during the filling of the cylinder. Your inspector filled that cylinder."

"You have no proof. Paulie assures me he did nothing wrong. Terry tells me he is needed because of the inexperienced concrete supplier."

Maintaining a civil tone with Mr. Norton had become a challenge.

"You should be concerned why your inspector did that. He is the threat to the project's concrete quality, not Shaffer Concrete. Refuse my request and I'll exercise my right to appeal the decision to the Meadville Board. I want a meeting with the full board or Paulie gone."

Mr. Norton was angry and not used to challenges from a contractor. He told Mike that he was not pulling Paulie and would notify the Board that RBO had requested a meeting to discuss personnel matters on the project.

Following his call with Norton, he called Ann back and asked her to come by the office in the morning. She agreed. He then called his father and advised him that the core and cylinder tests show the concrete was good.

"I don't know whether it was sabotage or incompetence on the inspector's part, but I asked Mr. Norton to remove Paulie as the concrete inspector. Norton is fighting the request, so we have a meeting with the Board scheduled for Tuesday to resolve the matter."

David C. Brown

## Chapter 5

The next morning Ann arrived with a box of donuts. She was in a cheerful mood and a delightful sight, her hardhat tipped back on her head. Mike half expected another Ohio State joke from her, but instead she turned serious and thanked him for helping to verify their concrete wasn't the problem. He assured her he was confident she would have done the same for him had the table been reversed.

He was considering whether to make known his relief over not being on opposing sides of a defective concrete cost-assessment dispute, when Steve's dog intruded with a sniff of Ann's leg, catching her attention. The mutt's breed was a mix of Labrador retriever and coonhound. Mike reckoned the friendly old mutt had learned that human personalities tend to occur in three broad categories with respect to dogs: kindhearted, malicious, and apathetic. The stray had recognized Steve was an easy touch.

"Who's dog?" She asked, bending down to greet the elderly black mongrel with a gray muzzle, which caused its tail to wag madly.

"He was hungry and friendly so I gave him some food. I don't know who he belongs to," Steve said.

"He is a nice dog. He doesn't jump or bark. Anyway, what can I do for RBO?"

Before answering, Mike explained Steve had a weakness for stray dogs.

"On the last three projects, Steve has managed to attract a stray dog. He ends up taking the dog home, although one ended up living at the Columbus office. But back to business, Mr. Norton has taken exception to my demand for Paulie's removal. We're asking the Board to resolve the matter. I need your help to fully understand the cause of the bad cylinder in order to explain it to the Board members."

Ann was enthusiastic over Mike's willingness to fight for Paulie's removal and offered her help.

"The bad concrete will be easy, but something else needs to be addressed with Mr. Norton. Remember I was asking about the steel sticking out of the footing the other day?"

Mike nodded. Steve paused in eating his donut. Ann had their attention.

"Well that basin wall detail only shows a single mat of number four-rebar on eighteen inch centers, both directions. Not to bore you with retaining wall design, but unless Norton and James has discovered a new and miraculous method to reinforce concrete, those walls will collapse as soon as they are loaded. They are completely unreinforced. Someone made a major design mistake."

"Show me on the drawing."

Sure enough Ann was right, no rebar, and Steve and he had both missed the error. That mistake meant the cost for the rebar wasn't in RBO's bid, and since a lot of rebar was missing, the cost would be high.

"Don't pour anymore footings. They lack the necessary vertical reinforcement to tie the wall and floor together structurally," she added.

Mike could kick himself for not noticing the missing rebar. Now change orders to the contract will be necessary. How Norton and James would respond was anyone's guess. The missing rebar effectively halted the project until the matter was resolved. He called

Terry. While they waited for the project engineer to arrive, they had donuts and coffee, though the mutt passed on the coffee and just had an extra donut.

Terry was in a foul mood and, on entering RBO's office, exclaimed, "What she doing here?"

"That's not your concern. What I want to know is why the basin wall detail doesn't show any reinforcement. Who is going to pay for RBO's crew downtime while Norton and James corrects their design mistake--and pays for the current footing removal?"

Surprised by the information, the engineer rushed to the drawing table and examined the wall cross-section detail. An irritated Mike fumed over his rude behavior towards Ann.

"What are you talking about? There's rebar shown."

Mike was astonished at the lack of Terry's structural knowledge revealed by that remark.

"I don't claim to be a structural designer, but even I know the rebar shown couldn't reinforce a sidewalk. This is a twenty-five foot high wall supporting equipment, retaining twenty feet of sewage water, and earth-fills. That wall is not a sidewalk slab. So what do you suggest?"

"Questioning another engineer's design is unprofessional. If you didn't like the design, why did you bid the job? My responsibility is to follow plans, not analyze them."

Mike could see Ann was having difficulties not commenting on the man's outrageous remarks and mind-set.

"What about our duty as engineers to protect the public? Are you going to advise Mr. Norton of the problem?" Mike asked.

"No." Terry stormed out of the office.

"Well, at least the jerk didn't take that last cream-filled donut," she said, "Though I'm amazed by his behavior."

"Steve, check on Westfield's engineering license, while I call Norton."

Ann's information so surprised Norton, he was actually civil. The consultant promised he'd immediately check the drawing and call him back.

In the meantime, temptation won and she scarfed the last cream-filled donut, her second one. While they waited for Mr. Norton's returned call, she offered that RBO needed to find a bright engineering student to help keep an eye on their worthless consultants this summer. Mike agreed.

"You're right. We messed up. Thanks for discovering the problem before the wall was poured," Mr. Norton said.

"Ann Lane is the one who discovered the problem."

"Is she RBO's engineer?" Mr. Norton asked.

"No, she is Shaffer Concrete's engineer, and she advised me this morning of the problem."

"She's the one Paulie complains about. Can I speak with her?"

"Sure. Ann, Mr. Norton would like to speak with you."

Shen gave him a questioning look, before taking the offered phone. The conversation lasted for about ten minutes with many comments on transfer of moments, shear, lateral reinforcement, and load factors. She was smiling at the conclusion of the talk as she handed the phone back to Mike.

"She is one knowledgeable young engineer. Forget Paulie. He's history. I'll have the drawings corrected by the end of today. You figure the added cost. We'll take it Tuesday for approval. Ask Ann to attend. I would like to meet her. Will this resolve the issue?"

"There's the existing footer without the rebar. It'll need removed and replaced. Who's paying RBO for that?"

"Crap . . . I'll work out something. Just remember you're an engineer and ought to have caught the mistake. Charge only your extra cost to replace the footing. No profit."

"We'll see about that, in the meantime I'll be looking for the new rebar information."

"Mr. Norton seems a lot nicer than I thought he would be," Ann said.

"You're right. Yesterday he was an unreasonable asshole. Now he's worried about the missing rebar and lawsuits. I wonder which one is the real Norton. He requested your presence at the Board meeting."

"Sure, I'll go. I've wanted to attend one of their meetings. They have a fair amount of concrete business over the year, which all goes to Ace now. I'll ask them to consider bidding next year's work." She added on noticing Mike's concerned look, "Only if your business goes okay. I won't stir the pot until they approve RBO's change order."

The Woodbrier brothers met at Sam's private office located over the four-car garage at his Conneaut Lake home.

"Paulie got himself fired," Sam said. He filled his brother in on the details of the testing lab's discovery of the silica gel. Then the Shaffer girl discovered Norton and James's mistake in their wall design in time to correct it.

"She's a hero with everyone. Shaffer is golden. We can forget about having them removed as RBO's concrete supplier."

"We should have hired her. So now what," Lou asked.

The brothers sat in thought for several minutes with their cigars and coffee. The issue they contemplated was how best to obtain, without paying a fair price, control of Shaffer's mining permit and the ten-million tons of gravel reserves located under his property. Their options were to eliminate his engineer-manager, pay a fair price, or find and permit another gravel deposit.

Sam knew his brother favored eliminating the Lane woman, but he harbored concerns she might prove to be a dangerous adversary. He reminded Lou they were wealthy, with much to lose if they ended up as defendants in a murder trial.

"Perhaps the prudent course is reining in our greed."

"Rein in, are you going soft?" Lou asked.

"That's right, brother. Our greed is going to trip us up someday. Why not pay a fair price. Hell, we could even hire her to run it. We'd still make plenty of money with no legal exposure."

"Not as much as we could without them. Paying fair prices. . . What's with you today?"

"Don't forget, Owen, word is he's getting interested in her. He could cause a lot of trouble." Sam added. "The Pine Tree air-duct deal is pending."

"Yeah, well, maybe he needs to be a suspect in her demise. It would make Jake's job easier."

"Did Sal have any suggestions? He comes from a long line of murderers."

Lou brought his brother up to date on his plan. Sal had set up a meeting with a Russian who could provide the services they sought. Sal would vouch for each party's identity to alleviate concern of a sting operation.

"How's Sal's attitude?" Sam asked. "Still on your case?"

"Yeah, he brought it up after all these years. Makes no sense. How many people has Sal popped? I know of three."

"Sal lost a baby daughter shortly after that. He's Catholic. Maybe he felt God punished him for his involvement. He told me once that not offering to take the baby was the most shameful thing he'd ever done."

"You're joking, the same Sal that gutted Albert over the shortages? Superstitious fool, there's no God, only luck and might. I should have wrung her neck."

"Christ, don't talk that way," Sam said.

"The meeting is scheduled next week, since we don't have the luxury of time. My goal is to arrange a plan for the prompt elimination of the girl. Then force the old man into a distress sale."

"We tried a similar approach a year ago and thought the problem was solved. Then she showed up. Is she a random consequence or a warning not to tempt fate again?"

Sam's remarks made Lou laugh. He jokingly asked if he'd been sneaking to church with Sal. Then, when his brother didn't answer, while gathering his hat to leave, Lou added, "You had best hope I'm right that there's no God or Hell. I'll let you know how the meeting went with the Russian. Then we'll make a decision."

After his brother left, Sam contemplated the consequence of their professed wish for no God. It meant no hope for salvation, only death and the end. He'd always believed that you were either the hunter or the prey and right and wrong depended on the situation. Power defined your worth and place in society. Did that make him a bad person in God's eyes? Wasn't that the way nature worked, survival of the fittest?

Sam knew it was too late to change and start worrying about their behavior, but lately he found himself wondering about whether such a thing as an immortal soul and God existed. He watched the boaters having fun out on the beautiful lake through his office window. How had they managed to arrive at the need to murder a beautiful and talented young woman for some sand and gravel?


The Meadville Board meeting was on the second floor of the Crawford County Annex building. The five-member board sat behind an oak table at the front of the room with their secretary-recorder to the right with her own desk. Mike admired the Board's heavy oak table while wondering about its age and weight. A wall clock and an old slate board graced the wall behind them.

Mike knew from the bid opening the Board members were a surprisingly diverse group. The oldest member was a friendly engineer fighting cancer, Mr. Bear, who looked like a Scot who appreciated a good whisky. The youngest Board member, an attractive African American woman, was a full-time elementary school teacher. The balance of the board consisted of two middle-aged men and one woman of indeterminate ethnic heritage. Sorting out proper ethnic labels for people in America was getting complicated. The diversity of the board members implied a liberal progressive community that Mike believed was good. He looked about for Ann and Mr. Norton.

He located her in front of the room talking to Mr. Bear. She had finally forsaken her overalls and hardhat for a sheath dress that showed her shoulders, arms, and stopped a couple of inched above the knees. Mike realized this was the first time he had seen her in something besides work clothes. He wasn't sure as to the color of the dress Ann was wearing-- reddish, fuchsia, pink --but it complemented her hair and skin tone to perfection. The results left him astounded. He had known from that first meeting in Columbus that she was a striking woman, but the transformation that simple dress had made in her appearance was awe-inspiring. He couldn't take his eyes off her; then again, a quick glance around the room indicated no one else could either. Mr. Norton's entrance broke the spell.

"Hi, Mike. Have the change order ready?" Mr. Norton said and glanced toward the front of the room. "Oh my--don't tell me-- that's Shaffer's engineer talking to Mr. Bear."

"Yes, that is Ann Lane."

Mike and Mr. Norton went up to make his introduction to Ann and drop off copies of the RBO change order for the added steel rebar reinforcement to the basin walls. Ann came back to his seat and sat beside him. She smelled wonderful, a vanilla fragrance.

"You cut a spectacular sight in that dress Ms. Lane." Mike whispered, which earned him a smile.

Mr. Norton was an experienced performer in front of boards and commissions, but he still ran into heavy going explaining how the error happened. The Board wanted assurances his engineers had thoroughly reviewed all the drawings for other mistakes. He explained how a CAD system error had deleted the rebar layer in the final printing. After blaming the mistake on software errors, he extolled Ann for discovering the problem and introduced her to the room.

"The Board should be aware of what a talented engineer works for Shaffer Concrete and how focused she is on their project. We're all in debt to her for pointing out the oversight."

The compliment and room applause turned Ann a delicious shade of pink. The Board, after short discussion, approved the change order. After the meeting concluded the two female Board members came over to talk with Ann. Mike waited for them to finish; he had invited her out for a beer.

The bar was several blocks from the Annex. The bar-restaurant was similar to several Mike had noticed in Meadville, an old two-story residence in which the lower floor had been converted into a neighborhood bar-restaurant with several tables and a small kitchen in the back. This bar featured spaghetti and several brands of draft beers. The youngest patron in the bar when they entered was at least two decades older than Mike, but the atmosphere was friendly and welcoming. A ball game playing quietly on the wall mounted TV provided a peaceful background murmur.

They traded family information while having a cold beer. He learned she had two older brothers, a younger brother and sister. They were all Purdue graduates, except her sister who was a sophomore at Indiana University. Her mother was a math teacher, and her dad was a farmer on the 900-acre family farm. Her parents were Purdue and Ball State graduates. Mike was impressed with her family's education. The discovery she did not currently have a boyfriend or husband in her life delighted him.

Ann pried out of Mike he had two older sisters, Linda and Abby, both lawyers and married with kids. His father was a Penn State graduate, and his mom was an Ohio State graduate and lawyer. He had three nieces and one nephew: a small group compared to twenty some in Ann's extended family of Lanes. She learned he was staying in an older motel along US322 that rented rooms with a kitchenette unit.

Mike's desire to know this single woman better required he do something before the evening ended.

"I'm going to canoe down French Creek and do some fishing this Saturday. You should join me. I'll fix us a nice lunch."

Ann cheerfully accepted his invitation and told him Mr. Shaffer had bragged about the quality of the walleye pike in French Creek. She wanted to catch a couple during their canoe trip.

"They're the best fish for eating," she added as they parted.

Mike, amazed by how eager he was for Saturday to arrive, had a hard time finding sleep that night. He couldn't get Ann out of his thoughts.


Betty Deere, that freshman in education from Edinboro, had managed to obtain Jerry Woodbrier's cell phone number and had called accusing him of drugging and raping her.

"Betty, I'm not that kind of guy. Remember, all we did was talk about that magazine article."

"Yeah, I remember that, and you getting me a drink. Next thing I remember is waking up in my car with everything sore. You gave me roofies and raped me, you bastard."

"I'm sorry you think such nonsense, but I'd say you just drank too much or your date did something. I didn't."

Jerry, to his relief, quickly discovered Betty hadn't been to the police, and she had delayed having a doctor check her for several days. The examination was inconclusive and useless to prove a rape had occurred. She admitted that.

"You may get away this time, but I'm putting the word out about you so other students know you're a sneak and sexual predator."

Jenny Lowell's disappearance had made many of the students leery and Jerry couldn't afford her warning other students about her suspicions. He needed a lawyer to scare Betty into silence. To get a lawyer, Jerry had told his father about Betty's threats and lies. She was just a vindictive date who didn't like him dropping her for another woman. His father wasn't interested in his son's women problems, but he did okay Jerry using the company's lawyer to contact the Deere woman. The lawyer had called her and threatened legal action if she persisted in her lies and defamatory remarks. Jerry had heard nothing more from her.

The Syrian had called the day before inquiring if they had any new video. Jerry assured his best customer that a keg party on Seminole Drive was coming up that should provide an opportunity for more rape videos. Paul had his eye on two cute Allegheny College students, one named Lucy, last name not yet known, and Helen Smith. They planned to give the girls starring roles in videos.

The Syrian had a connection to several XXX bars in New Jersey. The smut dealer, who Lou had introduced them to, bought every pornography item Jerry and Paul offered for sale. He always paid cash. However, during the phone conversation, the Syrian had made clear that if they couldn't, or wouldn't, make a snuff video, he planned to take his business elsewhere. Jerry had assured the Syrian that he would soon have one. After hanging up on the Syrian, Jerry pondered the risks of a snuff video. Paul wanted to make one. Jerry was still working up the nerve, however if they did, he hoped that bitch Betty was the star.

Ann brought her boss up to date on last night's meeting, the concrete testing, and problems with the rebar, but not the planned Saturday fishing trip. She suggested he visit his friend Mr. Bear and ask for a chance to address the Board over bidding next year's concrete. Her boss liked that idea and promised to invite Mr. Bear to lunch tomorrow and get his thoughts on how best to approach the French Creek Sanitary Board. He cautioned her that the manager of the Board's current Meadville wastewater treatment plant was a golfing friend with Sam Woodbrier. She should expect resistance from the manager to her request requiring future ready-mix concrete supplies be bid.

Ann had another talent she didn't advertise; she was an accomplished shot with a pistol. Her father had given her a 45 APC Springfield Model 1911 pistol--not the fanciest semiautomatic pistol available, but a proven and dependable weapon. Her father worried about her living alone and wanted her to be able to defend herself. She had a Pennsylvania pistol carry license and kept the pistol in her purse or in a camera case in situations where a purse might raise questions.

The back gravel pit provided her a convenient place to practice after quitting time. Ann liked shooting fifty rounds at a session. She usually target practiced once a month. She could hit a paper dinner plate at fifty feet, seven out of seven shots, time after time. She would be a lethal opponent in a fight, if she could get to the pistol, but then that was the weakness in any self-protection effort. Her father's advice was to understand reaction is always slower than action, so she should minimize surprise by keeping her doors locked and staying aware of activity in her surroundings at all times.

The next morning Steve told Mike his father had called the previous day. Mike called him at 9 A.M. about the missing wall rebar that Ann had caught and told his father that the Board had already approved the change order. After his son had finished with his news, Mr. Owen relayed a request from the son of his old friend Bill Hopkins, who had died in a Kentucky plane crash. Hopkins had helped him survive the recession with a timely million-dollar loan in 1991. Bill's son, Mark, had a friend in the Purdue University physics program who was after a summer job in the construction industry, preferably one involving process equipment and structures. Their Meadville project would be perfect for Mark's friend, and Mr. Owen wanted to help by hiring the student, Frank Arthur.

"You know anything about the kid?"

"Only that he's 19-years-old and will be a senior in the Purdue physics program this fall."

Mike reckoned the kid could at least count, was literate, and might be helpful in keeping an eye on Terry. They agreed Frank would report Monday to the Meadville office. His father would handle getting word to Frank.

Meadville's weather tends to be partly cloudy or rainy, but occasionally blue sky made a passing appearance. Saturday was a lovely sunny day. *The weather and company could not be better*, Mike was thinking as Ann and he slid the canoe into French Creek at the Bicentennial Park public access in Meadville. Earlier they had left Ann's truck at Shaw's Landing. A boat access point about ten miles downstream, where they planned to end the canoe trip.

Pennsylvania rightfully considers French Creek an ecological treasure. The stream starts in the southwest corner of New York and flows through the northwest corner of Pennsylvania to the Allegheny River at Franklin, Pennsylvania. Mike knew from the geological information in the construction plans that the French Creek 800,000-acre watershed was a glaciated plateau created by the most recent glaciation period, the Wisconsin, just fifteen thousand years ago. The glaciation was also the source of the rich gravel deposits Ann used in her concrete.

"Did you know the creek has 27 species of mussels?" he informed his date.

"Like clams?" a surprised Ann asked.

"Mussels and clams are all the same thing to me, though I suspect mollusk experts wouldn't agree. Let's try to find one on the trip."

Ann was in the front of the canoe as Mike pushed off the bank and smoothly slid into the back seat. She cut an attractive sight in her blue runner shorts and top. *She is everything I could wish for in appearance. Please let our personal-chemistry mesh*, Mike thought, no he *prayed*, as he started paddling downstream.

French Creek consisted of a series of pools several hundred feet in length separated by short, swift rapid sections and bends. Some of the pools appeared to be ten to twelve feet deep, though algae limited visibility to five or six feet. Trees along the riverbank, undercut by erosion, had fallen partially across the stream, adding interest to the passage. The first part of the trip was through part of Meadville, then Kerrtown, past the old wastewater treatment plant, and under US 322 bridges that marked the end of the residential area. Next, they passed the new plant's construction area. Schools of large carp lazed just below the water surface in several pool areas. About a mile south of Meadville, in a shaded pool, two large Northern Pike watched them float by, more proof that French Creek was teaming with fish. Ann was eager to try her luck on the walleyes.

"Mike, let's stop above this rapid section and try for a walleye."

They brought the front of the canoe around and headed for a small beach area. As the canoe dragged bottom, Mike, then Ann, jumped out of the canoe into the cool water and, though slipping on some of the moss-covered rocks, they easily shoved the canoe onto the sandy shore. The small beach was a peaceful location. If Mike hadn't known better, he would have thought they were miles from civilization.

Mr. Shaffer's advice on catching French Creek walleyes was to use a weighted spinner with a worm and then cast the spinner so it landed where the fast current enters the next pool. The goal was to hold the rig where the current was still strong enough to spin the spinner.

Ann carefully baited the spinner hook with a large worm. To put her boss's advice into action she waded across the shallow above the rapids to the other side of the creek and cast her bait. To stay out of her way, Mike fished the other side of the stream channel. Mike saw her suddenly jerk her fishing rod and, smiling gleefully, waded back across the creek to Mike's location.

"I got something. Help me land it."

Her *something* was an eighteen-inch walleye. While she was admiring her fish, Mike got a hit and dragged in a ten-inch red-fin sucker.

"Now that's more like the fish we catch in Wildcat Creek back home. Are you going to keep him?" Ann inquired.

"No, I only keep what I'm planning to eat." Mike eased the hook out of the red-fin and released him in the creek.

They both baited again and went back to fishing for another fifteen minutes with no bites. Mike decided to float on down the creek and find another location that appealed to Ann. They alternated between floating and paddling for another several miles until they were a mile below Wilson Shute and found another spot that Ann liked. The creek made a concave curve at the bottom of the rapids and the current had undercut the riverbank, making a deep, shaded pool. Erosion had carved a ten-foot cliff in the creek bank, which was made of clay and sand-gravel layers.

Fist-size holes perforated the cliff face in which birds had built nests. The graceful birds zoomed back and forth across the water before returning to their nest holes. Mike ventured they must be some kind of swallows. Ann, after a careful look, declared the birds to be cliff swallows. Mike teased that she was just guessing because the birds were nesting in a cliff of sorts.

"Nope, mister big city boy, they have a squaretail. Barn swallows have a fork tail."

Ann waded across the creek for a position that allowed the current to sweep her bait into the undercut area of the bank. She had a hit within a minute of casting. She crossed back to his location for assistance in landing another nice walleye. Ann was glowing with her success in catching two large walleyes.

"My boss knew what he was talking about. Will you take a picture of the two walleyes?"

What a pleasure to find a woman who likes fishing and wading creeks. He couldn't help thinking of the contrast between women while positioning a radiant Ann so the sun was shining on her face and the walleyes. He snapped several pictures. He could never imagine Charlene wading creeks or baiting a hook with a live worm.

"Are you going to cook those fish?"

She was. He realized this magnificent woman was definitely the optimistic sort. She had brought a plastic bag and a sharp knife to clean and fillet the walleyes. Ann went to work cleaning and filleting the fish while explaining her plan to store the bagged fillets in the drink cooler ice while they finished their adventure. Later she was going to invite a handsome construction engineer to her humble apartment for dinner.

"Who's the lucky engineer?"

"Mike Owen. You heard of him?"

"Oh yes, but I heard he's not much of a fisherman, only catches suckers. Fresh walleye might be wasted on him."

"Maybe—but us Hoosier girls do try to enlighten Buckeye boys whenever we can. Good for neighborly relations."

Mike loved this repartee and they continued the banter as she cleaned the fish and expertly filleted them. She added they were not the only ones to benefit from her success. Raccoons were in for a treat, if they discovered the pile of fish guts before the crows. She cleaned the knife with sand from the creek. Mike realized this lady would be very much at home in a wilderness as he waded into the shallows above the rapids in search of a mussel-clam. He found one, about the size of a small moss-coated soup bowl and carried it over to Ann. He watched her examine the mussel closely and even take a sniff.

"Can these be eaten?"

"I figure if the clam was cooked, though the meat would probably be tougher than rubber bands."

"You think he has a pearl inside?"

Mike had read up on the freshwater mussels and told her fresh water pearls existed. The endangered Northern Riffleshell can form a pearl and lives in French Creek. As to which mussel was a Northern Riffleshell, and how many mussels would have to die to find a pearl, he had no idea. However, he didn't figure Pennsylvania would approve of killing a bunch of their endangered mussels to find a pearl.

"You're right. Murdering a handsome fellow like Mr. Clam here for a piece of calcium carbonate and conchiolin would be a crime."

Ann waded back into the creek and returned the mussel to the creek bed, while Mike laid out the lunch he had prepared. He wasn't sure how she would respond to his lunch after promising something nice. He had forgotten his promise to supply lunch, until this morning, as he was leaving the motel room, and ended up raiding his emergency ration stash in the room. Lunch was two cans of Beanee Weenees, two maple-favored moon pies, and two diet Pepsi's in a brown bag. Ann came back to the canoe and asked for her lunch, which Mike gave her. He was relieved when she laughed after looking in the bag.

"Man, this is quite a lunch. What's this---a spoon---why you thought of everything! Did lunch take long to fix?"

"I got up early to fix everything. I wanted lunch to be special. Something you would remember."

"You have indeed succeeded, Mr. Owen. The moon pie is a rare treat," she said and started laughing again before settling down to eat.

The dining area was a gravel bar where they had dragged the canoe. A piece of driftwood provided their seating, part of a large tree trunk worn and weathered to clean gray wood. Looking around the area they found numerous clam shells and several beer cans. *Why do people litter?* Mike wondered as he basked in the sun by his lovely lunch date.

The rest of the trip was equally enjoyable and they reached her pickup as the last of the light faded and stars were appearing along with the mosquitoes. Mike promised to email the fish photos to her by morning, as they parted after transferring the canoe to his truck at the Bicentennial Park.

Back in his motel room, he downloaded the pictures and emailed them to Ann. Several minutes later, he received an email invitation to lunch the next day, Sunday, at her apartment. He accepted by return email.

Mike recalled at the last moment that a small gift might be appropriate for a woman who invited you to her home for dinner. He stopped at the Giant food store and purchased a small bouquet of cut flowers.

Ann's apartment was the upper floor of an old two-story house off Henry Street in Meadville. It was in serious need of a new coat of paint and the gutters needed repaired. The neighborhood was near Alleghany College, and though rundown, it appeared to be a safe and peaceful area. Henry Street was another old brick street in need of some tender loving care. Tree roots and leaking sewers had created a series of speed bumps and ugly concrete patches. The curbs, cut sandstone pieces, had deteriorated from years of weathering and salt. Repair of the brick pavement and sandstone curbs would certainly enhance the neighborhood and might encourage the residents to repair their homes. The realization that none of these steps were ever likely to occur in the old neighborhood made Mike pensive.

She lived in an upper floor apartment that required climbing a long, enclosed, and dark stairwell. The apartment had an old wooden door with a spy hole. Ann greeted him at the door in a yellow sundress that was every bit as attractive as that fuchsia dress she had been wearing the other night. His flowers were a hit. That girl looked great in dresses, he concluded, while examining her apartment for additional insight into Ann's personality.

Her apartment had a mudroom with a washer and dryer in the first room to the right where she kept her boots, work jackets, hardhat, and coveralls. The larger room was a kitchen at one end and living room-TV room at the other end. The bedroom was off the kitchen with a bathroom between the mudroom and the bedroom. The rooms had the old-style windows and high ceilings with molding that Mike wished he could have seen new. Multiple coats of paint now obscured the ceiling's fancy scrollwork. The multiple glass panes that formed each window had waves and imperfections. Mike figured the panes were the original glass and the house had to be a hundred or more years old.

The furnishings looked new and the rooms very clean. Magazines and newspapers were neatly stacked beside a chair in front of the TV. Mike spied the *Wall Street Journal, Fortune, Barron, Civil Engineer, O, The Oprah Magazine, People,* and *The Weekly Standard*, and reckoned he was safe to assume she was a conservative business-type politically. Based on the several books shelved by the TV, Ann obviously liked history. Mike then examined the pictures she had sitting on various shelves while waiting for her to finish with her cooking.

"Who is the big guy in the army uniform?"

"That's my older brother, a captain in the Special Forces in Afghanistan. He'll be home within the month. The other pictures are my parents and younger sister and brother."

Her family was nice looking, which explained her attractive appearance. He idly examined the various books piled on shelves and the views from the different windows. The little kitchen table was set for two, with his flower gift in a vase for a centerpiece. The aroma from cooking was making him hungry.

"I baked the walleye and potatoes. The potatoes will be a few more minutes. For desert I couldn't find any Moon Pies, so I baked a blueberry pie, which I hope will be satisfactory."

Curiosity made him incautious. "Is the pie a Mrs. Smith or a Ms. Lane blueberry pie?"

"The canoe trip lunch made me realize I was in the company of a gourmet with--ah, *special tastes*--so I baked the pie from scratch using Mom's old recipe."

Mike was getting a bit uncomfortable with this turn in their conversation, but Ann was smiling, so he concluded she was just teasing him.

"I'm impressed. This is shaping up to be the best meal I've had in years. Is it ready?"

It was, and they ate. The fresh walleye was great and the baked potatoes with butter and sour cream complemented the fish. Part of the meal's enjoyment was watching Ann, a neat eater who daintily worked her way through the fish and potato, a small bite here, a quick dab of sour cream there, never dropping a speck during the process. It was a stark contrast to his place setting, which looked like a small bomb had exploded in the center of Mike's plate.

Her tabby cat had come out of hiding and was sitting on the floor watching her every bite. Mike took mercy on the poor cat and slipped it a piece of fish while Ann was distracted with serving the pie. The blueberry pie was wonderful. He had two pieces.

Afterward they sat at the table and talked shop, deciding during the course of their discussions to push the basin construction hard over the ninety days. The basins represented 80% of the concrete demand, which along with the concrete required in the adjoining utility work would consume 95% of the project's 15,000 cubic yards of concrete. A rapid completion of the project would help him meet his father's conditions for buying RBO and remove the employee-employer stigma troubling him with Ann. Winning Ann's good opinion was rapidly elbowing aside his original and only goal of making the 10% net profit requirement in his father's agreement for selling RBO.

During the course of their after-lunch discussions, he told her a young Purdue student would be starting Monday for summer employment. Ann wanted to know the student's background. He told her the student was a nineteen-year-old boy from West Virginia who had completed his junior year in the Purdue physics program.

"How did you find him?"

Mark explained the family connection through the son of his father's old friend and banker, though his father's friend had been more in coal investments than banking. His father had asked him to make a job for the student and he did.

"Wonder why a physics major would want to spend a summer working on a sewage treatment plant?" Ann said.

Mike added that Frank was also pursuing an engineering degree and likely wanted the experience. She started cleaning off the table, and he helped her by drying the dishes and taking out the trash. The afternoon ended. For a mad moment, Mike wished some magical event could occur to allow them to spend the rest of the day in her bedroom. But the magic failed to appear--nothing happened. He thanked her for a wonderful meal and left without a kiss.


The apartment felt empty after Mike left. Ann sat petting her tabby cat, thinking. How far should she go to satisfy her desire to know everything about him? What was proper? She worried he might think she was just trying to get more concrete business. Did Mike have any strong feelings for her? She enjoyed his company and wouldn't be adverse to a more physical relationship, but feared making a wrong gesture that might give him an erroneous impression.

He liked those old Victorian houses. Maybe she should ask him out next weekend to show him that beautiful, old, abandoned red brick farm house with eighty acres of land she had found just north of Venango. A property Ann was thinking about making an offer on.

Then she had an awful thought: what if Mike found out about that episode with Jerry Woodbrier? Guys like Jerry always ended up telling a friend, who in turn told someone else until every gossiper knew about it. She wouldn't care except Jerry would never tell what actually happened; he would be too ashamed to. He'll make up some tall tale that made him look good and might make Mike wonder about her probity. And why, after a year, had Jerry called and now wasn't returning her call? Ann's terrible mistake had been not calling the police that night.

What should she do? Her cat had no advice.

## Chapter 6

Ann breezed in at lunchtime to check on the status of the next concrete pour.

"Numbskull is out inspecting the first vertical wall form," Mike said. "After that, he promised to check the rest of Basin No. 1's footing forms. Assuming, always a dangerous thing, that all the forms pass inspection, Shaffer should plan on another five hundred cubic yards of concrete for Friday."

"Ah, are you referring to Mr. Westfield?" She asked. He nodded and smiling she added, "I'd hoped it wasn't the red-headed boy with Larry?"

"That's the summer intern from Purdue, Frank Arthur. He seems like a nice kid."

"What's his provenance?" Ann asked with a mischievous smile.

"What's his origin? I assume from some female."

"I deserved that for trying to upgrade an Ohio State graduate's vocabulary. I'll ask him directly."

Their laughing woke the black mutt in Steve's office. The dog padded in to check the disturbance. Ann petted it while taking notice of the dog's new collar, license, and rabies tag.

"Blackie you old cutie, your yellow collar goes well with your gray whiskers and you're all legal." Blackie's tail was a blur of motion as she finished petting him and left, throwing Mike a last smile and leaving a delightful scent in the room.

"Discover anything interesting about the kid, let me know. Don't forget the concrete for tomorrow," Mike told her back.

Larry checked in prior to quitting for the day.

"Mike, that summer intern is sharp. He actually knows Topcon equipment and how to layout. I want to start him on the CAD system. If he can tie fieldwork notes into the project's reference system and drawings, it would be a tremendous help."

"That's a lot of responsibility to put on a summer intern. Are you sure?"

"I will be tomorrow. I also want to start two layout crews. I'll use him on the simple layouts, like the pump station pit. That'll get this project rolling," Larry said.

The next morning Mr. Shaffer was teasing and pestering Ann. She had shown him the picture of the two walleyes.

"Who took the picture?"

"Mike did." She reached for the photo and Mr. Shaffer handed it back.

"Mike as in Mike Owen from RBO Construction?"

"Yes." The mutt nudged Ann's leg. It wanted out and she opened the office door.

"Nice looking walleyes. What did you do with them?"

"I ate them. They were delicious." Ann was starting to wish she hadn't shared the pictures with her boss.

"I know Walleyes are good eating. Those are big fish. Did you eat both of them?"

"No."

Mr. Shaffer, still looking at Ann's photo, smiled at her answer.

110

"Did Mike help you eat them?"

"Yes."

"Who cooked them?"

An exasperated Ann spelled it out; she had cooked the fish and invited Mike for lunch on Sunday, since he had invited her on the canoe trip that had provided the opportunity for her to catch the walleyes. It wasn't a date or anything, just a fishing trip between business associates.

"Of course, just business, I understand. I've only met him once. Is he a decent person?"

"Yes and very proper and fun to be around, not the typical rich man's son. And before you get any wild ideas, we're not dating. Besides I figure he has plenty of women in Columbus."

Mr. Shaffer reckoned he had pestered his beautiful concrete technician enough and told her to let him know if she would need any extra trucks on Friday. RBO had scheduled a huge five-hundred-cubic-yard concrete pour on Friday. After Ann left, he decided that his wife had it about right: there was a powerful attraction developing between his concrete tech and Mike Owen. He laughed at her apprehension that the Columbus girls were serious competition.

After assurances everything would be fine, the two surveyors cleared out of Mike's office. He then left to check the first large concrete pour, hopeful Ann might also be on site. Basin No.1 was a busy site. A crew was pouring wall footings, and another crew with a large concrete pumper was pouring the wall forms. The new Norton and James inspector and Ann were making test cylinders near the concrete pumper. The project engineer, Terry, was down by the footing pour, watching the activity and smoking. Mike headed over to meet him.

Terry, by way of greeting, commented on how much activity was required to place three hundred cubic yards of concrete in one pour. So far everything was on track, but Terry worried the wall crew was loading the forms too quickly. He reminded Mike of what Mike was well aware of, twenty-five feet of fresh concrete put a lot of pressure on the bottom form ties. If the form ties broke, allowing the forms to fly apart, the released concrete would make a royal mess.

"What cheerful thoughts, how is Shaffer's concrete today?" Mike asked as he looked again at the wall form.

"It's okay. Also Jake plans on installing electrical conduits and sewers tomorrow and needs grade controls first thing."

"I'll take care of it," Mike said and walked over to the wall pour and Ann.

Meadville's Italian heritage had resulted in a number of local pizza and Italian restaurants, and Mike planned to sample all of them over the summer. The Pizza Villa was this evening's choice. He ordered two slices of pizza with the sweet pepper strips. He had discovered the delicious sweet pepper strips at a local sub shop. While he waited for his order, he examined the other patrons and available places to sit. The place had very limited seating.

The indoor dining area had four tables with four chairs at each table. Three of the tables were full. A lone young woman sat at the fourth table reading a textbook while making notes between bites. An Allegheny student, Mike figured, and he asked to share the table with her. She gave him a brief smile.

"Sure, have a seat, Mr. Owen. I'll be done in a minute."

"Thanks, have we met?"

He slid the chair back from the table with his foot and flopped down while trying to recall where he might have met this woman.

"I'm Katie Gambone and help my father with the roll-off trucks. I've seen you at the sewer project."

"Okay, I met your father the other day. Is that a physics book? Are you studying for a physics test?"

Mike had a bit of pizza while she considered her answer. He had looked into a set of clear, dark, almost black eyes in a very attractive face. Her attire consisted of all-black, long-sleeve, loose-fitting sweats that effectively concealed the shape of her body. No hardware protruded from her lips, eyebrows, or nose, so perhaps her all black outfit did not imply a gothic life style. Her teeth were white and perfectly shaped. The Gambones had a nice, well cared for daughter, and his opinion of John notched up.

"Alleghany College requires their neuroscience students to understand basic physics," Katie said. "I have a final test next week."

"Physics gave me trouble."

"It's a challenge. I never quite resolve why a doctor needs physics."

Mike suggested that Alleghany might want graduates to understand physics in order to comprehend the concepts that their equipment and tools are based on, magnetic resonance imaging, for example. His comment caused another scrutiny from her before she nodded in agreement.

Two loud-talking men entering the order line distracted them and the other patrons. The larger of the two was a man that Mike estimated to be about his age and height. He was slightly sunburned and had longish, brown hair that was already starting to recede and seriously thinning on top. A heavy sloping brow, bushy eyebrows, and closely set gray eyes gave him a vaguely hostile look. He could have been a powerfully built man, but the cumulative effects from bad habits and lack of exercise had left him puffy and lacking muscle tone. Though from his aggressive demeanor, he still considered himself a tough man. Mike figured the guy had likely been one of those kids that were big for their age, had become accustomed to dominating their peers in school, and developed a bully's mindset. The thug looked familiar.

"How's the genius trash girl doing?" The big man had noticed Mike and Katie. A sly look crossed the thug's face. "You're wasting time with the queen. She's not into men."

"My dad's right. You can fancy it up, but white trash is still white trash," Katie said.

"Ah, a garbage truck driver's daughter calling someone white trash. What a joke."

"You still doping girls, Jerry? I heard Betty Deere reported you."

Katie's accusation wiped away Jerry's good-old-boy façade. A kid that had been waiting behind Jerry and his pal tried to slip around them in the line to place his order. The boy probably figured he was more interested in gabbing than ordering pizza. Jerry grabbed the kid's shirt and jerked him back.

"Wait your turn, punk."

Mike had only wanted to satisfy his hunger for pizza, not get in the middle of some local bad blood as he watched Jerry's pal, a squat troll, of a man rough up the kid.

"Hey pal. Go easy there. You'll hurt him," Mike said.

Jerry's pal threw the kid on the floor. Jerry walked over to Katie and Mike's table and asked if they wanted to do something about his friend's effort to maintain order. Mike had a slow-to-stir temper, though when finally aroused, his temper's ferociousness was difficult to control. It had caused him legal issues in the past, but not tonight. He was having difficulty taking the jerk's implied threat seriously. The guy reminded him of his sister's Shih Tzu fussing at him. The troll on the other hand looked dangerous. Their antics had ruined his appetite. Mike might as well rain on their parade, and fished out his cell phone while verifying with Katie that Meadville had 9-1-1 services.

"You're calling the police?" Jerry asked.

"Sure. They get paid to deal with morons."

That Jerry had no interest in talking to the police was obvious as he looked around the room at his hostile audience. He gave Mike a mute f-you, and told his pal they needed to find a place that served beer. He then hurriedly walked out the door.

The kid had a bloody nose. Katie went to him and wiped his nose, while asking if she needed to call his mother. The kid recovered quickly, didn't need his mother, and went on to order his pizza. Mike then asked who the jerk was. He was Sam Woodbrier's only kid and his pal was Paul Taylor, his cousin.

The next morning Steve handed Mike a note that Pine Tree Construction had called and was installing electrical conduit and sewers. The note reminded him of Terry's complaint regarding lack of survey control marks. He told Frank who was in the office to check with the foreman, Jake, and verify he has the controls his crew needed.

As Frank started to leave, Mike, wishing to help Pine Tree, instructed him to inform Jake that if he needed concrete to call Steve. Jake could avoid a partial load surcharge by adding Pine Tree's few extra yards of concrete to RBO crew's large footing pour. Frank acknowledged the instructions and hurried out of the room.

Frank found Jake at the sewer installation site and related his boss's suggestion. The foreman, a wiry older man with an evil-looking cigar clinched in his teeth, had a mood to match his cigar.

"Sonny, I'm not buying any of that crap Shaffer calls concrete so your boss can bang their concrete tech. If I need concrete, I'll call Ace."

Frank wondered where companies found jerks like Jake and who the concrete tech was as he started toward the north pump station excavation. He remembered the question on controls and turned back.

"Need any benchmarks, horizontal references?"

David C. Brown

"Are you asking if I have enough controls for this section? Where does RBO find you kids? Do you think my crew would be digging if they didn't have controls? If I need anything, I'll call."

Frank's earlier instructions from Larry were to over excavate the pit for the pump station about a foot and then use sand to bring the bottom of the excavation to final elevation-grade. The pump station was a massive concrete box that came in sections designed for stacking on top of each other, and the first or base piece would arrive in two days. Mike didn't want to handle the eighteen-ton base of the pump station twice, so Larry's orders to Frank had been to have the excavation ready for setting the base.

All the action and responsibility RBO's job required suited Frank just fine. The Pine Tree excavator operator, a young black man, was sitting in the cab of the excavator, waiting for instructions. The excavation needed to be twenty feet deep and had the potential to be dangerous from the excavation walls collapsing and burying a worker. Frank knew from his mining experience one proven way to avoid that danger.

"You've been digging in this material. Reckon a one-to-one slope will be stable for the walls of the excavation?"

"An engineer who asks an operator for his opinion, how refreshing, yes, Red, one to one will work fine in this sandy gravel."

"Thanks. Give me a minute."

The summer intern calculated the extra width needed to have a twenty-foot square bottom after measuring the ground elevation and some pencil scratching in the field book. The top of the hole would have to be a sixty-foot square, and that he told the operator required excavating fifteen hundred cubic yards of material and hauling it out of the way.

The one fifteen-cubic-yard rock truck assigned to the excavation will make for slow process. He walked back to where Jake was working and told him the excavator needed another rock truck hauling excavated material.

"Make the excavation walls steeper. That'll reduce the volume of the excavation that needs hauled. One rock truck is sufficient," Jake said.

"The excavation would be dangerous. It needs to be sloped back to be safe."

Frank noticed the rough irregular bottom of the trench the Pine Tree Construction crew had excavated. Three men were placing sections of pipe on pieces of rock and mud clods to bring the pipe bottom in alignment with the laser beam used to control the grade line. Jake, in front of the crew cementing the pipe sections together, had been busy piling up more rock supports at eight to ten-feet intervals.

Having read the pipe installation specifications, Frank knew a sand bed shaped to grade was called for under all pipe in order to cradle the pipe during covering. What Pine Tree was doing was all wrong. When the trench was backfilled, the pipes would sag and possibly break from the weight of the fill on the unsupported sections of the pipe between the piles of rock.

"Jake, stop what you're doing. That bedding is not spec."

"What's your problem, kid? First you over-excavate and now you're the expert on how to bed pipe?"

"It's apparent you're not. Take that pipe out and start over with a sand bed as required by the specifications."

Jake moved surprisingly fast and stopped a few inches away. In a threatening voice, he told Frank to go play with his Legos or whatever.

"Quit bothering men trying to work. Otherwise, I'll have to spank you and send you home."

Frank, amused by the threat, smiled and said, "Regardless, only correctly installed pipe will be accepted. That is not acceptable."

David C. Brown

The rest of Jake's crew had come up to stand with Jake. One of the younger laborers gave Frank a malicious look as he stepped in front of Jake.

"You talk tough for a kid. You better leave before you get hurt," the younger laborer said.

The big laborer, leaning on a shovel, told the young laborer, who he had called Jerry, to let Jake handle the inspector. Jake, thoroughly aggravated, snapped at the big laborer to shut up. Frank reckoned Jake had now pissed off the big laborer and the odds weren't so unequal. Frank set about stirring the laborers' animosity toward their foreman by explaining that the problem was their foreman's instructions.

"Jake has you installing the pipe wrong. Probably on purpose, in order to turn a job that should require twenty hours into an eight-hour project. Save Pine Tree a bundle and screw you guys and the sanitary board. Take a break while I find the project engineer."

The laborers were muttering among themselves. Jake and Jerry looked murderous as Frank walked off to find Mike and Terry. He heard Jake tell his crew to get back to work. Mike and Terry were at the footing pour talking to a remarkably fine-looking woman in coveralls, boots, and hardhat. Frank now understood whom Jake had referred to earlier.

"Excuse me, but Jake has a problem with the pipe bedding that needs to be resolved."

"Are you talking about him setting the pipe to grade and then adding the sand backfill for the bedding?" Terry asked.

"Yes, he's doing it wrong and going to mess up the pipe. The spec is very clear. The bedding is placed, graded, and then the pipe installed."

"Don't worry about it, kid. I've already talked to him. His method is okay, but I'll check later."

"What are you saying, Terry? You approved Jake's half-ass approach for bedding pipe?" Mike asked.

"I'm the engineer for the project, and I'll decide what is right. I don't want any more meddling in my decisions."

Mike knew a student questioning Terry's judgment had made him angry. But the project engineer had already repeatedly demonstrated his incompetence, whereas Frank appeared competent and honest.

"Frank, get the camera and meet us at the piping site. Hurry, Terry, let's go see this method. Ann, see you later."

Jake and a young laborer were waiting at the sewer pipe installation site. The pipe crew was unenthusiastically fitting pipe together behind them. Mike recognized the laborer with Jake was the man he had seen at the pizza shop, Sam's son.

Jake started whining to Terry that he had told the kid that was an approved bedding method. The kid wouldn't listen. The nonsense irritated Mike. Even Terry wouldn't have approved that crappy installation method.

Frank arrived with the camera. Mike told him to take a bunch of pictures showing the sewer pipes draped over rocks.

"Get Jake and Terry in the background of some of them," Mike said. "Terry, tell your fool of a foreman to either do the bedding in accordance with the specs or for him and his crew to vacate the site."

Instead, Terry told Jake to wait. Mike now knew something was seriously amiss with Terry and Pine Tree.

"I'm getting Mr. Norton on the phone and find out who's running this project. There is nothing wrong with that method of pipe backfilling."

"No, to the contrary, there isn't anything right about your method of backfilling and regardless, the specifications set the conditions of acceptable work," Mike answered, not bothering to hide his disgust.

Terry called the consultant's Pittsburgh office from RBO's office. While they waited for Mr. Norton to be located, Frank stuck his head through the conference room door a couple of minutes later and gave a thumbs-up signal. Several minutes passed until Mr. Norton answered the phone, and Terry launched a major bitch session. RBO personnel constantly questioning his authority was threatening to undercut his effectiveness in managing the project. Mr. Norton needed to put manners on Mike Owen and his minions. Mike could hear Terry's muddled and unpersuasive explanation of why the bedding method he had approved was fine. The fact that Mr. Norton was even listening to the absurd explanation added to Mike's bewilderment. Why did the consultant continue to tolerate such a pathetic example of a project engineer?

After several minutes and "Yes sirs," Terry smiled and handed Mike the phone. Mr. Norton, with no greeting, angrily assaulted him. He had already told him before he didn't appreciate contractors telling them how to inspect their work. Clients hire consultants to ensure a contractor didn't cheat and built the project in accordance with the plan, blah, blah.

"Was he clear on not harassing his inspectors, or did he need to get Mr. Owen involved?"

Mike figured Norton was the one who wasn't clear on the issue.

"Don't say another word until you check your email for three pictures I just sent. After you looked at them, we'll continue this discussion." Mike waited on hold for several minutes during which Terry became increasingly nervous.

"What am I looking at?" Mr. Norton asked.

Mike explained that he was looking at photos of his engineer's idea of pipe bedding, a rock every five to ten feet to hold the pipe to grade. He went on to ask Mr. Norton what he expected would happen when Pine Tree Construction dumps the backfill on the pipes. No response was forth coming from the consultant and Mike said.

"They'll sag and break from lack of bedding support under the pipes. I will not tolerate such inferior workmanship."

"You're right. This is a bit rough looking, not the best bedding I've seen."

"It's one more example of why I don't think Terry is capable of being the project engineer. This is a complex project. If you really believed this is acceptable bedding, and in accordance with your specifications, put your approval in writing and give the Board and RBO a copy."

"I need to talk to my engineer. I'll be on site tomorrow. Now let me have him back."

Terry, looking ill, took the phone and issued several "Yes sirs," after which he hung up the phone and stormed out of the room. Mike wondered if his behavior meant that Jake was going to fix the bedding and called Frank into the room.

"Thanks for bringing that mess to my attention. Check on Jake's crew and let me know if they are correcting the pipe bedding."

Frank called fifteen minutes later to report a second rock truck had arrived at the pump station excavation and Jake was correcting the pipe bedding.

Lou Woodbrier met the Russian and his driver at Sal Gambone's tree-trimming business garage in Monroeville near the Pennsylvania Turnpike exit. Sal's job was to guarantee that everyone was who they claimed to be and arrange their meeting in a safe spot. Today, that was Sal's Monroeville garage. With everyone satisfied concerning his arrangements, Sal excused himself and waited out on the lot in his car.

The Russian gangster wasn't what Lou had expected. A few inches shy of six-foot, maybe a hundred and sixty pounds, the gangster looked like a well-groomed American businessman. He spoke English better than Lou did and without a trace of a foreign accent.

Lou figured there was no need to beat around the bush.

"I need a young woman eliminated. The police need to believe her death was the work either of a random sex-crazy fiend or from her boyfriend's jealous rage. Can you help me?"

"Yes, I have just the person for the task. Of course, which scene happens will depend on circumstances. What is your time period for results?"

"As soon as possible and still do it proper. What period would you estimate is needed?"

"A few days will be required to arrange travel and brief him on the project. His English is not good and he will need a driver and car. Will that be a problem?"

"No, I have a driver."

The Woodbrier brothers had speculated on what a murder was worth now days. Lou, not in the mood to haggle, asked, "What's your fee? How's it to be paid?"

"It's twenty thousand dollars. Ten thousand dollars upfront, cash of course. The second half of the payment, another ten-thousand-dollars, on the day my man arrives in Pittsburgh. Sal will hold that payment for me. Should the boyfriend cooperate and we're able to take him down along with the woman, I want an extra five thousand dollars."

Lou muttered he was in the wrong business as he reflected on the Russian's price. He nearly told him to forget it, and then agreed.

On a more sober note, the Russian pointed out the obvious: murdering people can be dangerous work. Things can and do go wrong. If things did go wrong, he did not want his man arrested and talking to the authorities. Lou didn't either.

"I only know one way to assure a person doesn't talk. Is that what you're suggesting? I can be slow in understanding subtle messages."

"I believe we're on the same page, as you Americans say. Now do you have the pictures and background information on the two subjects?"

Lou handed over an envelope with pictures and information on Ann Lane and Mike Owen. While the Russian was studying the pictures, he counted out a hundred new hundred-dollar bills.

"They're an attractive couple. Put the currency in this folder. Who's the driver and contact?"

After stuffing the hundreds in the Russian's expensive-looking handbag, Lou gave him a picture of Paulie and a prepaid cell phone with Paulie's number programmed in the memory.

"Tell your man to call. My man will meet him," Lou said.

They parted and went their separate ways. As Lou drove west on the Turnpike toward I-79, he reflected on how damn expensive and complicated this method was compared to an old fashioned hit-and-run with a car. Tomorrow he needed to contact Paulie and get him on board as the driver. Lou was having second thoughts about the part of making sure that the Russian's killer didn't talk in the event things went wrong: That was asking a lot of Paulie. More money to pay, he will expect several thousand dollars for his troubles, especially if a killing becomes necessary. Lou mulled over his various options and commitments as he entered the tollbooth to exit onto I-79 north.

As he passed the Grove City rest area, he thought of that abandoned baby and Sal's censorious remarks. His business partner, Sal, was a hypocrite. Apparently helping to murder a twenty-something young woman was okay, whereas killing a month old girl was taboo.

## Chapter 7

Mr. Norton's scruples were flexible, but his work ethic was solid. Already on I-79 at 3 A.M., the corrupt consultant headed north out of Pittsburgh to Meadville for a 5:30 A.M. meeting with his project engineer. The traffic was light and he was at Terry Westfield's apartment a little after 5 A.M. knocking on the door. He wasted no time on pleasantries.

"Are you by yourself, no woman in the bedroom?" Terry nodded, pausing to light a cigarette.

"First, do you understand you're in this to the end?"

"I know. Lou has made that clear."

Mr. Norton wasn't confident his engineer did understand and elaborated that he shouldn't count on Sam and Lou Woodbrier giving people second chances.

"Those two prefer to eliminate problems. They're already in an evil mood over losing the concrete business to Shaffer. Let me have some of that coffee."

"But Paulie only did what Lou ordered," Terry said.

"You and I know that. Who knows what Lou thinks? However if Pine Tree doesn't perform as expected, we'll be held accountable."

Mr. Norton figured Terry did fear Lou, but as usual, his project engineer had been quick to blame others for his problems and start whining. His defense for yesterday's screw-up was that no one would have figured a summer intern cared about pipe bedding.

"If only Jake had given the kid some song and dance about the rocks being a temporary fix to check the pipe fit. Any nonsense probably would have satisfied him. But no, he had to insult the kid. Sam's son's big mouth didn't help."

"Jake's your responsibility, you recommended him for the job. Blaming him won't protect you from Lou's wrath. How do you drink this swill?"

Mr. Norton dumped the coffee in the apartment's kitchen sink while adding that Terry needed to get with the program and help calm concerns at the morning meeting.

"I'm worried that bedding deal will have Owen apprehensive. He might wonder if a scam of some sort was underway at the site."

"He's too green to figure out our plans for the air duct material."

"So you think. We need Owen's focus off Pine Tree's pipe bedding," Mr. Norton said. "Or air ducts. It needs to be on bedding the concrete technician."

"I wouldn't mind that goal," Terry said.

*Lord, how did this moron managed to graduate from an engineering school.*

"Jake needs to act contrite and you make sure he knows what contrite means. Some apologetic behavior on your part wouldn't hurt either. After the meeting on the pipe bedding, we'll meet in Pine Tree's field office to review the request for changes in the material specifications on the basin air ducts."

Sam Woodbrier had an opportunity to take advantage of a Russian supplier's deal on cheap chromoly pipe. First though, someone from Pine Tree needed to submit an "or equal" request to the Board for approval. Norton had the request ready for Jake to pass on to Terry, but first he wanted to make sure they understood their parts before making the submittal.

"The other item is a replacement for Paulie."

Terry had no suggestions, but offered to ask around. In closing, before walking out, Norton added, "I prefer RBO and Woodbriers not know of this meeting."

Mr. Norton wondered if his sure bet was about to explode. There was considerable money at risk in his deal with Lou Woodbrier. Their agreement was a kickback of five percent of Pine Tree's invoices or about four hundred thousand dollars. Out of that money, he had to pay Terry and several other people their cuts. He had originally hoped for a net of three-hundred-thousand dollars from the kickbacks, but now with Owen's suspicions aroused by Paulie's attempted sabotage of Shaffer's concrete and Jake's crappy bedding, he feared their swindle might fall apart. He thought of that old aphorism "The best laid schemes of mice and men go often astray."

Mike considered his options for protecting RBO's reputation and financial interest as he waited for the Norton and James personnel to arrive. Their behavior puzzled him, and he could not understand Terry Westfield's behavior at all. He had never encountered consultants or a project engineer who seemed so indifferent to quality assurance and control. Yet they were ready to throw Shaffer off the site at the first imagined problem and their own inspector almost certainty sabotaged the concrete test cylinders. Maybe the meeting would clear the air.

A cheerful Mr. Norton arrived first, and then Terry and Jake. Those two looked concerned. Larry and Frank were in the next room listening while preparing their field notes for the day's layout survey.

Mike wanted them available if needed. Steve would take notes of the meeting and sat beside him. The two guises of Mr. Norton's' persona had Mike leery. *Why would the consultant be cheerful at a meeting called to question the competence of Norton and James personnel? Well we will see how long the smiles last.* He brought the meeting to order.

After brief greetings, Mike expressed his concerns over Pine Tree's unacceptable workmanship the previous day on the pipe bedding and Terry's alarming defense of the clearly improper work. He realized a few subcontractors take short cuts, if allowed, and for that reason, he was not as alarmed over Pine Tree's attempted shoddy workmanship as he was over Terry defending it. His behavior had raised serious concerns over Norton and James's choice for a project engineer.

"I don't believe your project engineer has either the ability or desire to provide the necessary over-sight of the quality control and assurance required for this complex project," Mike said. "I'd like to hear your thoughts on your project engineer's performance and what you suggest to alleviate RBO's concerns."

Terry was beet red. The cheerful Mr. Norton was gone.

"The Meadville treatment plant is the third large project where I have used Terry as the project engineer. His first two projects finished on schedule and in budget, so I'm certain he has the desire and ability to be a satisfactory and effective project engineer. As to your concerns about Terry's alleged defective performance, part may be bad chemistry. Or maybe it's anxiety. This is your first large project. It's only natural that you worry, want a perfect project."

"You're suggesting my anxiety caused your engineer to defend Jake's shitty bedding. . ."

"No, no, that's not what I meant. Please, we all know that work was unacceptable and it was rectified. I'm saying, unless there is another specific defect to address at this meeting that in the future we all agree to try harder to work out issues as they arise. I'm sure Terry is willing."

"Mike, I admit I can be a bit abrupt, even unfriendly at times, but let's try to work together and make this a good project," Terry hastily offered in response to Norton's cue.

"He's right Mike. Give him a chance. However, Jake's workmanship yesterday was unacceptable. Terry will be on top of the work going forward."

"Mr. Owen, I promise Pine Tree will be extra careful in the future," Jake added.

Mike almost asked Jake if he meant extra careful in hiding his crappy workmanship.

"Have we covered your concerns, Mike?"

Placate, that was their goal. Mike realized that going forward the protection of the French Creek Board's investment and RBO's reputation would depend on him, not Norton and James.

"Time will tell. You're correct. I need to be specific in any future complaints. Thank you for coming."

They all shook hands and filed out of Mike's office. Mike watched Mr. Norton stop and introduce himself to Frank and remark on his excellent work yesterday of discovering the improper pipe bedding. He was asking Frank about being an engineering student when Mike quit paying attention to their conversation. He was now fully cognizant that Dennis Norton was a smooth operator and knew how to charm the opposition. Then he turned to tease Steve and lighten the mood.

"What a long meeting. Did you have enough paper for all those notes?"

Lost in gloomy thoughts, Ann halfheartedly tidied up the lab bench and desk, and tossed the rat a clean rag to use for its nest. Shaffer's business was booming, and the RBO project was adding an extra thousand cubic yards of concrete sales to the weekly total. She was pleased with the results from her efforts to win the RBO contract and the financial boost the new business gave the Shaffers. Her melancholy mood after accomplishing her goal was from a developing conflict regarding her future.

Ann had wanted her own business for as long as she could remember and now believed the Shaffers would sell their concrete business to her for just about any reasonable offer. Her problem was Mike Owen. He was nice and fun to be around. He was smart and attractive, and she was in love with him. She recognized her dismal mood was likely traceable to the potential dilemma of having to choose a career or love.

Ambition was a two-edged sword. When the RBO project finished next spring Mike would be moving back to Columbus to take over the family business. Shaffer's business depended on the gravel deposit and their established customer base in the Meadville-Franklin area. Ann could make a good living from the business, but Shaffer Concrete was a small business, and like all successful businesses, it required a full-time and committed management. She could hire a capable manager to run her business, and she could live in Columbus and provide oversight. But then she wouldn't be running the business, and because of Shaffer's small size, the manager's salary would take a large percent of the profits.

If only Mike was a local businessman or a professor at Allegheny College, then there wouldn't be a where-to-live issue. Ann suddenly realized she'd eaten six donuts while brooding over her dilemma. *Get a grip, or I won't fit in my jeans.* She pitched the remaining donuts from her desk, one at a time into the trash barrel. None missed. The rat arrived as the last donut landed.

Mike's thoughts about her were a mystery. Perhaps she was mistaken about the reason for his behavior, and he felt nothing more than an appreciation of her as a useful subcontractor that was saving

RBO several hundred thousand dollars. Ann dearly hoped otherwise and knew only time would resolve their relationship. She drove to the project to meet RBO's summer intern and catch up on Purdue news, maybe even see Mike.

Frank was at the north pump station excavation checking the elevation of the sand layer that formed the concrete base foundation pad. The next day Mike planned to install the pump station on the pad. It needed to be right. Terry and Jake were waiting for Frank's verdict when Ann walked up. He told them the elevation checked. Terry in turn told Jake to take his laborers back to the sewer bedding and call Frank when it was ready for inspection.

"Terry, what are you doing? Throwing your responsibility to verify Jake's work on Frank?"

"Pine Tree is RBO's sub, not Norton's. The kid's providing controls for their sub."

"Doesn't the Board pay you to independently verify the contractor's final elevations?"

"You worry about concrete, I'll worry about elevations. And for your information, my responsibility is to check the pump station elevation when it is finished. I don't provide construction layout, which is what the kid is doing," Terry said. He ground out his cigarette and stormed off.

Ann folded the tripod while Frank packed the level in its case. She carried the tripod on the walk back toward the office, and cautioned Frank on letting Terry off the hook with his checking of Pine Tree's work.

"Terry was correct today. I misunderstood what you were doing. I'd apologize if he wasn't such a jerk," Ann said. "Just you remember working with Jake's crew is fine, but don't confuse that with the final certification measurement and taking responsibility for approving the final work. That's Terry's job."

Frank understood and thanked her. She learned his goal was a PhD in physics to go with his engineering degree. He planned to focus on muon-catalyzed fusion of deuterium research.

"Muon. . . Is that the heavy electron?"

"Yes. Do you like physics?"

"Not really, I suffered through it to get my degree. Why are you working construction, for the engineering experience?"

Frank explained his desire was to broaden his knowledge of construction before settling into the four-year PhD program, and Mike had been kind enough to give him that opportunity. Plus the work paid well.

The wall forming crew foreman, at Mike's suggestion, had opened another box of new wall-ties, the steel wire devices used to hold the concrete forms together. The foreman had concern that the twenty-four-inch wall ties appeared tampered with. They both knew if the wall-ties broke during a concrete pour, the wall forms could fly apart and possibly severely injure or kill a worker. The cleanup from a failed concrete wall form was a race against the clock because the concrete will still harden.

Mike had never given the actual wall ties much consideration because wall-ties failures usually resulted from poor form design, i.e., too few wall-ties used to support the load. He had never heard of wall-ties failing from being defective, though he supposed that currently anything was possible.

He saw Ann with the summer intern and walked over to show her the wall tie with a small groove neatly cut around the wire strut of the wall-tie. He knew a wall tie resisted the pulling apart or tensile loads in the form from the wet concrete, and the strength of that resistance depended on the cross-sectional area of the wire. He figured the wall tie wire with the groove was a sneaky method to reduce the wall tie strength by half or more. Mike was fortunate his foreman had noticed the alteration to the wall-ties.

"Ann, have you ever seen a wall-tie with grooves cut in the wire like these?" Mike asked her and then added, "You think they're unsafe?"

"I don't think using them would be wise."

Mike and the foreman finished checking the wall-ties and found both cases of the new twenty-four-inch wall-ties had grooves, over two hundred wall-ties. They debated whether the factory had messed up or the groove was the result of sabotage. The foreman wondered aloud who would be against a wastewater treatment plant upgrade.

"Maybe the same party that put a hundred pounds of sugar in two of my concrete truck drums to weaken the concrete." Her remark surprised Mike.

"Are you saying Shaffer was sabotaged even before those test cylinders and you didn't say anything?"

Mike's tone of voice had her defensively answer that she had always figured Ace was responsible for the sugar and the attempted sabotage was an effort to make Shaffer lose the concrete contract due to weak concrete. She never thought they would harm RBO because that would just kill their golden goose. Besides, she had no proof and feared RBO might decide Shaffer wasn't worth the hassle and have Ace supply the concrete.

A pensive Mike watched Ann drive off. Her fear wasn't groundless. He paused in his contemplation to order a laborer dispatched to Pittsburgh with the defective ties and instructions to return with undamaged wall-ties. The forming crew foreman, a trusted employee of RBO, agreed to Mike's request that he personally check each wall tie before allowing it to be used in future wall forms. Having resolved the immediate work stoppage, he wandered back to his office lost in thought. Terry's remark last week about overloading the wall forms and his discovery of sabotaged wall ties today had him convinced some party was deliberately endeavoring to disrupt the project.

Mike agreed with her opinion that the Woodbrier brothers and Ace were behind the sugar in Shaffer's concrete mixer truck drum and the test cylinder sabotage. Both those acts related to Ace trying to screw over Shaffer for the project's concrete business. But sabotaged wall ties, what's their purpose? What possible benefit could a failed wall form be to Ace or Pine Tree? Or were the tampered wall ties just malicious vandalism by a wrathful employee at the manufacture's factory? He needed answers; his reputation was at risk along with his father's opinion of his abilities.

Where to look for answers eluded him. The project appeared to be progressing well. Basin No. 1's concrete floor and walls were finished, and the crews had moved to setting up Basin No. 2. The air duct piping for the first basin would arrive Monday and installation would start the next day. The north pump station, electrical conduit, and sewers were progressing well. By all metrics, the project was ahead of schedule and under budget. He should be feeling satisfied with the project's progress, but instead he had a nagging undefined apprehension that serious troubles were developing that he was ignorant of and could wreck his plans.

"Frank, have you read the specifications for the project, especially the ones dealing with materials like piping?"

"Yes, but I've not finished the electrical equipment. Some of the sections make my eyes glaze over, they're so dry."

"Good . . . I mean I'm glad you have read them."

Mike had decided to check the material installed by Pine Tree against the requirements in the project specifications. The basin air-ducting material consisted of stainless steel pipe, manifolds, and control valves and represented about forty percent of Pine Tree's bid of eight million dollars. Norton and James was required to certify the material meets the project specification requirements, but he wanted a second independent verification that the material was as claimed. He cautioned Frank to make every effort to verify the material without getting Pine Tree and Terry in an uproar. While Frank was verifying the material, he would have Steve check on the blowers and electrical control panels. One thing to watch for, he advised both men, was the clause "or equal" being exercised to change the material in the bid to a supposedly better material. If anything doesn't look right they were to inform him, no matter how minor the discrepancy.

"Is something amiss?" Frank asked.

"I don't know of anything. I just wish to double-check and avoid problems."

Mike regretted snapping at Ann and wondered if she would go to dinner with him. The only way to find out was to call her. She was receptive and suggested they meet at that quiet restaurant-bar they went to after the Board meeting and that way they could go as is after work.

Waiting for their food, he told her about having words with Jerry Woodbrier at the Pizza Villa and meeting Katie Gambone. The information caused an unexpected reaction in her she paled. Her eyes got a faraway look for a moment, and then she scrutinized him as if searching for some hidden intent behind his remarks.

It dawned on him that Ann must have had some past encounter with Sam's son. After a moment of silence, she asked about Gambone's daughter, having never met her. He described Katie and relayed her comment regarding Jerry doping girls and Betty Deere, which further upset Ann.

They had the house spaghetti dinner. A preoccupied Ann barely touched her food. On the drive back to his motel room Mike reflected on her behavior; something was clearly bothering her. Did he have any business prying into her affairs? Probably not, but Ann was too captivating and appealing to allow her reluctance to discourage him. He intended to discover what troubled the lady and help.

The following week Sam and Lou Woodbrier met Dennis Norton at his Pittsburgh office to discuss the Meadville POTW project and a possible "brown field cleanup" near Butler, Pennsylvania. Norton and James was located in a new office building at Robinson Town Center near the Pittsburgh airport. Sam was impressed with the large office where several engineers were working at CAD stations on design work and another dozen or so people busy on phones and meetings. Lou and he tended to forget Dennis actually ran a respected consultant firm. If only people knew.

Dennis started the meeting with his concern over the RBO personnel checking project material against the specifications, instead of passively accepting Norton and James findings. He trusted everyone present appreciated that could be a potential problem for the air duct material. They had started double checking material after discovering two boxes of sabotaged wall-ties.

"Owen is suspicious and wary of Terry and Jake . . . and probably me. Those wall ties were the final straw. Was that your brilliant idea, Lou?"

All three of them were robust middle-aged men used to issuing opinions and orders, not receiving them. Lou was getting red from Norton's implied criticism.

"Owen was already suspicious from your engineer's lame handling of the pipe bedding issue." Lou said. "He needed something else to worry about. That's the reason sabotaged ties made sense. If he worried about his form design being faulty, if he had to clean up failed concrete wall forms, he wouldn't be worrying about air duct material."

"If this, if that. . . The point is he found your sabotage, and he's now alerted and looking," Dennis said.

"I'll admit I misjudged him. I figured, after the first week, he'd be spending more time in Columbus than Meadville. He's not the typical rich man's son," Sam said.

"I think that hot Shaffer girl is the attraction, not commitment to project management," Lou said.

Their discussion moved onto the Butler "brown field" site project for cleaning past contamination from a chrome-plating operation. Sal's brother, John Gambone, was considering the purchase of a small landfill in West Virginia. If John did go ahead with the purchase, he might be receptive to disposing the contaminated Butler soil at a reasonable price. Lou offered to check.

Paulie was working on a concrete curb project near Grove City and just off the I-79 exit ramp, when Lou called and told him they needed to meet at the Franklin airport parking lot at 5 P.M. He arrived a few minutes ahead of time and watched Lou's black Mercedes wheel in and park several spaces to his left. Paulie stepped on his cigarette after he exited his truck and walked over and got in Lou's car.

He had done several unlawful and well-paying projects for Lou over the last five years, but this would top them all.

"I want you to help a person kill that miserable bitch. Her murder needs to look like a sex crime," Lou said. "A friend of a friend will do the nasty part, but he needs your help. He's flying in from Serbia, can barely understand English."

"Who is he? Is the guy any good?" Paulie asked. He didn't like the sound of this, a lot of potential blowback working with foreigners.

"He's supposed to be an accomplished murderer and rapist. His name is Karl. You need to pick him up at the Pittsburgh Airport."

Lou wanted him to assist Karl until the job was completed, and then make sure the man left the country. The assassin would arrive tomorrow on US Air at 2 P.M. and with any luck, they could deal with the girl that evening. Karl could then fly out the following day.

"He has her picture and information. Will you handle this?"

Paulie, though a venal soul, couldn't help wondering what the world was coming to when his boss would consider being an accomplished rapist an important talent for his hired assassin. Lou sounded eager for the kill and unlikely to squabble over pay.

"A car is required and I want three thousand."

"Okay, but no more than two thousand for the car. Also, if he messes this up, you need to make sure the man is never captured by the police."

Lou's last qualification changed the assignment totally in Paulie's mind. The guy sounded dangerous. He might be the one that ended up dead. The thought made him extremely nervous and cautious.

"Will Karl need any . . . ah . . . tools for this job?" Paulie asked to stall deciding if he wanted anything to do with Lou's scheme.

"Yes, take that tool-bag in the back seat." Lou cautioned that the items in the tool-bag, along with the tool-bag, were clean and in the clear plastic bag. "Don't you handle the bag and items, as that might leave forensic evidence for the police. In fact, use a glove to carry the outer bag, Remember one of the items in the bag is a loaded 9-mm pistol, keep that in mind if you needed to put him down."

Paulie thought *Lou always did a fine job of stating the obvious.* It never failed to irritate him due to the implied lack of experience. His annoyance and indecisiveness evaporated when Lou handed him five thousand dollars in hundreds for expenses and his trouble.

"Karl is going to have all the fun. Shame there's no way for us to watch. Others will handle his payment. You have any other questions?"

"If the worst occurs, can Karl's body be traced back to you?"

"No."

Back on I-79, Paulie realized finding a clean vehicle was critical in the event Karl's plans went amiss. His best source for such a vehicle was his bookie. He turned on to I-279 and drove into Pittsburgh.

The bookie had just the type of vehicle needed, a reasonably priced vehicle that would clear a police license inspection and still be untraceable. A couple hours later Paulie headed home in a decent running dark green Camry.

Mike's reason for having Steve and Frank independently verify material was due to RBO's contract with Pine Tree Construction. The contract required Pine Tree Construction to supply all material for the items they installed. His logic had been the contractor would be more careful handling the material if the damaged or lost material cost had to be borne by them. Pine Tree had obtained a better price for the Type 316-stainless steel air manifolds and ducting called for in the aeration basins. They had bid both supplying and installing the air ductwork for $3,200,000.

The best price RBO could find for the stainless steel material was $2,400,000. Mike had calculated the installation would cost RBO another million dollars, so Pine Tree had won the work for both supplying and then installing the air duct. At the time, he figured they wanted the work and were willing to take a minimal profit on the air duct portion of the project. Now he wasn't sure of their motive.

The weakness with the subcontractor supplying the material was quality control. The consultant's project inspectors were to verify the subcontractor's material met the project specifications. If they didn't do a proper verification that the material met specification, the subcontractor had every incentive to substitute substandard and lower-cost material to increase their profit.

If the subcontractor did substitute lower quality material and it failed, RBO and the consultant, in this case Norton and James would be ultimately responsible. Mike did not want RBO's reputation damaged. The questionable trustworthiness of the project consultants and their project engineer was one source of his growing apprehension.

His summer intern, Frank, had discovered Allegheny College girls. He was in Mike's office when Ann stopped in to check the time he would be by tonight. Frank, in a chatty mood, told them about being at the library helping one of the girls with physics homework, when he had noticed the old Jenny Lowell poster at the library. He asked Ann if she had been here when the student disappeared. The question caught Mike's attention, and before she could answer, he asked if there were any other missing girls listed.

"No, she was the only one," Frank answered.

Ann then explained she had moved to Meadville about a month after the Lowell girl disappeared, but remembered hearing her mother on the news, the anguished pleas for information about her only child. She told them the whole Jenny Lowell affair had depressed her, and she remembered being disillusioned such a thing could happen in a small town like Meadville. Mike noticed the pensive Ann was back. She told them she had to get back to the concrete plant.

Frank's question had Ann wondering why Jerry Woodbrier had called. She had returned his last call and left a message, but he had never called back. She had concluded he was playing some perverted mind game. Mike and Frank's remarks and the calls all served to remind her what a scary night that date with Jerry had turned into. She shuddered to think what he had planned and what might have happened had she not woken up, though in the end she had the last laugh on that bastard. Mike relating about meeting the creep at the pizza place had shaken her. What would he think of her if Jerry told him some twisted version about that nigh and who was the Betty Deere that Gambone's daughter had mentioned?

Mike had been to Ann's apartment on Henry Street for that fish lunch and looked forward to seeing her cheerful place again. This evening his thoughts were on security in general, and he couldn't help evaluating how safe the apartment might be. The door at the bottom of the stairs to Ann's second-story apartment had an old-fashion-skeleton key lock that might keep a small child out, but not a crook. The dark, unlighted wood stairs creaked loudly with each step. The noise from the old wooden stairs should alert the apartment dweller she had a visitor approaching. The upper door was also a flimsy old wooden door, but at least had a modern-looking lock and a spy-hole lens. He knocked.

Ann opened the door and cheerfully greeted him. She wore a simple black Jersey dress that would have been at home in the most sophisticated society. The dress and her pixie hairstyle complimented her winsome figure. Mike found himself staring at her and not returning her greeting after she had opened the door. After his momentary lapse of manners, he recovered and praised her appearance.

"Ann, you're a sight to behold. You're beautiful."

"Flattery will get you everywhere, Mr. Owen, but Shaffer is not lowering the concrete price," a pleased Ann responded.

"Damn, and here I was going to feed you and try for a ten percent discount. Well maybe next time."

141

David C. Brown

In truth, concrete and business were the last things he was interested in this evening. His thoughts focused on knowing this lovely woman better. In a more serious vein, he asked if her neighborhood was safe since that door at the bottom of the stairs wouldn't offer much protection. And that stairway was a potential deathtrap during a fire. He worriedly inquired if there was another entrance.

"Why, you act concerned. I'll have you know this apartment has a very high tech back entrance, a window."

A bemused Ann explained the bedroom window opened onto the back porch roof where there was a wood ladder for use in an emergency to get off the porch roof. Curious, he asked for and received her okay to enter the bedroom to check the window exit. He verified the window actually opened and then checked the access to the roof area. After closing the window, he was careful to latch it.

"Well that exit would work for an agile person like you." Then glancing around, Mike decided Ann's bedroom was a cozy looking nest.

"Meadville's a calm place. In a year I've never heard of any troubles around this neighborhood."

"Good, ready to go?" Her tabby cat rubbed against his leg and meowed. He took a moment to bend down and pet the cat before leaving.

## Chapter 8

The architecture of the restaurant displayed Rocco's success. The original restaurant had started in the first floor of a two-story residence. An added one-story cinder block building to the rear provided additional seating for a flourishing business. Paving the front and side yards had created an off street parking area for their customers. The cuisine was Italian. Ann and Mike decided on the shrimp primavera with artichokes over fettuccine and a side of steamed asparagus. The bread, salad, and house wine complimented an excellent meal.

Ann, as he was discovering, was an elegant and neat eater. Mike watched her carefully spread a uniform layer of butter over a piece of bread, and then used the knife to cut it into halves, before sampling with a small nibble. She followed the bread with a small bite of salad greens. Next, she extracted a shrimp from the primavera sauce, consumed it, and followed with a fettuccine noodle she had carefully wound around the fork. Next, her attention focused on a difficult black olive that resisted her efforts to spear it with the salad fork.

"I won't tell anyone if you use your finger," he said. He had devoured his meal before she had finished her second shrimp. He teased her. "Didn't your mother ever warn you not to bolt your food?"

143

"Now that you asked, I don't believe she did. Obviously your family limited eating to one-minute periods and then removed the plates," she cheerfully countered.

Mike would have been content to sit and watch her all night. Ann finally finished and declared Rocco's meal as excellent. They left after complimenting the owner on the meal. On the trip back to Ann's apartment, he pondered if he dare kiss her when they got to her apartment. He felt foolish worrying over such juvenile issues, but then no woman had ever enflamed his desires like this marvelous female beside him and he didn't want to make a wrong move that would upset her. They both had a busy day scheduled tomorrow, and the time was now 11 P.M. Best to drop her off and get some sleep was his pathetic decision as he pulled into a space in front of her apartment. Ann had no qualms though and gave him a quick chaste kiss.

"The evening was lovely Mike, thanks. Oh--stay put I'll be up the steps in a flash."

He had been exiting to walk with her to the apartment, instead sat back in the seat. Before closing the Cherokee's door, he said. "Waving from the kitchen window, that way I'll know you're safe."

"You're sweet. I'll do that," Ann said. She closed the passenger door and disappeared up the apartment stairs.

He watched the light go on in her apartment, but no Ann came to the window. The lack of her appearance puzzled him. Crossing to reach the window would only require a moment. Could she have forgotten that quickly? Should he check?

He waited another minute, no wave, and exited the truck and eased over to the outer door. A quick look showed the stairs were clear and went up to her apartment door and knocked. No response, but he could hear another door close and prior to that the sound of something being dragged across the floor. An icy fear griped him. Something was seriously amiss. Should he call 9-1-1?

"Ann, say something or I'm kicking in the door," he shouted from the hallway.

He paused for several seconds and gave the door a hard shove with his leg. The door flexed and popped the striker out of the wall frame, but the chain held. Another hard kick sent the door crashing open against the wall. Ann's ripped dress and bra laid on the floor. Dread filled him as he eased in farther. No one was in the main room so she had to be in either the bedroom or bathroom. Where was her assailant? Her apartment was dead quiet. He could faintly hear a TV playing, either in the lower apartment or in one of neighboring houses. The bathroom door was open and the room empty. He tried the bedroom door, locked, and knew he should call the police because something was seriously wrong. Calls take time, and Ann might be dying. He gave the bedroom door a hard kick.

The bedroom door flew open from his kick and before he could regain his balance, a large crew-cut man leaped from the bedroom door and grabbed his neck, smashing Mike's face with his forehead. He caught a momentary glimpse of Ann lying naked and unconscious on the bed bleeding from a head wound. Then he was on his back on the kitchen floor with the big stranger on top choking him, the man's grip unbreakable.

Already feeling faint, Mike frantically struggled to break the chokehold. Keeping the stranger from crushing his larynx required both hands. He didn't dare reach for his pocketknife, but did manage to knee the stranger in the crotch. His reward was a grunt from the guy and a momentary reprieve from the choking. He reached his knife, but couldn't unfold the blade with one hand as the attacker redoubled his choking effort. Mike was near passing out. Death was near if he didn't manage to break the chokehold.

The bedroom door exploding open snapped Ann conscious. She remembered opening her apartment door and a sudden pain.

145

Where were her clothes? Who's fighting? Something was terribly amiss. Where was her pistol? Was it in her purse by the front door? Then she remembered she had left the pistol home in her camera bag, which thankfully was lying partially open on the floor near her. She couldn't get her left arm and hand to work. It acted broken and the pain was intense as she rolled off the bed hitting the injured arm. The pain help clear her vision and she saw a large man and Mike struggling on the kitchen floor.

Ann dragged herself toward the camera bag, remembering that the pistol did not have a round chambered. She used her right hand to pull her pistol out of the camera bag. Her left hand was useless. The empty chamber was a serious, maybe fatal problem for her and Mike. Her pistol was a 45 APC Springfield Model 1911auto and it was single action. Her pistol would only fire if she pulled the slide assembly back to cock the hammer and then allow the slide assembly to fly forward, chambering a round. After that, all that was required was to keep pulling the trigger until the gun was empty. She could cock and load the Springfield in her sleep with two hands; with one hand, she was nearly helpless.

Now past frantic, Mike dying in the next room, knowing she would be next, her only hope was to somehow get a round chambered and the hammer cocked. Holding the pistol vertically against the edge of the steel angle that formed the bed frame, she carefully pushed the pistol down, catching the pistol bolt-slide assembly on the top edge of the bed frame, as the barrel slid down the outside of the steel bed frame angle. Keeping the front edge of the pistol slide assembly hooked on the bed frame without catching the barrel was difficult. Ann, on her knees beside the bed, desperately pushed the pistol down and twice the slide assembly started to cock back, but then the edge of the slide assembly popped off the bed frame, slamming nosily back against the empty barrel chamber and failing to load a round. The noise of her effort was bound to alert the stranger. He could disarm her in a second if he heard and noticed her efforts.

The realization that she'd never leave this room alive if she failed to chamber a cartridge and cock the pistol madly played repeatedly in her thoughts. On her third attempt, she had the bolt face past the cartridge, just a hair more to be sure, then a *click* as the hammer locked back, fully cocked. What a glorious sound! Never in her life had a sound been more welcomed and hope returned. *Don't get careless,* she cautioned herself. The bed sheet was now jammed against the slide assembly injection port. She had to clear the bed sheet or the bolt-slide assembly could jam on the edge of the fabric as it slammed home. With a prayer, Ann violently jerked the pistol clear of the bed covers and off the frame edge, allowing the slide assembly to slam home against the barrel chamber with a cartridge. A loaded and cocked automatic pistol, hope surged in her heart.

She stood up shakily and saw Mike was turning red and beating ineffectively at his attacker with a closed pocketknife. She quickly, but carefully stole up to the stranger and though her hand was shaking nearly uncontrollably, she managed to put the pistol barrel against his head by his left ear and screamed, "Stop!" Then she remembered Mike was under him and adjusted the angle to assure the bullet missed him.

He had been unaware of her presence. The assailant reacted quicker that a snake, lashing out at her during the moment she needed to adjust her aim. She fired. The muzzle blast was deafening and the bullet ripped the assailant's left ear, and thankfully missed Mike. It buried itself in the floor. The stranger had kicked her hard in the leg, sending her sliding back into the bedroom doorframe, as the pistol cycled another round into the chamber. She was dazed, the pain from hitting her left arm against the floor threatened to overwhelm her, but she had a death grip on the Springfield and never lost her focus on her assailant. The madman, similar in size to Mike, but with a round face with small closely set brown eyes did the unexpected. Instead of leaping after her, he shook his head as if to clear his thoughts, and incredibly made a hold-it-motion with his hand while calmly getting to his feet. He pulled out and held up a badge with his left hand, while drawing a black automatic from his belt with his right hand. He even smiled reassuringly at Ann who noticed his teeth looked in poor condition.

"Put the gun down. Police," his forceful accented voice demanded.

His tactic reminded her of a snake hypnotizing its prey. Then Mike buried his now opened pocketknife blade in the assailant's left leg. The assailant howled and violently backhanded him with the pistol, sending him sprawling. Ann shot, hitting the pistol instead of his chest. Still her bullet did the job. It devastated the assailant's right hand before he could get off a shot. The stranger swore as his black automatic pistol flew across the room. Hate radiated from him as he stepped toward her.

She feared he wanted to get close enough to deliver a killing head kick, but Mike's knife was stuck in the assailant's leg, causing him to stumble and hesitate. She watched the hateful expression transform into disbelief and pain as the assailant realized her pistol was rock steady and pointed at his chest. Time was now her friend as she considered where best to shoot him to assure he stayed down, but alive for he had much to answer for.

The stranger must have finally realized the game was up with his right hand and pistol now useless. He panicked. His sudden move startled Ann. She almost shot him in the back before taking a quick aim at his right leg. The bullet buckled his leg. He screamed a foreign-sounding curse and fell through the apartment door with a loud thump.

Mike was on his hands and knees on the floor gagging, which she took as a good sign of his recovery. Ann called 9-1-1 and then peered cautiously around her apartment doorframe to see if her assailant was gone. The stairs were sprayed with blood, but clear of a body. Let the police worry about the bastard. She went back to check Mike. Her left arm throbbed and felt like it was on fire. She suddenly realized she was naked and Mike was staring at her. He had a bloody nose and horrible-looking marks on his neck and face.

Salvation had been Mike's reaction when a gunshot exploded in his face and the choking stopped. He didn't know what was happening, but was determined to stop the assailant and with his other hand now free, he had the knife unfolded in a flash. He saw a leg beside him and stabbed. His reward was a crushing blow that knocked him flat. Another shot exploded. Then a third shot rang out and the assailant was gone. An angelical Ann was standing naked in front of him with a wounded-broken arm and a large pistol in the other hand. Blood was dripping off her chin as she talked on her cell phone while he got to his feet.

"Who was that guy? Are you okay?" He asked her as he got up rubbing his neck. "I thought I was a dead man until that gun went off. You saved my life. Is that broken?"

"I think so, I can't move my hand. I have no idea who he was."

Mike asked her what had happened. Ann told him she remembered stepping into her apartment and heading to the window, then the next thing she remembered was the bedroom door banging open and fighting. He then reminded her she was naked and had called 9-1-1. Before the police arrived, she needed something to wear, and he offered to help, since her arm wasn't working.

"What do you want me to fetch?"

"I need a pair of panties from the bedroom and that gray robe hanging in the bathroom."

He helped her put on the panties and then the robe as she carefully worked the pistol through the sleeve of the robe. She told Mike that with one hand, she couldn't put the pistol's safety on, and she was not disarming until there were police in her apartment. Ann then went searching for her cat, while Mike lost in admiration for her was thinking what a sight. Even beaten up she was beautiful. The sight of her naked had sure gotten his thoughts off dying.

Paulie's evening had become a nightmare shortly after three gunshots from the apartment. At first, he had gleefully watched Mike Owen get out of his car and enter her apartment, thinking the rich boy was playing right into their hope of involving him with her death. The Serbian mercenary could handle Owen with one hand tied behind his back and Paulie decided to remain in the car. Then after the gunshots, he reckoned the man had decided to get it over with quickly. The assassin rolling out of the stair door onto the sidewalk startled him and an awful feeling that plans had gone dreadfully wrong assaulted him as he tossed the cigarette and started the car to intercept his partner in crime.

Karl had managed to get to his feet and stagger down Henry Street to the corner for pickup. His right hand was a bloody mess and both legs and the left ear were dripping blood as he flopped into the front seat with a deep moan and awkwardly closed the door with his left hand. Paulie was in a panicky state. The man's hand, a horrible mess of flesh and small bones, revolted him, but he remembered to drive carefully and not attract attention. Two blocks away a police car raced by with its lights flashing. He headed for US 322 south and Franklin.

"What happened? Are they dead?"

"Talk louder. I can't hear. I need a doctor."

"Did you kill them?"

"No, the girl had a gun, crazy damn country. She shot me before I could kill her. Find me a doctor. Now!"

He realized Karl had lost his pistol along with the use of his right hand and therefore was unarmed. He reached down beside his seat and the door for the loaded and cocked 9-mm pistol, brought it up and shot his passenger four times, as he drove past the city limits toward Franklin. Karl screamed something as he tried to grab the gun, before dying. It was an appalling turn of events. Now he was a murderer. He needed to dump the body.

A shaken Paulie turned off US 322 toward Geneva and found an overgrown field off a gravel road. He dragged the heavy body into the weeds for about fifty feet and abandoned it, and then drove very carefully to Pittsburgh, all the while praying he didn't run into a DUI checkpoint. The car was a bloody mess with two bullet holes in the door panel. Fortunately, the bullets had not penetrated the door or shattered any windows. His bookie was not going to be happy with the car's condition.

The Meadville police were very professional, securing the two pistols. They separated Ann from Mike by sending her to the hospital to check for rape and treat her broken arm. The young policeman wiped a pad over Mike's hands for gunpowder residue. He asked him to remain for the detective.

Detective Larkin arrived after a few minutes, introduced himself, and consulted with the patrolmen. The detective looked old enough to have studied under Sherlock Holmes: a soft-spoken older man with unkempt white hair, bushy-eye brows, and blood-shot eyes.

"It's late, Mr. Owen, and you have had a traumatic experience, but I would like to ask several questions while everything is fresh in your mind. Do you want a lawyer?"

"A lawyer, why?" The detective's question startled Mike.

"A formality Mr. Owen, I always ask before I start. Now how did you come to be here tonight? Wait a moment."

A couple of new people had arrived, another uniformed policeman and an older woman in a white lab coat named Ruth. After receiving instructions from the detective, they started gathering evidence. The detective returned his attention to Mike. The lab people were taking pictures and blood samples, as he told Detective Larkin about Shaffer concrete, RBO working on the French Creek project, asking Ann to dinner at Rocco's, dropping her off, the lack of a wave from the window, his attempted rescue, and Ann saving his life. During his narrative, the detective had used a recorder along with taking notes on a pad. The man reminded him of a newspaper reporter.

"Asking her to wave was an amazingly fortunate request you made. Are you familiar with firearms, Mr. Owen?"

"Yes and enough Mr. Owen. I go by Mike."

"Mike it is. Have you ever shot the US Army 45 automatic pistol?"

"No. I have shot Ruger 9-mm automatics. Just a minute, I need to get her."

Ann's cat looked in from the outer stairway. He knew she was worried about it and went over and picked it up. The cat was purring as he returned to his chair.

The detective commented on the cat being friendly and then continued to quiz Mike on automatics. Did he know a pistol that is not double action, even with a chambered cartridge, required cocking the hammer, before the pistol could fire? And without a chambered cartridge, a person had to pull the bolt back against a powerful spring, and then allow it to fly forward to chamber a cartridge.

He did. Would he agree that requires some effort, but was not difficult with two good hands, but it's more or less impossible with one hand. Mike agreed.

"So how do you figure Ann managed to cock the pistol with one hand?"

"Beats me, I'm just thankful she did."

"Yes, looking at your neck, I'd say you are. Now again, how did you get free?"

"You will have to ask Ann."

The detective made a turned-up hand motion that conveyed a desire for more elaboration. Mike speculated that she appeared to have ordered their assailant to stop choking him, which made the assailant go after her. How her first shot missed, Mike didn't know. His focus was on getting air, but remembered seeing her setting against the wall with the killer looking down at her. He had snapped open his knife and stabbed the man's leg. The killer then turned and hit him. After that blow, Mike was in a daze, but remembered there were a couple of shots and then the guy was gone.

"You have never seen him before tonight, don't know him?"

Mike was tired, nauseated, worried about Ann, and irritated with the repeated questions.

"No, I have never seen the man before tonight."

"The assault has every appearance of a rape and Ann will be checked. Did you have intercourse with her this evening?"

"You're a real piece of work Detective, and it's obvious you haven't heard anything I've told you about tonight. The answer is no!"

His comments had irritated the policeman, who responded.

"I'm skeptical. Your story is too neat. This event has the characteristics of a man discovering his woman with another man and getting in a fight. You would have to agree, two men fighting over a beautiful woman is far more common than a random attack by a total stranger. However, two items lent some credence to your statements. No gun residue on your hands and the torn dress laying there on the floor by the door. Perhaps the attack happened just as related. I intend to find out."

"I'm sure she will be impressed with your brilliant deduction that it was all her fault for having jealous lovers. This thinking passes for detective work in Meadville. I will offer one insight for you to consider in pursuit of your theory--Ann Lane is the one woman I've met that could be a virgin, quaint as that may seem today."

"I'll keep that in mind and think you should call it a night. Where can I find you tomorrow?"

"I'll be in the area. Call my cell phone or stop at the RBO office trailer. She will need some clothes. Okay if I get something for her to wear?"

"Ruth, could you gather up a set of clothes for Ms. Lane. She's my next interview. I'll give them to her and even let her know you suggested it and rescued her cat."

Mike headed to his motel room with the tabby cat. He needed to clean up, and then check on Ann. He called the Shaffers and advised them of their employee's assault and that she was in the hospital and needed to contact her family. They recovered from the shock, had many questions he wasn't in the mood to answer, but promised to later. Mr. Shaffer agreed to contact Ann's family. Then Mike sat down for just a moment to rest.

The nurse forced Detective Larkin to wait until the doctor had set Ann's arm and returned her to a room. The doctor cautioned him to keep the questioning short. The detective knew she was still under the influence from the medicine and he would have the advantage in an interview.

"Why didn't you shoot your assailant with the first shot?"

Ann explained in a weak voice that her goal was to make him quit choking Mike, but not kill him or Mike with a careless shot.

"I didn't realize how fast and strong he would be. He was after me the instant he became aware I was up."

"You fired a warning shot?"

"No, when I told him to stop choking Mike he struck me. I shot, but had to miss Mike. In the process I only nicked the assailant."

Ann explained how he had claimed to be a policeman and what happened.

"Why did you want him alive? Did you know him?"

"No. I wanted him able to tell the police who he was and why he had attacked me. He looked like a soldier."

In response to the detective's request to describe events, Ann relayed how she had opened the apartment door, stepped into the room, and next woke up on her bed naked from the noise of the bedroom door flying open. The killer had assaulted Mike and while they were fighting, she found her gun and he knew the rest. He asked if she kept the gun loaded, and she related her struggle to chamber a cartridge. The nurse had told him the assailant hadn't raped Ann.

"You're very fortunate Mike came when he did."

"I'm lucky to be alive and to think I thought he was being over protective to suggest waving from the window."

"Have you known each other long?"

She related how they had met because of the Shaffer contract with RBO, her concerns that the attack might be related to the sugar in the Shaffer mix trucks, and tampered test cylinders.

Detective Larkin thanked her for the information and told her about the clothes Mike had suggested she would need, adding that he had her cat. His information earned him a sweet smile. He realized Mike was a lucky man. The detective's had spent his life dealing with evil, foolish, and self-destructive behavior. This woman was none of those. He could forget the lover-triangle. The crime looked more like a hired hit for an unknown reason, though Ann suspected some connection to the concrete business. He wasn't ready to go there yet, but it did appear that someone had attempted to disguise the attempted murder as a random sex crime. Probably to shield the reason a party wanted her dead. Discover that reason and he would find the guilty party.

Standing back in front of Ann's apartment, he was amazed at the impressive blood trail from the apartment to the corner of Henry Street where it ended. Ann had nailed her assailant good. So there was a fourth person with a car involved, which would fit with the hired killer theory. He knew none of the area hospitals had reported patients or victims of gunshot wounds. A body found abandoned along some side road was the more likely conclusion to this search. In the meantime, while he waited for the body to surface, he needed to determine who would benefit from Ms. Lane's death.

Mike woke with a start and realized he had been asleep for several hours and the time was 4:45 A.M. He and the cat went to the project first thing where he found Steve, Larry, and Frank talking about the shooting and attack on Ann and him. He cleared up a couple of the wilder rumors, told the three of them to run the project and keep her cat safe until he returned. Steve put the mutt out.

The Meadville Medical Center, a fair-size hospital, was Mike's next stop. Mrs. Shaffer was there with Ann, who had an impressive cast on her left arm and looked radiant notwithstanding her bandages. He received smiles from both women as he entered and exchanged greetings. Mrs. Shaffer thanked him profusely for saving her Ann, which he attempted to correct by explaining she had saved him.

"Mike, my mother is coming into Erie on the 10 A.M. flight out of Indianapolis. Do you have anyone who could pick her up?"

"Yes, Frank could get her. What does she look like?"

"Mom is an older, smaller version of me, just slightly heavier. Frank will be perfect. They can talk math."

He sent Frank to Erie and then listened as Mrs. Shaffer and Ann discussed a temporary stay at the Shaffer home until she found another apartment to rent. She didn't want to consider returning to her old apartment, the memories and blood were too upsetting. Mike had to agree. The violated apartment could never be comfortable.

The attack on the Lane woman was the lead news story that morning, and Lou was a worried man. He had met a very tired and nervous Paulie at the Grove City curb project for the details on the previous night. Now he had to explain to the Russian that Karl wasn't coming back. After all the risks, effort, and expense, the girl was still alive and the police were involved. Detective Larkin might look like an Alzheimer-impaired relic, but Lou knew from some past narrow escapes that the old man was capable of figuring out the crime. He also knew discovery of Karl's body wouldn't be long, and in the body were several of Paulie's 9-mm slugs in addition to the ones from the girl or Owen.

Lou chided himself for not thinking to check on whether one of them had a carry permit, though he was still amazed Karl didn't make short work of them, pistol or no pistol. Some accomplished killer. No wonder Serbia lost the Bosnian War. With Karl's body, the police and Larkin will know the girl's attack was a failed hired hit and start wondering why anyone would wish to murder her. What a fiasco. Twenty-five thousand dollars gone and a police investigation, the resentment gave him indigestion.

The doctor told Ann he was going to hold her overnight because of the blow to her head. Otherwise, except for a broken arm and two ribs, she was in good shape. Mike wasn't sure if the doctor's remarks were an attempt at medical humor. Her mother's arrival precipitated an emotional reunion. Mrs. Lane knew all about the attack and was horrified with how close her daughter had come to losing her life.

"Why would anyone want to hurt my daughter?" she asked the room.

He was wondering the same thing. Mrs. Lane finally settled down, allowing introductions, which precipitated another outburst as she hugged and tearfully thanked Mike for saving her daughter.

"Mrs. Lane, please. Your daughter saved me."

Mike knew he owed his life to the Lanes raising a brave and capable daughter, but the emotionally charged atmosphere stopped him from voicing his thoughts. After a few moments to settle his emotions, Christ, he had almost cried, he told them if they needed anything to call. Otherwise, he'd stop this evening.

Mike hunted Frank up on arriving.

"How did Mrs. Lane know those details of the attack?"

"Cell phones, she knew more than I did. I didn't know you kicked in the door."

"Well, keep it to yourself. I am going to see about tomorrow's concrete. You need to check Pine Tree's work. Call me if there are any issues."

## Chapter 9

Mike had never met Mr. Shaffer and found him in the maintenance building. A heavy man, bent with arthritis, he waved for him to come in. He had been finishing a conversation with another employee who was his mechanic based on the oil and grease-stained coveralls.

"You have to be Mr. Owen, Ann's fishing partner. I'm Mr. Shaffer and this is Tim, Ann's right hand man."

"A pleasure to meet both of you, is the five hundred cubic yard concrete order set for tomorrow? Normally, I would pester Ann, but she's under the weather."

Mr. Shaffer laughed and explained he needn't have bothered for she had already called him once and Tim twice to remind them not to mess up tomorrow's order.

"My engineer was pissed her unreasonable doctor wouldn't release her," he said. In a more serious vein, he thanked Mike for saving her. "I couldn't have handled the loss of another young person."

"I'm sorry about the loss of your son. It happened two years ago?"

"Almost to the day, he died in a car accident. Tim, excuse the two of us. I need to discuss some personal matters."

159

After assuring Mike that all would be ready with the concrete delivery, the foreman left.

"Okay if we use first names? Mine is Ted." Mike nodded yes. "Are you familiar with the sabotage we have been putting up with?"

"I am now. She just told me a couple of days ago. Do you know who did it?"

"I do. The sugar was probably put in the trucks by Gambone's roll-off driver when he emptied the roll-off box that morning."

"Why that jerk, and to think I passed on Waste Management."

"It's more complicated than that," Ted said. He then related that two days before the sugar incident, John had stopped in to check on their satisfaction with his service.

"He talked to Ann, since I wasn't here, and warned her to be extra careful with any concrete going to your project, but offered no explanation. Ann, being Ann, acted. She found and removed the sugar, and then decided to sit on the information, figuring whoever had placed the sugar in the concrete couldn't know if they had been successful until the first test cylinders didn't failed."

Ted paused to get two bottles of water out of a small refrigerator in his office and gave one to Mike, before continuing.

"The first test cylinders passed, then the next set of cylinders failed and that was when everyone got involved. She feared RBO would just switch concrete suppliers to avoid the hassle. She was very happy when you made Norton and James retest and acknowledged the possibility their inspector may have sabotaged her test cylinders."

"I'm glad it worked out. The irony is the footing still had to be replaced, even though the concrete was fine, because of Norton and James design error," Mike said. "Norton wasn't happy, but RBO got paid for removing the footing."

"Who stood to benefit if Shaffer lost the contract?" Ted asked. "Not RBO, they would be paying twenty-five dollars more per cubic yard of concrete. Ace was the logical person to benefit from us losing the contract."

Mike agreed and asked. "How did the engineer fit in the scheme? The only quality control he ever showed any interest in was your concrete. Pine Tree could do substandard work all day long and he wouldn't care. Even his boss, Dennis Norton seemed indifferent until I made an issue of an item."

"You, of course, know Ace and Pine Tree are owned by Woodbrier Construction?"

"Yes."

"Then I would guess they have some understanding with Dennis. A cash kickback or some favor to the inspectors if certain conditions are met, but nothing that can be proven."

"I suspect you are right on both counts, a kickback that can't be proved."

Mike also figured Gambone must have owed the Woodbrier brothers a favor for some past under-the-table deal and paid it off by placing the sugar in Shaffer's trucks. His conscience must have bothered him, and he warned Ann.

Ted agreed that explained the thrash man's behavior.

"Sam is not dumb. He knows the RBO concrete business is no longer available. Hurting Ann would never change that fact."

"Don't overlook vengeance. With someone like Lou Woodbrier, vengeance is always a possibility," Ted said. "I wouldn't put anything past that man. Any chance the attacker was just some crazy asshole and she was a random target?"

"He appeared to have a plan that included her rape and death. He was a fit man, reminded me of a soldier. I don't think it was random."

Mike elaborated on his theory he was to be the fall guy for her murder.

"Damn, if your interpretation of the assailant's actions is correct, then the attack was no random event. It was a hired hit. And not over," Ted said.

"If I was gone, Terry and Norton could run the project as they saw fit. Who would benefit? Pine Tree for sure and the Woodbrier brothers. Who benefits with Ann dead?"

"This place would fold if something happened to her. I can't run it. My health wouldn't allow it. We would be heartbroken if something happened to her. She's like a beloved daughter."

"If you had to sell, Ace would be the likely buyer?" Mike asked.

"Probably, although with the demand for fracking sand, other companies might be interested."

"Is the business so profitable that people would commit murder?"

"It's a good business, but still a commodity business, and if Ace raised prices much, someone else would set up a ready mix operation and compete for the work. So I can't see them killing to put Shaffer Concrete out of business."

"What about the gravel and sand mine? Ann said you had millions of tons of gravel. Would that be of value to Ace?" He asked as he paced around the office.

"Sure, and there is considerable interest in the sand. But, there are gravel deposits all over the valley."

"Not with the necessary surface mine permits," Mike said, "Which I understand are expensive and difficult to obtain."

"I know whom to ask. Let's meet tomorrow after lunch. I may have an answer."

Ann finally had the hospital room to herself and her thoughts returned to the previous night. The attacker's purpose was her murder. But why, that question needed answered if she was ever to enjoy a life free of fear. She wished Mike were here. She wanted his thoughts on the reason for the attack. What -- he was!

"Feeling any better, Ann? I brought you a diet coke."

She smiled while scooting around to sit up in her bed and received the offered drink.

"Thanks have a seat. Your neck looks frightful. Does it hurt?"

"Not much. What about your arm?"

"No pain. I can move my hand again. Did Detective Larkin talk to you? He was here last night asking a lot of questions along the lines of whether I knew the attacker."

"I know, he seemed convinced your attacker was another boyfriend. I was a jealous ex-lover that stormed your apartment. In the end I thought I convinced him that wasn't the case, but apparently not."

"What was the reason for the attack? Do you think it was just a random bit of bad luck?"

"No, I think it was a planned attack. Do you have an enemy that would wish you harm?"

"None I can think of."

"Maybe the police will figure it out. Have you decided where you're going to live?"

"I'll stay with the Shaffers for a while. They have a big house, and I believe them when they say I'm welcome."

"You're right." Mike told about meeting her boss while checking on the big concrete order.

"They said you had already called them several times to remind them of RBO's large concrete order. I'm curious, have you ever thought about buying the business? Everyone credits you with making the place a success."

163

Ann lost her cheerfulness. "I've been thinking about a lot since last night. I'm not sure what is best for me. I'm feeling sleepy now and need to rest."

"I'm sorry. I should have realized. I'll call you tomorrow. Goodnight." The sudden change in mood surprised him.

She lay awake for a long time in the semi-dark hospital room, lost in thought. The issue she couldn't resolve was what Mike thought of her. He was everything she had hoped to find in a man--brave, looked good, smelled good, had a sense of humor, smart, and even rich--*Ah stop!* She scolded herself, *you sound like you're considering whether to purchase a prize boar hog.*

Ann knew she loved Mike. The real question for her: was it a one-sided love? Her thoughts returned to Shaffer concrete and her lifelong desire for a business. If she bought Shaffer, that meant staying in Meadville. Did she want business obligations tying her to Meadville when Mike went back to Columbus? If only she knew his feelings toward her, then she would know better which path to follow. She felt like tossing convention out the window and asking: "Mike, what are your feelings toward me?" Her grandmother would be horrified.

Jerry and his pal Paul were in the Green Lizard bar sorting photos from the party. The new roofies had been worth the price, and the girl hadn't a clue she had been a performer. Their mystery buyer would pay well. The rich pervert had wanted photos of white girls. They had eighteen pictures from the party in high quality RAW format to put on a DVD. Jerry was confident the "Syrian" would pay eighteen hundred dollars, a tidy profit from a fun weekend.

"What are your thoughts on trying to make a snuff video?" Jerry asked his partner. "The man is offering six-thousand dollars for a video showing a bloody death. He wants the victim to be young and white. He also wants us to kill her by evisceration after we rape her.

The girl didn't need to be pretty, just alive at the start and dead at the end."

"It would be messy. Where would we dispose the body? The police would go crazy on discovering a gutted corpse. It would light a fire under them, so the body would have to disappear forever."

"What about that farm near Frenchtown with the old house that Uncle Otto wants you to demolish with the dozer?"

"Yeah," Paul said. "That is a perfect location. Even better my uncle wanted the hand-dug water well located behind the house filled in, a perfect place to get rid of a body."

Jerry liked the location, and even had a girl in mind: Helen Smith, who liked to party. Paul thought her a good choice. She went to local bars by herself and would be easy to grab.

Their talk turned to the shooting on Henry Street. Who had been involved? The best they could sort out from the news articles was that her boyfriend, Mike Owen, had saved her bacon. *What a shame,* thought Jerry, for Ann Lane was responsible for the most humiliating night of his life and had stolen his backpack. Fortunately, she must have thrown the backpack away. Otherwise, they wouldn't be sitting here tonight. Maybe she'll die from an infection. He hoped that Paul never discovered the truth about that night and his missing camera.

The stainless steel air duct started to arrive on site that Monday. Jake used extra care in unloading the pieces and placing them on wood blocks. Then he covered the ducts with plastic sheets, which made Frank curious.

"Jake, they're stainless steel. Why cover them? You afraid they'll rust."

"They're easier to assemble when clean."

Frank was pleasantly surprised Jake had a sensible explanation and went back to checking the compaction of the sand-gravel backfill around Basin No. 1 in preparation for installing the first air ducts. He returned an hour later to watch the next set of manifolds get unloaded and examined one of the shipping manifests that Terry was gathering up. The writing was in a foreign language.

"Terry where is the pipe from?"

"Kazakhstan and Russia. They export a lot of stainless steel now days. Nice looking material, won't you agree?"

Frank agreed the air duct did look impressive and went back to the trailer to inform Mike the air duct was arriving on site. He also told him the material was from Kazakhstan and Russia. Surprised by the information, Mike realized that must account for Pine Tree's low price and vowed to remember foreign suppliers on the next project. He wanted a copy of the spec sheet for the stainless steel duct and sent Frank to find one.

Terry told Frank the analytical information went direct to Norton and James since everything was in Russian. He would have them fax a copy to Mike.

Frank wandered over to the unloading operation and watched a wood crate with several four-inch diameter nipples being set beside the large individual duct sections. The crate, partially submerged at some time during the voyage, had two nipples with a water line and a light rust coating.

"I need to show this rust to Mr. Owen and then I'll return it to the crate."

"That just stains from the crate bands rusting when the crate got wet," Jake offered as a rationale for the rust of the nipple.

"That makes sense."

At the office, Frank related the information that the consultant would fax the analytical information. He also added that some of the stainless steel air duct pieces either had rusted or been stained. Mike digested that information and then asked him if he was free this evening.

"Yes."

"Good, after Pine Tree leaves at five o'clock, get one of those stained nipples and another piece that's rust free. You need to take the two pieces of stainless steel to International Testing this evening."

Mike then called International Testing and arranged for the testing to determine the type of steel in the air ducts. He had cautioned the lab that the contractor wanted to use the pieces if they met specification, so only drill a small hole to obtain enough material for their test. The lab manager assured him the pieces would be repairable and if he delivered the samples by 9 P.M., results would be available by noon. Mike had a key to Pine Tree's storage lot and they quickly found two satisfactory samples for Frank to deliver. He told his young surveyor to save all his receipts. RBO would reimburse his expenses.

In his office bathroom cleaning up, Mike mulled over where to eat. The phone rang. Detective Larkin asked if he had time to look at photos of a body that a game warden had discovered below Wilson Chute in a field.

"Should Ann come?"

"I was going to call her next, but if you prefer to call her, please do. Meet at my office in an hour?"

Mike knew the doctor had released her from the hospital around 2 P.M. and she was at the Shaffers. He called and told her that the detective had pictures of a dead man who he thought might be their attacker. He had requested they look at the photos.

"Okay, but wouldn't the police use DNA from the blood to verify whether or not he was the assailant?"

"I would think so, but that process must take time, and the detective figures we're a quicker answer. Plus knowing the detective, he'll use it for another opportunity to ask more questions."

"How wonderful," she grumbled.

"Want me to pick you up? He wants to meet in an hour."

Mike knocked on the Shaffer's front door fifteen minutes later. Her boss answered the door and then Ann appeared wearing a light tan coat draped over her broken arm. He resisted the urge to wrap his arm around her and instead just stared at the beautiful sight as she returned his intense study.

"Ahem. Do you have a key?" Mr. Shaffer asked.

"I do. I wouldn't want him kicking in your door," she answered, which broke the spell and everyone laughed as she flashed them a smile.

Mike helped Ann into his Grand Cherokee while wondering if she felt for him the attraction he felt for her. Unfortunately, he wasn't sure enough to ask and feared rejection. He wasn't clear when he had realized she was the woman he wanted as his wife. The quandary for him was, in matters of the heart, caution could be poisonous. He needed to consider her appraisal of his hesitancy. She likely had pending decisions involving major, life-altering commitments such as buying Shaffer Concrete. He wondered what to do during the drive to the City Building and while parking across from the boat ramp where they had started the wonderful canoe trip.

Detective Larkin's office was a small room with a window that looked out on the back parking lot. Mike was surprised at the impressive array of modern computer equipment on his desk, better equipment then RBO had. The desktop had two large computer monitors and a keyboard arranged on it with a powerful Dell computer on the floor beside the desk. A fax machine, printer and copier combination unit sat on the file cabinet. The phone was in the top right hand desk drawer--to save desktop space Mike guessed. Reference books lined the shelf along one wall. Two chairs were available for visitors. Several pictures and awards hung on the other wall with a clock to complete the office décor. One picture showed a very young Larkin in a police uniform beside a 1964 Ford police car. The guy must be in his late seventies, Mike calculated.

He had half expected a hand-operated pencil sharpener and yellow pads, maybe even quill pens and an ink well. The detective was apparently a relic who believed in staying current with technology. Mike reminded himself not to judge people on appearance. The detective read his thought.

"You think only young people use computers? Be a gentleman and help Ann move that chair so her cast isn't hitting the desk."

Mike, embarrassed, tried to explain his surprise wasn't an age issue, but that Meadville supplied their officers with such fine equipment. The old man laughed at his lame excuse and Ann, the traitor, was struggling not to laugh.

"Most of it I bought and paid for on the advice of my technical advisor who also keeps me up to date on the latest and best software. Those reference books are there because I like to verify the information from the internet. An age thing I suppose, but a harmless habit."

Mike asked whom his technical advisor was and if he was expensive. His technical adviser was his sixteen-year-old granddaughter who demanded he buy her the same software and equipment, so she was rather expensive.

The detective turned serious, opened a folder, and handed them several face pictures of a man found earlier that day.

"Someone had dragged him about fifty feet into an abandoned field off the gravel road by Wilson Chute. Animals had chewed off part of his face, but there was enough of his face to identify him."

Ann and Mike passed the four pictures between them.

"I believe he is the man I shot. What killed him?"

"What about you, Mike?"

169

"Yes, he's the guy."

"He died from four 9-mm bullet wounds."

Detective Larkin then explained the blood work would confirm their initial identification by connecting him to the apartment blood. The man had taken a pounding, prior to the fatal 9-mm wounds. He had three 45-caliber bullet wounds, a knife wound, and cut and bruises consistent with falling down a long stairway. The 45-caliber wound locations matched Ann's description from the other night. The later and fatal point-blank 9-mm wounds suggest a partner covering his tracks.

"I'm proceeding on the assumption that your assault was a hired hit. He entered the country that same day through the Pittsburgh Airport as Karl Karadzic from Serbia. Do either of you know Karl Karadzic?"

Ann and Mike both answered no.

"Interesting, think what this cost the person who wishes you ill, Ms. Lane."

The detective made clear he was no expert on hiring international killers, but speculated that at least ten thousand dollars would be required for the services of a person like former Captain Karadzic of the Serbia Special Police Group. Who, he added, was a suspected war criminal in the Bosnian war.

"Why anyone would spend ten thousand dollars to have you murdered? Care to enlighten me. I've been up front this evening with you."

Ann had told Detective Larkin earlier about the RBO concrete contract and her suspicions that Ace was behind the sabotage. However, by now the RBO contract was over half completed, and the company would be unlikely to give the business to Ace if she was suddenly murdered. So she couldn't imagine any sane business reason for Ace hiring a murder.

Mike then related his theory on why Karl didn't instantly kill him. The assassin had known who he was, and had made a quick decision to switch from a random sexual assault-murder to a lover's fallout. He wanted him alive and framed for her death.

Detective Larkin liked his theory.

"If Karl had killed you, Ann and your death is just another sad story. Your father would have stepped in to handle the daily project management until your replacement was hired. But with you alive and charged with her murder, that would have been a major distraction."

"What an evil man," Ann said. "What was the point?"

"I suspect to take his father's focus off managing the project. Have him focus instead on helping his son avoid prison and disgrace. How Machiavellian, the cunning and duplicity leaves me breathless. I never realized building a wastewater treatment plant was such exciting business. So who benefits from Ann's death and RBO unsupervised?"

Mike suspected the Woodbrier brothers. Lacking proof, he kept quiet, but promised the detective they would give the question a lot of thought.

On the drive back to the Shaffer home, Ann was unusually quiet. She had never given a thought to why the assailant didn't kill Mike out right. That he could have wasn't in doubt. That he had taken the effort and care only to choke Mike unconscious was the reason she had time to recover and load her pistol. And had she failed, the assailant would have murdered her, and left the man she had fallen in love with as the prime suspect in her death. His reward for worrying over her safety and investigating her failure to wave from the window would have been disgrace and possible prison time. All so, an evil person could gain some unknown advantage.

The final pour in Basin No. 2 was today, and Mike knew the pour would complete half the concrete required by the project. He spotted Ann supervising one of Shaffer's laborers making test cylinders and checking the entrained air content. The previous night they had discussed how best to answer questions about her broken arm from the crews and drivers.

Ann wasn't in the mood to discuss her near-death experience with strangers. She had come up with the nonsense that it was a police matter, and she couldn't talk about it until the investigation was complete. Mike thought her idea would keep the men's natural curiosity at bay until she felt ready to discuss the matter or they forgot about it.

Terry was waiting for him with analytical reports on the stainless steel air ducts. The reports were in some language he couldn't read other than the numbers.

"Can you read these reports, Terry?"

"No, but the Pittsburgh office had someone who did. The material meets specifications. Jake is going to start installing ducts this afternoon."

Mike didn't share Terry's confidence and asked if he had sent samples of the material to International Testing for verification of the Russian or Kazakhstan information.

"Your boss specified Type-316 Stainless, which I always thought was unnecessary for air ducts, though it will last forever. I want to be sure that the Board is getting what they're paying for."

"I'll have a sample sent to the lab to verify the material is Type 316," Terry offered and hurried off to find Jake and obtain a sample.

Mike had Frank checking and counting the air duct sections. He walked over to Basin No. 1 to examine the delivered air ducts, and check on Frank. Instead, he encountered Jerry Woodbrier removing the pieces of air duct from pallets. He was using a four-foot pry-bar to snap the steel bands that secured the air duct material to the wood pallets. He looked up from breaking bands.

"I heard your girlfriend's secret life caught up with her."

"Pardon me, what did you say?"

"I heard she claimed some assailant attacked her. Or did you catch her with another guy?"

Mike was confused. Was the jerk trying to provoke him or was he an insensitive moron. He opted for moron.

"It's a police matter, not open for discussion. Where is Jake?"

"Whatever, but I know she likes rough sex. The bitch likes to be smacked around."

Mike was wrong. This creep was trying to provoke him. His temper stirred to life, the coldness that precedes his aggression replacing his usual tolerance for fools. He turned back to look and saw a grinning Jerry holding the steel pry-bar like a batter ready to swing. He taunted him with a come-here hand action.

"What's matter, you sweet on that nympho? Want to make something out of it, big-shot?"

Mike walked briskly back to the jerk, and without warning hit him in the face with a brutal blow from his right fist. A spray of blood from Jerry's nose resulted from his fist's impact, but though dazed, he still stood. He buried his left fist in the soft gut. That did the job. The man fell in a heap on the ground. The pry-bar clanged as it fell among the air duct pieces. The brief commotion attracted Frank, Jake, and a big laborer from the Pine tree crew and brought them running.

"Is he dead?"

"No, though I don't figure he will be of much help for the rest of the day."

Jake wanted to know why Mike hit his laborer, his boss's son.

"He can tell you. Frank, meet me at the office when you finish."

Mike walked off thinking about Ann's behavior when he had related Katie's remarks about Betty Deere and Jerry. Could there was some past connection between them, though he found the idea that a classy woman like Ann would have any use for a loser such as Woodbrier's son hard to believe, but everyone makes mistakes.

Or, maybe the attack on Ann had no connection to business. Maybe a rich sexual predator was working in the Meadville area and hired thugs to do the hard part of capturing and rendering his victims helpless.

"I have a special assignment for you. Search the internet and newspaper archives for information on Betty Deere and Jenny Lowell, along with anything on other missing girls from Allegheny and the Meadville area."

"Okay to spend some money on reports and archives searches?" Frank asked. "And may I ask why?"

"I'm curious. Get a company credit card from Steve to use. Use your judgment."

Word of a fight between Mike and Jerry swept the project site. The news made Ann very uneasy. Could Jerry have been stupid and said something to Mike about that night last year. He couldn't be that dumb, she told herself, but if he had what would Mike think of her? Time would tell. She did know what the concrete crew thought about the fight; they thought their boss threw a good punch for a college boy.

## Chapter 10

Mike received a call from Mr. Shaffer shortly after lunch asking him to stop by the office. He had information on the matter they had been discussing the day before. Mike, with Ann's cat, arrived at the same time as she did. Her cat had decided he was okay and lay calmly on the passenger seat, purring. He had hoped the relaxed cat would lift her spirits. Ann wasn't her usual cheerful self, but reserved as she accepted and placed the cat in her truck. After cracking open the truck's windows for air, she walked to the garage with him. Was her quiet mood because of his fight with Jerry? Surely, she didn't like that creep. Or was her arm hurting?

Her boss had been busy since their meeting yesterday, and now believed he understood the value of his business to the Woodbrier brothers.

"Our permitted gravel mine is Ace's target. Another year's production will exhaust their only gravel pit near Meadville."

"That will be a real cost burden for their Meadville operation. They'll have to haul in the gravel and sand for their concrete," Ann said.

They learned that Ace had never made a surface permit application on any other property, nor had anyone else. The four-hundred-acre Woodbrier farm a few miles south of Shaffer's plant that everyone had figured Ace would develop into their next gravel-sand operation had environmental issues. Mr. Shaffer's contact in the Pennsylvania Department of Environmental Protection had told him that a preliminary geological investigation two years ago found high groundwater tables and several wetlands that would severely limit any mining activity. The brothers had quietly dropped their plan for permitting the Woodbrier farm after that geological report.

"After next year, our gravel mine will be the only permitted operation within twenty miles of Meadville." Shaffer said.

"What about Taylor's sand pit out by Conneaut Lake?" Ann asked.

"Places like Taylor's didn't count. The DEP tolerates local operations like Taylor's pit that people and townships use for an occasional load of fill material. If the owners tried to install process equipment to separate the sand and gravel and created large disturbed areas, the department would close them down until they had permits and all the necessary environmental controls in place."

"So after next year, Ace will have to buy their concrete aggregate from competitors to make concrete in their Meadville and Franklin area plants," Mike said. "What is Ace's concern? The high cost of aggregate next year?"

"That's what I think. Ann you're up on costs. How is buying their aggregate going to affect their concrete costs?"

She put her coffee down and answered her boss's question with her usual detailed explanation.

"A cubic yard of concrete weighs roughly a ton and a half. The mix water, gravel, and sand account for most of that, so the cost impact per cubic yard of concrete to Ace will be the difference in the cost of a ton of purchased sand and gravel versus their mining and hauling cost. Their cost of mining and screening sand and gravel will be similar to ours, say $4 a ton. Then they already have an extra cost we don't have. Ace has to haul the gravel from their offsite mine to the ready mix plant and rehandle the material, say another $8 a ton. Since they are already handling the aggregate twice, those costs will reduce the impact of buying someone else's aggregate at $20 a ton delivered. The net cost increase to Ace when their mine closes will be $8 to $10 per cubic yard."

Shaffer interrupted her to explain to Mike the significance of the ten dollars per cubic yard cost increase to Ace. It would be serious money. The operation sold about a hundred thousand cubic yards of ready-mix concrete in the area last year. That ten-dollar increase per cubic yard in cost becomes a million-dollar hit to annual profit.

"Control of our sand and gravel operation would be worth a million dollars a year in cost savings to the Woodbrier brothers. Was that worth killing for, I hope not, but it is one explanation for the attack."

Mike was skeptical that in this day of billion-dollar deals and two-million-dollar vacation homes, wealthy businessmen such as the Woodbrier brothers would risk a murder conviction to save a million dollars, but then a million dollars every year was still a lot of money. What a muddle of possible motives for the attack.

"Sam and Lou are my number one suspects for the sabotage, but they've never expressed an interest in buying Shaffer," Ann added.

Mike pointed out that *someone* had hired a killer. He suspected Pine Tree Construction was working some fraud at the French Creek POTW project, though he would be the first to admit he didn't know what it was. The reason for bringing his worry to their attention was the Woodbrier brothers would be the ones to benefit.

"Anyone object to me telling Detective Larkin our thoughts?"

Mr. Shaffer gave a snort. "He's rather useless in my opinion, but I don't see any harm in talking to him. Ann, you're more involved. What are your thoughts?"

"The detective should be told everything. He's the only person with any real hope of catching the person responsible," Ann answered.

"I need to get back to the site. Basin No. 3's first footing pour is tomorrow and I need to check the forms. I'll contact the detective. Do you want to go, Ann?"

"Not unless he requires me. I want to spend some time with my mother."

The International Testing's report on the steel had come over the fax. Frank had the report on the two samples of stainless steel and gave Mike one of the several copies he had just made. The report identified the air duct steel as a chromoly steel with nine tenths of one percent chromium and a tenth of percent molybdenum. Type 316 stainless steel alloy generally contained ten percent nickel, sixteen percent chromium and two and half- percent molybdenum. The air duct material was not Type 316 stainless steel as called for in the specifications.

Chromoly steel was used for tubing that requires a higher strength than carbon steel, and though slightly more corrosion-resistant than carbon steel, was not considered a corrosion resistant steel. And Mike knew the chromoly steel, compared to stainless, was available at a much lower cost, since that steel contains no nickel, and a fraction of the chromium content in Type 316 stainless steel.

"You have any friends that understand Russian or whatever language that report is written in?"

"I might know a person, an instructor in the physics lab at Purdue that might help, Victor...something. He has an impossible last name . . . from Kiev, in Ukraine. He speaks Russian. I'll call him."

While Mike waited for Frank to call Victor, he called Terry and asked him the status of his test results on the air duct material. Terry told him tomorrow.

"Victor said he would look at it and call me right back," Frank answered as he finished feeding the last page into the fax.

Mike wanted to learn who started this fraud, the Russian manufacturer or Pine Tree. Victor called several minutes later, and talked to Frank for several minutes, verifying that the language was Russian and the material described was 4118 steel. The format of the report was different from the typical Russian analytical report. Victor thought that Kazakhstan mills use a different format for stainless steel. Regardless, according to Victor, the only way to know for sure was to send a sample of the material to a lab and test it.

"You should take none of those mills' paperwork at face value," he cautioned.

"I thanked Victor and told him I would buy the beer," Frank laughed before adding, "As soon as I turn twenty-one."

Mike, pleased with his young intern's abilities to find solutions, thanked him. He knew what 4118 steel was, that the lab was correct, and the foreign steel mill wasn't the problem.

"Tell Jake not to install any air duct until they have verification that it's 316 stainless."

Frank gave him a questioning look, but left to find the foreman. He was locking the office when Detective Larkin returned his call. They agreed to meet at the City Building in forty-five minutes.


Ann planned to spend the rest of the day with her mother, after leaving the Shaffer Concrete office, but first she went to the local sporting good-store to purchase a new pistol. There was no telling how long the police would hold hers for evidence. Besides, she needed a pistol suitable for single-handed operation, like a double

179

action revolver, and one that was small for easy concealment. The sport store had a large selection of revolvers, and she picked the .357 magnum caliber Lady Smith pistol by Smith and Wesson. She passed the State Police background check and paid for her new pistol and four boxes of ammo for practice.

The realization that her attack had not been a random event aggravated Ann. Another attempt on her life was possible, if control of the gravel mine was the assailant's target. Mike might also be in danger. Then she wondered where Jerry figured in all this and what had caused their fight. She'd never seen any evidence that Mike had a temper.

Ann changed her mind about going straight to the Shaffer home. Instead, she went back to their remote gravel pit and shot fifty rounds through the new pistol. It wasn't as accurate as her US Army 45, but at twenty-five feet, she could hit her five-gallon bucket-lid target five out of five shots. Equally important, she could reload the pistol using one hand and her lap. And the .357 magnum bullet packed a wicked punch compared to the 45 caliber round. The pistol needed a good cleaning, but that would have to wait until her arm healed, and she got the cleaning equipment from her old apartment.

At least she now felt safer, though her cat was thoroughly upset with all the gunshots. Her poor cat had been surviving on the men's lunch scraps at RBO's office. Ann reckoned her cat would appreciate some tuna. She stopped on the way to the Shaffer's home for several cans of tuna.

She looked forward to a visit with her mother, who she reckoned had a lot of questions about Mike Owen and their relationship. After taking a bath, being careful to keep her cast dry, and then a good dinner, Ann couldn't stay awake and deprived her mother of an opportunity to ask questions. Her last thoughts before falling asleep were to wonder how Mike made out with Detective Larkin.

Detective Larkin was working on the computer when Mike arrived, and after pausing for a brief greeting, he worked for another minute before wrapping up whatever he was typing.

"I often wonder how the world got by before these wonderful word programs. In the ancient days making a copy required carbon paper and onion skin paper. You know what carbon paper is, Mike?"

"I'm not sure, an ink-coated paper used with a typewriter so the key strike would imprint ink from the carbon paper on the second sheet under the one you were typing on?"

"You have the idea. Anyway, you called, so I assume you have an idea why someone wishes the lovely Ann dead?"

Mike related Mr. Shaffer's information. The gravel mine was worth a million dollars a year to Ace Ready-mix.

"I would suggest you call Mr. Shaffer direct, instead of receiving the information second hand from me, but he's not a fan of yours."

"Ted Shaffer has reasons to be unimpressed with my performance. Did you know he lost his only child, a son, about two years ago?"

"Yes, a car accident I heard."

Detective Larkin looked nonplused for a moment and then elaborated that he supposed his son's death could have been a car accident. The accident occurred just a few blocks from here on Chestnut Street. Bill Shaffer stopped at the light and a pickup rear-ended him. The impact was hard enough to pop the trunk lid on his Malibu and smash the taillights, but not trigger the airbag. He had jumped out to confront the other driver who in the meantime had backed up to free the bumpers and then started around Bill's car as if to run off. According to a witness, he tried to stop the driver who then swerved into him and crushed him against the open car door. The impact threw the door and his body into the gutter. The truck had then raced off. The police never found the driver or vehicle.

He paused at Mike's shocked expression, before adding his opinion that Bill's death wasn't a car accident. It was premeditated murder, though the record treats the death as an unsolved hit and run. Shaffer's son was a good man, and a geologist with a degree from Penn State. He was on the ball and had revived his father's concrete business. After his son's death, Ted lost interest, and rumor was he would sell Shaffer Concrete. Then Ms. Lane showed up.

"Three days ago a murder attempt was made against the current manager, Ms. Lane. Do you believe in coincidences?"

"Sure, random events that appear similar, but are not connected are coincidences. That's not the case here. Bill's death and her attack are connected--the removal of Shaffer's managers," Mike said.

The information that Woodbrier Construction dropped their plan for permitting their four-hundred-acre farm after an unfavorable geological report two years ago was news to Detective Larkin. The fact that Bill's accident occurred a couple of months after that decision inclined him to agree a possible connection could exist between the gravel mine, Bill's death, and Ann's attack. Proving the connection was the problem.

They sat in the office lost in thought until Mike asked if he had discovered anything about the driver for Karl. The old detective was in a confiding mood and enlightened him. The police had not found a trace of the vehicle or the driver.

"After I had interviewed Ann, I walked the neighborhood looking for parking spaces where a person might wait. From Karl's blood trail, I knew where the driver had picked him up. Two empty parking spaces that evening were in locations that would allow the driver to see the apartment entrance. A fresh Lucky Strike butt was in the street at the parking space with the best view of the apartment. So possibly Karl's driver smokes Lucky Strike cigarettes. Or not, but I still bagged the butt for evidence."

Mike decided to tell the detective about the possible fraud unfolding at the POTW project that may have bearing on this murder investigation.

"Pine Tree Construction has accidentally or on purpose, I'm not sure which, has taken delivery of chromoly steel air ducts instead of the type-316 stainless steel air ducts required by the specifications. The cost difference is approximately one and a half million dollars, with the chromoly being the cheaper material. I will know better tomorrow."

"I assume you believe Pine Tree hoped to substitute the cheaper material without anyone being the wiser," the detective asked.

"The fraud would have benefited from a distracted RBO management, and had Ann's attack been successful, I would have been seriously distracted."

"The Woodbrier brothers certainly appear to be the main benefactors of these attacks, but there is no evidence, zilch. Well, let's leave it at that tonight and see what tomorrow brings."

Detective Larkin sat in the quiet office and wondered what Dennis Norton's connection was to the fraud. Was Dennis in Sam and Lou Woodbrier's pocket? Who could put the Woodbrier brothers in contact with a Serbian hired killer? Who was the driver? He left at 1 A.M. for his home.

It was a night for his ghosts. His wife of forty-five years had died four years earlier from colon cancer. He missed her and the chance to discuss his cases with her for another perspective. Ann's attack would have intrigued her. Tonight though, the case haunting him was Jenny Lowell. How did she meet her end? The girl was a straight-A student in Allegheny's neuroscience program. Cute as a button and by all reports a friendly, decent kid from a good and loving family. He had never believed the runaway story. He prayed God would grant him the wisdom and evidence to see justice done for her before he died.

The next morning Terry Westfield was waiting for Mike in the RBO office trailer with his report from International Testing on the air duct material. The material was Type-316 stainless steel as per specification.

"I told Jake to start installing the Basin No. 1 air duct."

Had Terry actually cut a test specimen out of an air duct for the lab? No, Jake had given him one of the small nipples to send to the lab. Since all the pieces are from the same supplier, all the material would be the same, so the nipple ought to be representative of the air duct material. Mike didn't agree with that assessment and asked Frank to give Terry a copy of their test from two pieces of the air duct.

"That can't be right. The material is Type-316 stainless, not chromoly."

"Not based on those two field samples and the mill report," Mike said. "Tell Jake not to install the air duct until a lab verifies the material is Type-316 stainless."

Terry was angry and accused him of giving Pine Tree a hard time because he didn't like Jerry Woodbrier. Pine Tree had supplied the manufacture's documentation showing the material was Type-316, and he had sent a sample yesterday to the lab to double check. The lab would verify the material was stainless steel.

"You're being unreasonable. I'm calling Mr. Norton."

"That's a good idea, but first you need to countermand your order to start installing the air duct."

Mike told Frank to keep an eye on Pine Tree's crew and the air duct while he waited for the inevitable calls trying to convince him the air duct was specification material, or close enough not to care. The calls would be the usual sorry excuses from contractors caught performing substandard work, begging him to overlook improper work and material. He figured first Norton would call, then one of the Woodbrier brothers. The sad thing was the Board paid Norton and James to handle this type of material problem, not RBO Construction.

The first call was from Dennis Norton, and he used nice as his approach.

"Terry said there is an issue with the air duct material. You don't think the material is Type-316 stainless despite the manufacture's analytical report and the International Testing report. Why do you doubt them?"

"I sent two sections of the actual air duct to International Testing. The material is chromoly steel, not stainless, not spec."

"Chromoly is almost as strong as Type-316 stainless and will work for the air duct. The specifications allow substitutions. I can write the Board for approval."

Mike was disgusted with Mr. Norton's amnesia and reminded him of their February conversation when he was preparing RBO's bid. Asked why Norton and James had specified such an expensive material for the air ducts, Norton's response had been the French Creek Sanitary Board wanted a plant with low maintenance cost. Avoiding corrosion in the air ducts was an important element of that worthy goal.

"You even added that since everyone was bidding stainless steel, no bidder had an unfair advantage. Now suddenly corrosion is no concern," Mike said.

"We can change our minds. Chromoly will work fine for the air ducts."

"I won't argue if Pine Tree reduces their price to reflect the difference in cost between the two materials, and the Board's agreeable and acknowledges the new air ducts are not corrosion resistant."

"I'm sure the Woodbriers would be willing to knock twenty thousand dollars off the bid price and add painting the air ducts."

"I'll assume that was a poor attempt at humor. A reduction of $20,000 is a joke. I priced Type-316 stainless steel when I assembled the original bid. The stainless was $2,400,000. Chromoly is a third that price, or even less. What was Pine Tree's cost?"

"I haven't asked. I'm trying to keep the project moving and not waste a perfectly acceptable air duct."

"How considerate of you, but Pine Tree needs to reduce their bid more, like by $1,500,000."

"That is the most preposterous idea I've heard from a contractor. You can't be serious. Does your father know? I figure Pine Tree will be calling their lawyer." The angry Mr. Norton had resurfaced.

"Do Pine Tree a favor. Remind them that as a result of ordering the wrong air duct material, they'll quickly be in default of the no-delay-of-project provision in their contract."

"Don't take that attitude. It'll cause everyone problems, except the lawyers."

"I'm not especially worried. Pine Tree's performance bond of five million dollars will cover any expense to replace them, along with the extra cost to order the right material. However, the Woodbriers should be!"

"You're making a serious mistake. They will sue RBO."

"I'd suggest you caution them not to make this a bigger problem than it is now for Pine Tree with foolish threats."

Mike had a dial tone as his answer. He figured things were going to get interesting and harbored the hope that Sam's anger might cause him to make a mistake and help the police determine who ordered that attack on Ann.

*Speak of the devil* he thought as Ann and her mother came into the office.

"Hi, Mike. I was giving my mother a tour of the project and wanted her to meet Steve and Larry. We ran into Terry at Basin No. 3. He was in an evil mood. Have you been giving him a hard time?"

Mike noticed her mother looked right at home in those rubber knee boots Ann seems to favor. He told them about the air duct material mix-up, and Mr. Norton's negative response to his suggestion for correcting the problem.

"I reckon that's the scam you've been worrying about. Please be cautious. I'll catch up with you later," Ann added as they left the office, after taking time to pet the mutt, which sent his tail into an energetic wag.


Frank had been busy digging deep into missing girls from the area. Jenny Lowell was the only missing girl in the last five years from the Meadville area not accounted for. Jenny had vanished on a Saturday evening in March sixteen months ago, after attending a private party. A number of Allegheny students, with permission from the owner, had turned an abandoned farmhouse between Frenchtown and Tamarack Lake into a location for a beer keg party. Portable heaters and a small generator provided heat and electricity for the party.

According to reports, Jenny liked to party, didn't use alcohol, and usually drove herself, which she had that night. Police found her car near the Pittsburgh International Airport several days later in a back parking lot of the Blue Roof Motel.

None of the students recalled her leaving. The police weren't surprised that no one remembered her departing since over a hundred people at one time or another during the evening had attended the party. The amount of traffic generated by partygoers had even made one of the neighbors suspicious, and he had called the police. The

David C. Brown

police had checked around ten o'clock that evening and reported no problems.

Frank had two questions that needed answered: who owned the property and gave permission, and who organized the party. Someone did a fair amount of work rounding up equipment and buying food and beer. The internet had no additional information and Frank headed to the courthouse.

Dennis Norton had called Sam Woodbrier and told him they had a problem. He needed to meet with him and Lou. Sam had called his brother, who agreed to meet the two of them in Sam's private office over the garage at his home overlooking Conneaut Lake. He put on a fresh pot of coffee and sat at his desk to await his partners and admire the beautiful vista of the largest natural lake in Pennsylvania.

Lou and Dennis arrived at the same time and Dennis quickly explained the air duct issue. Sam fumed in response to his depiction of Owen's shocking demand for a price reduction of a $1,500,000.

"That's unbelievable. He can't be serious. It's not an acceptable resolution. You dreamed up the idea of switching materials. What do you propose?" Sam said. "For damn sure Pine Tree isn't reducing the price."

"That asshole is messing with the wrong people," Lou threatened.

"Let Dennis finish. You'll get your chance."

These moments caused Dennis to regret ever getting involved with the Woodbrier brothers. He had no one to blame for his predicament but himself and his greed. Since resigning was not an option, he soldiered on, explaining that now only several people were aware of the air duct material issue. To keep all their options open, they did not need to be involving lawyers, the Board, or suppliers.

188

"Mike Owen currently has the full picture," Dennis said. "Possibly he has told others, like Ms. Lane and his father. Being realistic, the only hope of containing the damage is for Owen to have an accident, and soon."

"And how will that help?" Sam said.

"First, if he hasn't told anyone, well, dead men don't talk. Second, if he has told someone, say his father, I'll have a better chance to initiate a resolution if Mike isn't there disparaging the solution."

"I like that idea," Lou said.

"I can buy time by telling Owen that Pine Tree agrees with his conditions, but needs a few days to lock in a stainless steel supplier. Ask him not to say anything about the mix up so the stainless steel supplier won't learn Pine Tree is desperate. Give the brothers a chance to negotiate a better price for the replacement air duct."

"You think he's that naïve?"

"I think he would agree to that," Dennis said.

"Okay, buy us some time. Tell him whatever you think will work. We'll get our lawyer on the problem. Plan to meet again next week."

He understood the brothers were not about to discuss a murder in front of him and gathered his briefcase and left. Dennis called Mike to tell him that contrary to his expectations Pine Tree was willing to make things right, but needed a few days to arrange a new supplier. In the meantime, the less he said, the better, to allow him an opportunity to negotiate with the Board on changing the air duct material and price. Mike was agreeable.

Mike had never met anyone that changed moods faster than Dennis Norton did. Still, he was having difficulties accepting the Woodbrier brothers were going to acquiesce to losing well over a million dollars. He was mulling over the implication of the call and possible repercussions when Frank entered the office to get a level rod for Larry.

"Hi, boss. After I drop off the rod, I'll be at the courthouse on the Lowell matter. In case you're interested, your old pal Paulie is down at the footing pour."

"What's that weasel doing on the site?"

"Besides smoking up a storm, he is after empty concrete test cylinders. Norton and James is the consultant for the Grove City job, and he is their inspector."

"I feel sorry for Grove City."

"The guy reminds me of my uncle. Has the same habit of lighting the new cigarette with the one he just finished. A serious chain smoker, smokes the old style short unfiltered Lucky Strikes. Can you imagine his lungs? They have to be a mess."

Mike thought, *Paulie.* He decided to play a hunch. After getting a small plastic bag out of the supply closet, he drove to the Basin No. 3 site.

When they arrived, the fired inspector was just getting in a red Norton and James Ford pickup. Mike watched him throw a cigarette on the ground while slamming the truck door. After waiting a moment, he told Frank to go distract the Norton and James inspector.

Frank, without a question or missing a beat, walked up to the inspector and asked him to come over and check the rebar spacing behind the wall form. The moment they were out of sight, Mike hurried to the parking area and carefully retrieved the butt. He called Detective Larkin and asked to meet. They agreed to meet in fifteen minutes at Walmart's parking lot.

"I have a possible lead on Karl's driver and a Lucky Strike butt that you should check for a match on DNA or whatever it is police check to identify people."

"Why your focuses on this particular cigarette butt?"

190

"He was the inspector involved in sabotaging Ann's concrete test cylinders. That along with him being a Lucky Strikes smoker, I thought made checking for a connection to Henry Street worthwhile."

Detective Larkin agreed and took the bag.

Mike called his father and found out Dennis Norton had not called him and proceeded to bring his father up to date on the air duct material controversy. His father agreed that Pine Tree was just stalling. No way, the Woodbriers would voluntarily replace the air duct and lose a million dollars.

"I want to make our lawyer aware of this potential problem. Get his thoughts on the best approach to dealing with Pine Tree to minimize delays."

His father sanctioned involving the company's attorney, and then asked if anyone else had attacked him or Ann. No attacks, Mike assured him.

## Chapter 11

"Can a plausible accident be arranged quickly? Remember he is already on Larkin's radar from that botched attack on the girl," Sam said.

Lou looked belligerent, and answered accordingly.

"Forget that line of reasoning. People get too clever. Karl's screw-up is a perfect example. He should have just shot them and been done with it. Now Larkin is wondering why anyone would want to kill Shaffer's concrete tech. You really think he isn't going to suspect an accident involving Owen?'

"So what do you suggest?" Sam asked.

"Knowing that, hit him. Nothing fancy, just leave no evidence."

Sam thought why indeed and switched his attention from his brother to watching, through the garage office's large window, Dennis drive off. After a moment to be sure the consultant had left the property, he returned his focus to his brother.

"I don't like this one bit. We're allowing Dennis to expose us to serious personal risks for a rather minor payoff with this air duct business."

"Minor? It's over a million dollars," Lou said.

"Plus, I'm not comfortable with Dennis having such damning information. He dreamed the scheme up to bid stainless steel air ducts."

"Well, it worked, forced everyone to bid a high price to cover the stainless steel cost."

"Yeah, I know. Use his position as the consultant to approve a switch to a cheaper material after awarding of the bid. The scheme would have worked, if we had been the general contractor instead of the subcontractor. Without RBO's collaboration the scheme can't work, even taking out Owen doesn't ensure success if other people start asking questions about corrosion and cost differentials."

"Dennis could pull it off if Owen was out of the picture."

"Maybe, but the federal funds involvement meant potentially serious audits at the end of the contract. One wrong question on why the air-duct material was switched, or how the cost adjustment was determined, could unravel the scheme."

Lou agreed and said. "If only Karl had been successful. His botched hit put everyone on alert. The police are involved. Paulie knows too much."

Sam was well aware that his brother, though uncomfortable with Dennis's inside knowledge, believed Paulie to be the weaker link. The inspector had been involved in two murders and if the police connected him to one of those murders, or some other dumb thing he'd done that they weren't even aware of, he would sell Lou out in a heartbeat.

That was his point, Sam told his brother. He wasn't comfortable with their exposure. The Shaffer gravel mine was the only item worth taking such risks. Still, he agreed that Paulie was a threat that they needed to address.

"Paulie's death would put Dennis on notice to behave," Lou said.

"You never know. It might scare him into going to the police. I'm considering instructing him to sort the air duct issue out on his own. Let him work out something with the Board and RBO. The prudent decision may be to risk losing a half million dollars, rather than trying to murder our way out of the problem."

Lou disagreed with his brother. Giving up on the air duct scheme was a sign of being weak, not being prudent. Their business associates would think they were getting soft.

"I'm relieved you agree he is a walking time bomb and needs to go. Instead of pulling back, I want him to try again on the girl and Owen. If he screws up again, a possibility since those two fought off Karl, I still figure the girl would be so terrorized that she'd go back to Indiana. Owen could go either way--get his back up or be reasonable. Regardless we're no worse off with the Pine Tree problem."

"That just put's Paulie deeper into our business," Sam said.

"Well my last step would be eliminating him. Plant evidence on him for the police to find that links him to the attacks. The police will know he isn't the end of the line, but what can they prove? Having a body with evidence linking it to the crime will help satisfy the public."

Sam didn't for a moment believe being cautious was a sign of weakness. Instead, it was a sensible weighing of risks and rewards. Lou's plan had plenty of risks and pitfalls: the girl had already proved she was no weak sister, Owen was surely on guard and likely armed, and Paulie was going to be leery.

"I'll concede that similar reckless risk taking, as just proposed, has made us wealthy," Sam said. "Then the risks had been necessary, but today . . ."

Sam had never forgot they were raised in that sorry shack behind the dog food plant in Kerrtown and considered white trash by the people who worked their parents for minimum wages and zero benefits. The local big shots were not about to cut them any breaks, and he felt they'd been justified in cutting a few corners to get started. Their ambition was to escape poverty, and become accepted by the local society and respected. They had been successful. Due to their wealth, they were accepted. However, a murder indictment would end their social acceptance. The kicker was they now knew most of the people they had initially considered social role models were pathetic losers. Without some rich and likely criminal ancestor, many of those same people would live a life of penury.

"We have much to lose. For that reason alone we need to heed the hardest lesson for successful people--what worked in the past may not work tomorrow. Times change and smart people change with them. Hiding criminal involvement from the police with all their new technology is becoming impossible."

"Not impossible, brother, you just have to be more careful," Lou said. He looked unconcerned.

"I wouldn't be surprised they already had proof Paulie was involved in that Henry Street attack. They just don't know who he is--yet."

"That's my point. He is too dangerous to leave alive."

"That's not my point. Remember a drop of your blood or a hair is like leaving a business card for the cops," Sam said.

"Yeah I know. So don't leave evidence."

"I'm inclined to support your idea, despite the pitfalls, because Paulie has to go and quickly. I like your idea to accomplish other benefits while getting rid of him. But then, brother, I want to tidy up all the loose ends and go straight from here on."

Lou agreed with Sam's opinions, except maybe the last part.

"Paulie is going to be skittish and need handholding. I don't see any option but to offer to drive for him or have him drive me. I'll have to be involved, unless you have another suggestion?"

"What about explosives? Blow up the damn car with them in it. The Arabs do it all the time. It can't be too difficult."

"Can be if you don't know anything about explosives and I don't."

Besides, Lou pointed out, explosives are not easy to find and time was limited. They needed to eradicate the problem, ideally tomorrow. He would entice Paulie with an offer of seven-thousand dollars for a double hit. That amount would maximize his greed and minimize his caution.

"I'll give him that fully automatic AK-47 rifle I bought from Sal last summer, along with two forty round clips. Even Paulie should be able to do serious damage to a stopped car with that kind of firepower."

Lou's last hit job had involved rear-ending the victim's vehicle and then running over the angry driver when he exited the vehicle to investigate the damage. That method wouldn't work with two people in the vehicle.

"I plan to force Owen's vehicle off the road, then pull alongside, and have Paulie hose down the car's occupants with forty 7.62 mm slugs through the windows. Then finish the job with a white phosphorus grenade tossed in the car. It would be a Baghdad moment in Meadville."

"Well, that ought to do it," Sam said.

He accepted Lou was the cowboy of their partnership, but also appreciated that an audacious action like this needs a quick and bold person to be successful. Despite the risks and weakness of his brother's plan, Sam had a great desire to resolve the issue.

"Find out if he's willing. I'll find out Owen's plans."

Lou, not concerned with failure, was happy, and parted in high spirits to track Paulie down.

The bookie had been livid with the Camry's condition and was currently after Paulie for another thousand dollars to cover the cost of disposing of the 1998 Camry. He thought the bookie's attitude unfair; he couldn't help that Karl had messed up. What else could he have done? He was thinking about calling Lou for the money when

Lou's call arrived. They agreed to meet at the closed public spring on old Route 8 south of Franklin in an hour.

Lou wasted no time. After brief greetings, he told Paulie he needed his help to finish the job Karl had failed to accomplish. Nothing fancy, a drive-by type operation with an AK-47, but they needed to do it tomorrow evening or at the latest, the following evening.

"I want you to roundup another clean car," Lou said. "You can shoot or drive your choice along with seven-thousand dollars for your troubles, five of it now."

Fear and greed warred in Paulie. He knew the bookie was serious about collecting the extra thousand and that Lou would be unreceptive to paying the extra money to the bookie if he refused to help. The simplest solution was to add the thousand to the cost for another vehicle.

"Sure, I'll help and handled the gun. The car is the problem, I figure that will cost several thousand after the last experience."

Lou knew he was being maneuvered on the car cost, but let it ride. He asked if the price included shredding the car afterward.

"I don't know. I'm not even sure my friend has another car."

Lou told him to request that added service during the arrangement of the vehicle, while he counted out an extra two thousand dollars to add to the five thousand dollars.

"I wanted two pistols for backup. Oh, by the way, have you ever fired a machine gun?

"Is it fully automatic?"

"This AK-47 is fully automatic. Two full forty-round magazines enough?" Lou asked.
"The more magazines, the better and I'd used the bump stock AR-15's, same thing. I need to find the bookie."

Satisfied with Lou's deal, he headed to Pittsburgh to find a vehicle. They had decided a heavy pickup truck would work better than a car. Lou would call tomorrow on the time and place to meet. The thousand dollars put the bookie in a helpful frame of mind and a ten-year-old Ford F-250 with Leroy's Garden-Lawn Service painted on the doors was soon located. Paulie didn't want any memorable markings on the pickup and had the name painted over with gray primer. The bookie agreed for an extra $500 to have the pickup shredded when returned, no questions asked. The vehicle cost came to thirty-five hundred dollars.

Frank had returned from the courthouse and worked on a topo map at the office for a half hour before calling Mike over. One of the numerous small black squares on the USGS topo map had a circle drawn around it in red pencil.

"That's the party house where Jenny was last seen. Otto Taylor owns the property, a one-hundred-eighty acre parcel."

Frank explained his dead end on the internet--numerous articles with the same limited information on Jenny's disappearance. There was no information on a Betty Deere. Mike took the copies to read and thanked him for the information.

Helen Smith, a dark-haired farm girl, was a sophomore Frank had made acquaintance with while in the Allegheny College library researching Jenny's disappearance. A lively soul, Helen had introduced Frank to the Goat Barn social scene. Both were underage, but managed to get past the doorman with Helen's fake ID card. After a couple of beers and two dances, they decided a dark country lane offered more entertaining possibilities and left.

Helen told him about a party that several Allegheny seniors planned for Saturday night at an abandoned farmhouse near Frenchtown. She invited Frank to go with her. He liked the idea and offered to pick her up at her home, a farm south of Meadville.

Mike had passed Katie Gambone driving a roll-off truck and told Steve to tell her when she came back across the scales that he needed to see her. He had just finished reading Frank's information on Jenny Lowell when she rushed in his office.

"Make this quick. I have to get the last load to the landfill," Katie said.

"Well, this will wait. I wanted to hear the Betty Deere story. There are no articles on the internet."

"I heard you and Jerry had a brief set-to. Is that the reason?"

"No, I'm just curious about her and Jenny Lowell."

"Meet me at Bows, six o'clock."

Katie was gone as quick as she had arrived. Steve told him how to get to Bows' bar. Before leaving, he called Ann to check on how her mother liked the area and asked how her healing was progressing. All was fine. He added he wouldn't be by this evening, but would like to take her out tomorrow night. Ann wasn't sure if her mother had a shopping trip to Erie planned or not. She'd let him know in the morning at the big pour.

Bows was a bar in a white cinder block building out SR 77 with a well-illuminated interior and loud music. The seating consisted of a couple dozen tables with three to four chairs each arranged around a dance floor. The décor was western with a lot of knotty pine and the obligatory deer heads common in the local bars. A comfortable establishment for a beer Mike decided and walked to the bar for one. Katie hadn't arrived.

A harsh looking man about his size and age tended the bar, and asked if he was Mike.

"My sister called and said she was running a few minutes late. She said to give you a beer."

He quickly learned the bartender was Katie's older brother, Tony, who was filling in for the sick owner, his uncle. Mike found a corner table and waited with his Miller Lite. A couple of the laborers from the project was at the bar and waved to him. Katie and another girl rushed in five minutes later. She told her brother she wanted two of whatever Mike was drinking and another one for him. She looked very at home in Bows with her jeans and boots. Her friend was a quiet person, unlike Katie, who radiated loudness. Both were cute girls. Katie's friend was about five feet four inches tall, with a lissome figure.

"Mike, Betty wasn't available. This is Lucy Kerbert. She heard about Ann's attack and that you decked Jerry. She wanted to meet you."

Introductions attended to, Mike explained the attack on Ann had made him realize no one was safe. He had thought her attack related to business issues that he hoped would be resolved shortly. Then he had learned about Betty Deere and another girl Jenny Lowell. He was curious if a sexual predator operated in the area. Perhaps business issues had nothing to do with Ann's attack.

Mike explained that he had no connection with the police, had no law enforcement background, and really had no business even involving himself in Jenny's disappearance. However, sometimes an outsider's perspective on an event can lead to new insights and resolution. So if Lucy didn't wish to answer his questions, he certainly would understand.

After they exchanged glances, Lucy told Mike to ask away. He started by asking what happened to her. She wasn't sure, but suspected a date rape. Lucy had heard about a keg party some of the older students were having at a home on Seminole Drive and went. These parties were equivalent to singles bars in larger cities, but better in that most of the attendees were Allegheny College students, and generally, the parties were fun affairs. Drinking wasn't her thing and she had limited herself to a couple of glasses of draft beer over the evening.

A big guy, an older English major who she learned was Jerry Woodbrier spent time with her. They talked about hooks in prose to grab the reader's interest and traded jokes. He at some point refilled their glasses and then things became fuzzy for her. She dimly recalled camera flashes while laying on a bed, though her memory of flashes may just had been part of a dream. Her next clear thought was sitting in her car dressed. The cold had awakened her and the house was dark. The time was three o'clock in the morning. She had a rotten taste in her mouth and a mild headache. When she got back to her room and undressed, her panties were on backward and her vagina was swollen and starting to ache.

"Did you tell the police?"

"I did. A doctor examined me and verified my suspicions, but there was no semen. Detective Larkin questioned Jerry and me along with several other students. They all professed not noticing anything improper," Lucy said. "That lying Paul Taylor told the police he saw me leave around eleven o'clock."

Lucy took a sip of beer ad continued, "According to the detective, the complete memory blank for the evening, other than the flashes, is typical of flunitrazepam anterograde amnesia. The detective said he'd ask around, but wasn't optimistic. Then a few days later Jerry stopped me in the library. He was mad that I would suggest he was capable of such behavior. I told him to stay away from me or I'll call the police. The next day Woodbrier's lawyer called to caution me of a possible lawsuit for slander. So I dropped the complaint and considered myself lucky nothing worse happened. I could have ended up being another Jenny Lowell."

"You figure Jenny was a date rape that went bad?" Mike asked.

Katie spoke for the first time since Lucy had related her story. "That's my bet. Jenny was a date rape victim."

Lucy nodded in agreement. Mike then told them about Frank locating the house where Jenny vanished. Otto Taylor owned the house, located south of Frenchtown toward Tamarack Lake.

"I need to learn who organized the party," Mike said. Lucy didn't know. Katie thought she might be able to find out.

"Otto Taylor is Paul Taylor's grandfather. Paul and Jerry are cousins."

Katie then told them one of her state police friends told the story about finding Jerry naked with his hands taped behind his back and blindfolded with duct tape last April. A female had called the state police saying a naked man was standing along a dirt road near Frenchtown. She had called with Woodbrier's phone.

Jerry claimed he had stopped to help an older couple with car trouble and they had robbed him, taken the phone. No older couple was ever located. Police found Jerry's car at Ace Concrete's Saegertown office. Her state police friend knew there was more to the story, but Jerry didn't cooperate and they dropped the matter.

The meeting wrapped up with agreement to stay in touch. If Katie could find out who organized the party Jenny attended, perhaps that information would give them a lead.


The third aeration basin neared half completion with the floor pour today, another five-hundred cubic yards of concrete. The pour progressed uneventfully. Mike found Ann with her arm in the cast enjoying the sunshine on a pile of steel concrete forms that offered her a seat with a good view of the pour activities.

"You're wasting your time with Katie. She's rumored to not be into guys."

"Do I detect a hint of jealousy?"

"You better believe it. I worked hard to save you," a smiling Ann answered.

Mike related his meeting with Katie and Lucy and watched his love's cheerfulness fade. Lucy's story had obviously affected her as much as it had him. To lighten her mood he told her Katie's story of a naked Jerry Woodbrier found along a gravel road. Ann's response startled him: she looked stricken. Then Mike knew. The reason for all Ann's past pensive behavior whenever Jerry Woodbrier's name came up, she was a victim of date rape by the bastard. He nearly demanded an answer before realizing what a sensitive issue he had stumbled into and how treacherous this terrain might be.

"Is there something you need to tell me?"

Ann gave him a beseeching look while slowly shaking her head in the negative. She stood up to walk off, just as Steve yelled that a lawyer wanted to talk to him. Mike needed to read the fax just sent first, before calling the lawyer. A moment after Steve's yell, Ann's phone rang. Mike heard Tim ask her to pick up a fan belt at the dealer for the small rubber tire loader. The batch plant crew needed the loader back in operation as soon as possible. Mike watched Ann hurry to her pickup.

The RBO attorney had faxed a copy of the letter she proposed to send to Pine Tree. The letter invoked the delay-of –project provisions and started the clock on the ten-day notification period to forfeit the performance bond and have Pine Tree vacate the site. Mike's goal was to use the letter to motivate Pine Tree towards ordering the stainless steel air duct and avoid delaying the project. The attorney's letter was fine with him, but Mike remembered agreeing to give Pine Tree a couple of days to negotiate with the stainless steel suppliers. He told the attorney to have everything ready to mail in three days if Pine Tree still dragged their feet on ordering the new air ducts.

Mike debated beating the answer out of Jerry, but figured that would more likely land him in jail, instead of getting an answer on

Jerry's involvement with Ann. Life in Meadville was proving dangerous. He needed a better method of protection than his fists. Next time he might not have Ann there with her pistol. His shotgun in the motel room that he planned to use for hunting the local ring-necked pheasants in the fall would do. It was a Remington Model 870 pump shotgun chambered for twelve-gauge three-and-a-half inch magnum cartridges. The gun packed a wicked punch.

A shotgun's size limited its handiness for concealment, but the 870's easily exchangeable barrels include one that was eighteen inches long. With the short barrel his shotgun was a versatile self-defense weapon and reasonably maneuverable in the confined space of his Cherokee. Mike reckoned the prudent response would be to buy a non-resident hunting license along with a box of shells and carry the gun in his vehicle. With a valid hunting license and the gun unloaded and in a gun-case there should be no legal issue. He drove to Wal-Mart and purchased a box of powerful high velocity No. 4 Hevi-Shot cartridges for three-and-a-half inch 12-gage magnums and the non-resident Pennsylvania hunting license.

Mike found Ann standing by the lower pond below the Shaffer screening operation watching her people perform. The concrete trucks were in line, with one loading under the batch plant. Two rubber tire loaders were hustling sand and gravel to the batch plant hoppers to keep up with the mixer. Many well-organized activities to watch as Shaffer raced to complete the five-hundred-cubic yard pour at the RBO project. He knew Ann was proud of her organization and rightfully so as he walked over to her. She looked worried.

"Hi Mike. Are you wondering what I am?"

"No, I know what you are--the finest woman I have ever met."

David C. Brown

"As you know, an interview with Woodbrier Construction brought me to Meadville. I quickly realized they would never hire a woman engineer. Nothing specific, just comments like can you handle rough men, would the dust and noise be a problem, comments along those lines concerning a woman being too weak for the rigors of construction. Sam's son Jerry was there and after the interview he asked if he could show me the area later. I had an interview with Shaffer that afternoon, and though I felt the Woodbriers wouldn't make an offer, I did want to see the area. I agreed to meet Jerry at Ace around six o'clock."

She then told about her interview with the Shaffers that afternoon. As he knew, it had gone well. She left with a job offer from Shaffer that afternoon.

"I was tired and took two caffeine tablets before leaving to meet Jerry. I knew from college that my body wouldn't react for at least an hour to the caffeine, and then I would be awake for half the night, but I didn't want to nod off after eating dinner. The weather was warm that evening for Meadville in April, and I wore a short dress. Jerry wanted to show me Ace's plant, and prior to the tour got them each a Corona and put a slice of lime in each bottle. The equipment was newer than Shaffer's equipment, but not maintained as well. After the tour of the plant in Jerry's new Ford crew-cab pickup, he offered to show me Woodcock Reservoir before it got dark. He knew from the interview that I liked fishing."

"I know."

"Woodcock is a beautiful lake and located a few miles from Ace's plant. I got sleepy in the warm cab. Nearly fell asleep during the short ride to the reservoir. That should have forewarned me, but the fresh air revived me on exiting Jerry's pickup. We spent ten minutes reading the signs and looking at the lake and dam. Then Jerry wanted to eat, and we headed to town."

206

Ann paused and looked him in the eye for a moment, and then continued with her story. Mike appreciated that none of this was easy for her.

"A flash woke me. I was momentarily confused, and then stunned to realize I was on a blanket in the pickup bed on my back, naked. Jerry was standing over me, naked with an erection. He was busy adjusting a camera. My left hand and ankle were fastened with nylon ropes to tie-down rings in the side of the truck bed."

"Christ, what'd you do?"

"I kicked the bastard with my free right leg, caught him squarely in his scrotum. He bent over from the shock, and I kicked him again, catching his jaw. That knocked him off the truck bed."

Ann's description of her harrowing night appalled Mike. "What if your leg had been tied, or handcuffed?"

"That doesn't bear thinking about. I'd have been helpless." Ann described her frantic effort to untie the ropes and free her left hand and leg. Free and on her feet, she saw Jerry stunned on the ground behind the truck.

"I worried how long I had to secure him. He was too big and strong for me to subdue. I discovered the roll of duct tape on the blanket, and decided to try securing him before he recovered. He started to struggle, but I managed to get his hands behind his back and taped together."

"What if you hadn't?"

"I'd have done something. Claw an eye, maybe run into the woods. He started whining he was just playing, and I had hurt him. I duct-taped his eyes and ears. Then I added more tape around his arms to tape them to his body. He could stand, but couldn't see and started asking what I was going to do, pleading for me not to call the police. I never said a word after the second kick."

"The feeling of power, satisfaction that swept through me was awesome as I looked down on that would-be rapist. I now know what David felt those many millennia ago."

"If you hadn't wakened. . ."

"That thought still haunts me. Or the other tie downs had been installed."

"Wait, what do you mean?"

"It was a brand new truck and only had those eye-bolt tie downs on one side of the bed. They're always installed in pairs opposite of each other, I figure whoever was installing them hadn't had time to finish before Jerry grabbed the truck. It was brand new."

Ann continued her story. She had decided no police while getting dressed as Jerry stumbled blindly around the truck crying for her not to leave him. Had she known of Jenny Lowell's disappearance at the time, she would have called the police and waited for their arrival. Instead, she found his truck keys and phone. The cell phone gave her the idea of calling the police. Let the creep explain how he ended up naked and tied.

Then she remembered Jerry had a camera and found it under the back of the truck, a digital Olympus. Ann knew next to nothing about how to operate his digital camera, but finally figured out how to turn it on and took a couple of pictures of Jerry. Why she bothered she wasn't sure except for a vague thought the pictures might prove her story if the need arose. She then put the camera in his small backpack and the backpack in the truck to take with her. She walked back to him and finally spoke.

"I told Jerry I would shoot him dead if he ever said a word. I was worried about the embarrassment. I should have been worrying about what he might do to another woman. I have prayed many times since then that my fear of embarrassment didn't cost another woman her life."

"I think you were in grave danger. Isn't the idea of date rape to get the woman unconscious with a drugged drink, have your sneaky way with her, then tidy up the woman and scene so she doesn't realize rape has occurred? Duct tape leaves sticky residue. Rope leaves marks. That he bothered to try securing you to the truck implied he thought you might wake. How could Jerry ever hope to explain your predicament if you woke up? He couldn't. I think he planned from the beginning to kill you if you woke up ahead of time."

"Surely he can't be that heartless and cold."

"Your experience convinces me that Jenny Lowell was probably a victim of a similar crime. She also woke up, but she died. If Jerry did that, the next one would be easier. You're very lucky. What did you do?"

"I shoved him off the edge of the farm lane and left him crying in the road ditch."

Ann called the state police when she entered Meadville's city limits and told them about seeing a naked man and where to find him. She parked Jerry's pickup at Ace and got her own car. She drove back to Indiana that night after a shower at the motel.

"I believe the caffeine saved me."

Mike was amazed and horrified by her story. By then he was hugging Ann.

"We better leave before they forget to add cement," Ann said.

Mike refocused on his surroundings and noticed the loader operator had slowed down, and drivers were watching them with smiles.

"You're right, let's get my Cherokee," Mark said. "Lucy remembered a flash. That along with your experience suggest the perverts must take pictures of the victims. You still have his bag and camera?"

"I do, but back home in Indiana."

"Jenny Lowell disappeared five weeks before your attack. If he was involved there might be evidence in that bag or on the camera connecting him to the girl."

"My father will be here the first of the week, I'll ask him to bring it, but I don't expect we're that fortuitous. Even Jerry's not that stupid to leave pictures of a murdered girl on his camera's card."

## Chapter 12

The productive day ended with Basin No. 3 finished, except for the end wall pour. Larry, with Frank helping, worked on the sludge digester foundation layout. Pine Tree was making excellent progress on the electrical and sewer lines connecting the process equipment to the different basins and pumps. The early August weather, as nice as the Meadville weather gets, had helped all the crews get ahead on their schedules, and that had Mike in a relaxed mood. He looked forward to picking Ann up at 6 P.M. for their dinner date.

Tomorrow night her father and brother would be in, and Mike figured she planned for him to meet the Lane family. He suspected Ann's mother had surmised his intentions toward her daughter. Mrs. Lane had expressed considerable interest in his opinions on political matters and children. The temptation to tease her was great, but he behaved himself.

Ann wore one of those short dresses that so became her. Her left arm cast was a jarring reminder the world could be a dangerous place, but regardless, the cast did not distract from her beauty. Every time he saw Ann, Mike was reminded how fortunate he was to have met her. Tonight she wanted to try a nice looking Italian restaurant on US322 a mile west of Meadville. Mike had promised no business talk or any discussion about Jerry.

The Shaffers's home was Alden Street in Meadville, an older residential section of town. Mike, in order to admire an old Victorian house, drove to Chestnut Street instead of using the more direct route down Arch Street to Main Street. They had just stopped at Chestnut and Grove for the light when a scruffy looking F-250 Ford pickup rear-ended them. The impact threw their heads against the headrests.

Ann snapped, "Damn fool drunk!" She opened the passenger door to get out and confront the pickup driver.

Mike had looked in the rear view mirror. The two men in the truck wore ski masks and the driver was reversing the truck. Was the driver fleeing an accident scene? Then he remembered Detective Larkin's description of Shaffer's son accident. This was no accident. He grabbed Ann's cast.

"Don't get out. Close the door."

"Why?"

"They're wearing masks. I'm turning left. Can't let them pull beside."

Ann slammed the door as he whipped in front of the pickup, just missing another collision. A short burst of gunfire and pieces of glass flying through the rear compartment of his Cherokee occurred as he fought to straighten the vehicle from the abrupt turn into Grove. The bullets eliminated any doubt of the pickup crew's intentions. Mike floored the accelerator to escape.

Ann had magically produced a small pistol. The bouncing vehicle and arm cast were interfering with her efforts to aim the pistol out the Cherokee's shattered rear window at the pickup. She managed to fire one shot at the pursuing pickup, but then the shooter cut loose with another long burst of bullets.

The shooter had some kind of machine gun as pieces of plastic, glass, fabric, and bullets ricocheted around and through the cab. Something thumped into the back of his seat. Pieces of Ann's cast hit him in the face; then Ann fired again. Mercifully, the bullets

212

missed Ann and him, but the Cherokee engine wasn't so lucky. Red warning lights glowed across the dash and the engine was missing and losing power.

Fleeing down Grove Street wouldn't save them. Mike knew the damaged Cherokee couldn't out-run the Ford pickup. He hit the brakes and whipped left into Clinton Court sliding sideways into a trashcan and tossing Ann hard against the door. The pursuing pickup's old brakes couldn't slow the truck enough for the driver to chance the turn. It slid by Clinton Court. A moment later the pickup, in a cloud of tire smoke, reversed back past the alley entrance and turned into street.

Mike remembered his shotgun in the backseat. To gain time to load his shotgun and obtain some protection from the next expected burst of bullets, he turned the steaming and knocking Cherokee off the alley through an old wood fence protecting a backyard garden to put a garage between them and the pickup. The engine seized up, stopping the Cherokee at the edge of the garden. They could hear the pickup coming up the alley. Ann and he would only have another moment to escape.

"Quick, run between the houses."

Instead, Ann jumped out of the vehicle the moment it stopped and ran to the corner of the garage. He heard her shoot again at the assailant's pickup. Mike hoped her shot caused the driver to reconsider accelerating up the alley. Her shot must have connected because he heard the truck slow. Then several bullets tore through the wood garage and slammed into the lower rear panel of the Cherokee, showering Ann and him with wood splinters and pieces of red plastic from the tail light.

Mike now had his shotgun free of the gun-case, and they both ran to the back of the small garage. Their goal was to keep the garage between them and the pickup as a shield. They heard the assailant's pickup tear around the other end of the garage and smash through the

213

remains of the garden fence. Ann had waited for the assailant's pickup to bog down in the soft garden soil and then she stepped back around the garage corner for another clear shot. Her bullet caused the driver to duck and stall the pickup at the garden fence back yard boundary. The remains of the garden fence, the soft ground, the lack of four-wheel-drive, and her shot had finally stopped the pickup from driving clear around the garage.

The shooter had jumped from the bogged-down and stalled pickup in order to run across the yard and flush them from behind the garage. At the same moment, the man living in the house with the garden started yelling from the basement door, distracting the shooter. The shooter's distraction provided Mike another moment to finish loading the shotgun magazine. In the excitement and running from the Cherokee, he had ripped the shell box. His hand shook uncontrollably, causing him to spill most of the shotgun shells on the ground behind the garage.

Mike finally managed to insert the third and final shotgun cartridge in the magazine. The driver had recovered from Ann's last shot and had the pickup running again. It sounded like the driver was turning the truck around. Mike figured the driver's plan was to block their escape through the alley while the shooter flushed them from the garage. Mike worked the shotgun's action to chamber a round. He felt his anxiety fade as he clicked the shotgun safety off, ready to defend Ann and himself.

"I can't believe I'm not shot," Ann said. "Only a piece of my cast is missing. Are you okay?"

"I think so. Watch the alley, the bastard is coming."

Unlike him, Ann appeared unruffled by the violence as she walked to the alley end of the garage to cover their back should the driver make a sudden move in that direction.

When Lou saw the passenger door open after rear-ending Cherokee he figured it would play out just as planned. Then the door had closed and Owens had made a sudden left turn into the side street instead of trying to run straight ahead or turn right into Paulie's line of fire. He was able to get off a short burst, maybe ten rounds, as the Cherokee turned, but obviously, the bullets didn't hit anything vital as Owen raced down the narrow street.

Paulie had a good target while the Cherokee was racing down Grove Street and emptied the magazine, another dozen rounds. The bullets were hitting the Cherokee because pieces where flying off. At the same time, to his amazement, that Lane girl shot back, and he heard Paulie swear as her bullet hit the truck. Then Owen had surprised him again by turning left into an alley. Lou couldn't get the old truck slowed down enough to risk the turn and had slid past the alley. He had to stop the pickup and back up before he could turn into the alley.

Swept up in the heat of the hunt, Paulie was yelling. "That bitch's shot nicked me in the leg. Hurry before they get away."

He switched out the empty AK-47 magazine for a loaded one as Lou pursued the smoking Cherokee up the alley. Owen turned off the alley before he had the magazine seated and could shoot. A moment later Lou saw the girl lean around the corner of the garage and, calm as could be, fired at them. A hole appeared in the windshield spattering glass in his face and causing him to slow. He yelled at Paulie to quit screwing around and shoot the bitch. Finally having reloaded the AK-47, he fired a short burst into the garage.

A moment later, they cleared the garage to find the Cherokee's doors open and no bodies. Wisps of dark smoke were leaking out from under the Cherokee's hood. No one was in the backyard and then she was firing at them again. Her bullet smashed into the cab side window, narrowly missing him and Paulie.

"Damn her! Where did she go? In the garage? End this. I'll get turned around," Lou told Paulie.

An old man had come out of the house that the backyard garden and fence were part of, shouting he was calling the police to report drunken hoodlums were tearing up his yard. Paulie got out of the pickup and snarled for the old man to mind his own damn business. Paulie fired a three-round burst at the old man to emphasize he wasn't kidding. The breaking the window and shattering chucks of the cinder block wall of the basement from the three bullets sent the old man diving back into the house, shrieking for his wife to get his rifle.

The shooter had been clever by firing a three-round burst into the corner of the garage while moving for a clear view of the garage's other side. The noise and pieces of wood from the three bullets tearing through the garage had startled Mike, but he held his fire until the shooter cleared the garage corner. The shooter's attention was concentrating on the rear garage door that his last burst had knocked open. Mike realized he had not noticed him standing beside the garage wall. On seeing Mike, the shooter shifted his aim.

Not hesitating, Mike fired at the center of the shooter's mass. The load of heavy pellets hit dead center in the shooter's chest and shoved him backward and causing him to fire a burst of rounds into the sky. The shooter tried to recover and bring the AK-47 muzzle back towards Mike who shot again. The second shot caused the shooter to drop the assault rifle and collapse backward onto the lawn.

Mike figured no need to call the police; those spent bullets landing back in the surrounding neighborhood would add to the wide spread alarm from the gunshots and would surely prompt many more 9-1-1 calls. He focused on finding a couple of the dropped shotgun shells to reload the magazine. Then he heard the pickup engine roaring as the other killer reversed the pickup back past the end of the garage. To rescue his partner Mike reckoned.

Lou heard the shotgun blasts and saw Paulie go down, and realized he could not leave Paulie alive for the police. The truck had just roared back over Paulie's chest with the rear wheels spinning when he saw Owen with a shocked look and a shotgun by the garage. Lou shifted gears, floored the truck's gas petal, and spun the rear wheels forward across Paulie's body. A load of pellets from Owen's shotgun slammed into the front of pickup and passenger door. The pellets sent a cloud of rust, paint, and glass dust through the cab. A number of shotgun pellets and fragments of the truck hit Lou's neck, arm, and hand. Then Lou saw in the rearview mirror the old man run from his basement into the back yard, he carried a bolt-action hunting rifle.

The shotgun blast had shredded Lou's reckless confidence and fear percolated through him as he realized his plan had failed. He needed to escape, but where could he hide the truck? The truck would be a trove of evidence connecting him to the shooting and Paulie. He remembered the company-owned rental property in West Mead, a fifty-year-old ranch house that had a double garage and was currently unoccupied.

Sod was flying off the rear truck wheels as he sought escape from the soft garden soil while fearing another blast from the shotgun. A heavy rifle slug plowed into the back of the pickup cab as the old man fired. The battered pickup roared back through the remains of the fence and raced up the alley. On exiting the alley, he forced himself to drive the speed limit. Lou drove the city's back streets to the property near the West Mead Elementary School.

Lou found the hidden house key, entered the garage through the house, and manually opened the garage door from inside. He drove the steaming and dripping pickup into the garage and hurried to close the garage door. The door had just closed when a police car went by with sirens wailing. Unfortunately, the house was in a neighborhood with other homes and foot traffic to the school. Lou realized the neighbors could easily look in the garage windows and see the truck. To hide the view he decided to tape newspaper over the garage windows. The truck needed a final hiding place. *But where?* He wondered, while calling Sam.

"I need help at the West Mead rental. Wear old clothes and boots. My helper is gone, and the others are still with us."

"I'll be there shortly."


Mike and Ann spent a tense minute convincing the old man they were victims like him, before Mike noticed the smoke. He had just finished putting the small engine fire out on his Cherokee with the vehicle's fire extinguisher when police arrived with guns drawn. The first police to arrive at Clinton Court weren't sure what had occurred. They called Detective Larkin while handcuffing Mike. Ann handed over her pistol to the wary older policeman while his partner held a gun on her. Mike noticed that a bullet had notched Ann's cast.

Ann presented a quandary for the policeman with her cast-- how to handcuff her. The policeman finally told her to get in the patrol car's back seat after taking her pistol. Ann didn't seem to think the policeman's order worthy of comment and serenely settled on the rear seat. Mike thought he might have detected a sigh of relief from her. The police then threatened to handcuff the old man if he didn't calm down and give them his rifle.

The mangled body wasn't touched, other than the younger policeman verifying the man was dead. The body has been both shot and run over. The Cherokee looked like it had been in a war. The garage had a dozen bullet holes. The old man became even more excited after discovering several bullet holes in his basement wall. A resident from Grove Street had walked over and told the policemen that his car parked on Grove had three bullet holes in the trunk and rear door. Of greater concern was the car's leaking gasoline. The older policeman called the fire department. Another neighbor ran over to tell the police his bedroom window had two bullet holes. Clinton Court had never had such an exciting evening.

Fifteen minutes later Clinton Court and Grove Street were full of police, news, fire, and emergency service vehicles. The old man appeared to have had a heart attack and an ES crew worked to save him. Several of the other police had remembered Ann and Mike from a week earlier and had them released. Mike told them an older blue Ford pickup was involved and had fled the scene. Everyone speculated on the motive and identity of the dead shooter with the AK-47 while waiting for the coroner and Detective Larkin to arrive.

Detective Larkin arrived with a middle-aged black woman, whom he introduced as Detective Tan. He informed the various officials that the coroner would be there in a moment. He then asked Ann to go with Detective Tan and Mike to wait by the Cherokee. He was all business with the police, quickly organizing a neighborhood canvas for witnesses and securing the various sites and evidence. Day light was going fast, which lent urgency to the effort of securing the sites and shortly, only Mike and Detective Larkin remained by the Cherokee. Ann and the other detective had walked off toward Chestnut Street.

"I assume this shot-up Cherokee is yours, Mr. Owen. What happened?"

Mike explained they had just left the Shaffers, headed for dinner, when a Ford pickup rear-ended them at Chestnut and Grove. He remembered the detective's description of Bill Shaffer's accident. That, along with the fact the driver and passenger wore ski masks, convinced him to flee by turning into Grove Street. As they had turned, the bullets started flying, eliminating any doubt about their attacker's intent. Then he realized his vehicle was crippled. Ann had a pistol, which along with his shotgun, would even the odds if they could get away long enough to load his shotgun and find a barrier to hide behind for shelter.

"This garage was the barrier. We ran around it to keep the garage between us and the pickup."

"Looking at the dug-up yard, I'd say the pickup wasn't four-wheel drive. That was fortunate, otherwise they could have zipped around the garage and run you down," Detective Larkin said.

"Maybe, by then I had the shotgun loaded. Regardless, at first opportunity I shot the guy the coroner is examining. I think he's Paulie. Then I watched as his partner drove over him twice."

"You know the guy?"

"He was an inspector on the project, works for Norton and James."

"Well, as they say, dead men tell no tales."

Mike explained his final shot was at the pickup driver trying to stop the madman, but No. 4 shot was for ring-neck pheasants, not pickups, and none of the pellets apparently hit a tire or harmed the engine. The pickup driver had fled up the alley.

The detective examined the Cherokee for several seconds.

"I count three bullet holes in the instrument panel, two bullet holes through the left side of the passenger's seat, an entrance hole in the middle of the driver seat, but no exit hole, which meant the seat stopped the bullet, and three bullet holes in the windshield about where your head should have been."

After examining all the bullet damage, Mike was amazed that all those bullets had missed them.

"It's a miracle you two weren't killed. Do you know the driver?"

Mike answered no. They waited in silence for the photographer and coroner to finish. The coroner was an intense young man and informed the detective the cause of death would have to wait on the autopsy, though the truck tire injuries would have been fatal, if he wasn't already dead from the shotgun wounds. In closing, the coroner added the body had a bullet wound in the right leg.

The detective removed a bloodstained wallet from the body's rear pants pocket.

"You're correct, the shooter was Paulie Pelosi."

"Did the DNA on the Lucky Strikes butts match?"

"Matter of fact they did. Now I'll officially match Pelosi's DNA to the butts, which will place him at the scene of the Henry Street attack."

Sam parked in front of the rental unit's garage, and then sat there for a minute to consider his options. Detective Larkin would suspect Paulie was hired help working for the party that wanted Owens and Lane murdered. The detective would start his investigation by interviewing Paulie's boss, Dennis Norton. Then he'd interview the Woodbriers because of their rumored interest in Shaffer Concrete and contracts with RBO. If they were fortunate, they'd have a couple of days to cover Lou's involvement.

The situation proved worse than he had feared. Lou had two pellet wounds on his right arm, a pellet in his neck, and glass fragments embedded in his right hand. The pellets appeared to have inflicted deep wounds. The Ford pickup had a flat front tire and a windshield with several pellet and bullet holes, a bullet hole in the passenger door, and numerous pellet holes in the right front fender. Both the rear and door windows were shattered and the cab was full of glass and blood spots. The rear-ender into the Cherokee had caved in the pickup's grill and the radiator had a bullet hole that had allowed antifreeze to leak out on the garage floor. He then noticed there was even a large hole in the tailgate from a bullet that had then exited the right side of the truck's bed, ripping another large hole.

"I gather Owen didn't take kindly to being rear-ended?"

"Yes, one might say that, but that woman is the hellcat. Thankfully, she didn't have the AK-47."

"Paulie is dead?"

"He went down from a shotgun blast and was run over twice, but I didn't have time to check his pulse."

"Any of the targets hit?"

"The Cherokee looked like Swiss cheese and was burning, so I don't see how they could have escaped being hit, but Owen certainly acted uninjured. I never saw the girl after Paulie got out. He may have got her."

"Your wounds need attended. How will you explain them to the police?"

"The police!"

"Hell yes, you think they won't connect Paulie to us through Norton and James, Ace Concrete, and Pine Tree. That pickup has to vanish for you, us, to have a hope of escaping legal entanglements with Paulie and the police. I hope none of the neighbors noticed your arrival or the truck. That shot-up, blood-spattered pickup screams crime scene. The truck needs shredded, but how do we get it to Gambone's operation? Can't load it on a car carrier--everyone could still see it."

Lou suggested cutting the pickup into pieces and putting the pieces in a roll-off box to haul it to the shredder. Sam feared the noise and smoke involved in cutting a pickup into pieces small enough for the two of them to load in a roll-off box would bring neighbors over to investigate.

"I can remove the top of the truck cab with a cutting torch, there would be little noise or smoke. We can push the trimmed truck into a thirty-cubic-yard roll-off box and the tarp would cover it."

Sam liked his idea and called Jake to have him order the largest roll-off box Gambone Disposal had for a morning delivery. He advised Jake to tell him it was for a remodeling project at the West

Mead rental. They were cautious about John's trustworthiness after that sugar deal.

Sal Gambone, they trusted. Lou would arrange for Sal's truck to pick up John's roll-off box and take it early Saturday to the shredder in Pittsburgh and then return the empty box. Next week Sam would have Jake call and say Lou had made a mistake and for them to remove the box. A complicated plan with more players involved than they preferred, but a workable plan for making the pickup disappear. They carefully covered the garage windows, locked up, and went to Sam's house to dress Lou's wounds and get some sleep. Tomorrow would be a busy day.

Mike found Ann and Detective Tan sitting in the detective's car. She drove them back to the Shaffer's home. The shot-up Cherokee was on the news and they faced a host of questions, most of which they couldn't answer. The only persons that had the answers were dead or hiding. Though they didn't dwell on the fact, Ann and Mike knew they had been incredibility lucky to survive. He borrowed Shaffer's extra car, an old Ford Escort to drive to the motel. Ann walked Mike to the car.

"You saved my life tonight when you grabbed my arm and kept me from getting out of the car," she whispered.

"Thank Detective Larkin. He told me that was how they murdered Mr. Shaffer's son and their ski-masks removed any doubt."

Meadville news was full of speculation on the two murder attempts against a young lady engineer working at a local concrete company. Were the police making any progress? Was it some kind of gang or mob war? The missing Ford pickup description listed it as an older blue F-250 with numerous pellet and bullet holes in the front right fender, a smashed front end, and missing door windows. A ten-thousand-dollar reward for information regarding the pickup's location was included with the description.

Sam thought the newspaper and news described Lou's pickup rather well. Any of their neighbors who happened to see the pickup would probably suspect it was the one the police wanted. Owen offering a reward for information made that truck even more of a danger.

The first order of business for Sam was to convince his mulish brother to see a doctor. Those wounds had dirt in them and peroxide was not a substitute for an antibiotic or a tetanus shot. Unknown to the Woodbrier brothers, one group was pleased with Lou's refusal to seek medical help. The Clostridium tetani that had existed in the manure and mulch dust in the door panel were busy colonizing the anaerobic depths of Lou's neck and arm wounds.

Jerry read the newspaper while waiting for the advanced English prose class to start. Why would Paulie be involved with Ann Lane? Someone wanted her dead besides himself. Who could he be? The girl certainly led a charmed life--two failed attempts on her life, but then he had learned the hard way she was lucky. As long as she was alive, he would never know peace. Those near misses with Betty Deere and Lucy Kerbert had brought him to the attention of Detective Larkin who had headed up the Jenny Lowell investigation.

The fate of his missing camera remained a constant worry. He had searched his truck and the site the next day and finally concluded Ann had taken his backpack and camera. To think he had called her to ask her to return the items; his stupidity even amazed him at times. Now her boyfriend was asking questions about Otto's place, which had Paul nervous and asking questions. He wanted to know why Owen hit him. Fortunately, Paul didn't know about Ann and the missing camera.

Paul was excited that he had agreed to a snuff video. Jerry's partner volunteered to be the butcher Saturday, promised to drag the death out to ensure many screams. They both wanted their first snuff video to be a quality product. Paul had the bulldozer ready for filling in the well. Five gallons of gasoline would eliminate the crime scene. Helen Smith would be their star.

Katie was riding shotgun with Ben, her father's most trusted driver, on the way to RBO's site for the Friday emptying of the trash containers. Ben was well aware Katie was John Gambone's pride and joy and that her father expected him to keep her safe and out of trouble while teaching her to drive trucks over the summer. Why her father thought a girl who planned to be a doctor needed to know how to operate trash trucks, he hadn't ask. She had been a fast learner. He knew Katie could now handle any truck, even a front loader. Passing her in-state Pennsylvania CDL exam in March proved that.

Today, while he was at the landfill dumping a loaded trash truck, Katie would load the other roll-off truck and have it waiting for him when he returned. On the way to the project, they talked about the attack on Ann and Mr. Owen. Katie couldn't imagine how anyone fired eighty bullets in a residential neighborhood, without killing or wounding someone. Ben corrected her by pointing out the guy had managed to ruin Owen's Cherokee and caused an old man to have a heart attack. Katie wondered what chance they had to find the pickup and collect the reward. He was of the opinion the pickup was now a pile of parts in some Pittsburgh or Youngstown chop shop.

It was a hot August day and Katie wore running shorts and a tank top with her hard-toe work boots and hardhat. She was a very pretty girl and presented an unorthodox, yet attractive sight in her work outfit. Ben was a father with three daughters, from ten to twenty years in age. He would never comprehend a girl's fashion tastes and knew to offer no comment on the need to wear pants to protect the legs and long sleeves to protect the arms. He figured attracting the attention of someone at the site, not protection, was Katie's purpose for her work outfit while still striving to satisfy minimum OSHA and father requirements.

First, though, they had to deliver a large roll-off box for a remodeling project, before going on to the RBO site. Katie could see the West Mead Elementary School down the road towards Meadville as she got out and operated the cable controls to drop the box on the driveway in front of the garage. Ben waited in the cab as she finished unloading the box. Before she unhooked the cable from the box and Ben lowered the frame and reeled in the cable, Katie checked the clearance between the end of the box and the garage door to make sure the roll-off box's door had room to swing open.

The unoccupied house had the garage door windows papered over, an obvious attempt to hide something in the garage, which made Katie curious. She took a moment to find an edge of a window not completely covered to look into the garage. The interior light was poor, but sufficient for Katie to see the garage contained an older blue Ford pickup with a missing rear window and damaged passenger door. Her viewing angle prevented determining what had damaged the door. The truck leaned as if it had a flat front tire. A favorite junker that someone has dreams of repairing.

They arrived at the construction site, and Ben turned the truck over to Katie. He then started the loaded roll-off truck waiting at the site and drove to the landfill. She went and found a full roll-off box and lined up the truck frame with box rails in preparation to load. She hopped out and hooked the winch cable to the box. The Pine Tree laborers saw her and whistled at her lissome figure. She smiled and gave the crew a wave and then concentrated on pulling the heavy steel box up the roll-off frame past the center of gravity of the box. Kathy skillfully lowered the frame, which tipped the box onto the truck, and then completed winching the front of the box into the truck frame lock at the back of the cab. Once done, she unrolled the trap to cover the top of the box to keep waste from blowing out.

"Need any help?"

She looked around and found that cute surveyor Frank smiling as he commented on her nice work outfit.

"Quit ogling, boy, and help me get this tarp on top of the load."

After securing the tarp, they stood on top of the trash and discussed the previous night's attack on Frank's boss and Ms. Lane and the missing pickup. They gossiped together about how lucky Ann and Mark had been to have a lousy marksman as their assailant. The shooter missing them eighty times was also source of wonder to Frank. He then jokingly asked whether they had earlier picked up a roll-off box with the shot-up Ford pickup. Katie went white and silent.

"Are you all right? Are you sick?"

"I know where that pickup is."

"Are you serious or kidding me?"

"I'm serious. Well, I can't be sure, but I think I'm right. We just dropped a roll-off box in front of a garage with an old blue Ford pickup parked in it."

Frank called Mr. Owen and told him Katie saw an old blue Ford pickup at a garage where they had just delivered a roll-off box. She thought that might be the pickup. Mike had him pass the phone to Katie.

"Katie, these people are killers. Have you said anything to anyone else?"

Mike hoped Katie realized this was a deadly serious matter as she explained a comment from Frank made the pieces click in place.

"The crazy bastard might be vengeful. For your safety, best he doesn't learn who told the police. I'm already on the lunatic's

227

radar. I can pass on your information to the police. That way no one is aware of your involvement until after the killer's arrest. You'll still be eligible for the reward if the tip proves accurate."

"Ben and I dropped a large roll-off box at a house just past the West Mead Elementary School about an hour ago. The pickup is in the garage."

"Thank you, Katie. Let me have Frank." A moment later: "Stay with her on site until I call back. Help her with the boxes."

Mike tried Detective Larkin, no answer, and then Detective Tan, no answer. He left urgent messages on each answering service. He reflected on what to do. They might be loading the pickup right now.

"I might know where the blue pickup's hiding. Can you ride with me? Preferably armed," Mike said.

"I can't I'm at the Pittsburgh Airport, waiting for my brother to arrive, but as soon as he's here, I can meet you." Ann wanted to know how he'd found the location, but he declined to offer that information. He gave her the address and promised to keep her posted.

Mike drove Shaffer's old Escort over to the West Mead Elementary School and found the roll-off box in the driveway just as Katie had described. Two cars had parked beside the roll-off truck and box. A stout man, wearing gray work-coveralls, was hooking a cable from a roll-off truck's winch to the box. Lou Woodbrier stood beside the box talking to the man who Mike figured was the truck driver. Where were the detectives?

He could hardly stop and drove on by. He noticed the Catholic Cemetery and turned in, winding around the narrow lanes until he reached a spot from which the garage was visible. He tried the detectives again, no luck. The roll-off truck started to leave. Mike called Steve and told him to find Larkin or Tan and have them call him. Steve should do whatever it took--go to the police department, their homes, whatever. If necessary, he should get someone to run the office while he was out.

The roll-off truck, a clean-looking Volvo FM tandem diesel, turned and headed toward Franklin. No one else left the house to follow, so Mike pulled out and followed at a safe distance, figuring the driver would head for Route 322. On they traveled, through Franklin and south on Route 8. Mike was sure the driver's destination was I-80, the question was which way the driver would go--I-79 south to Pittsburgh or west on I-80 to Youngstown, Ohio. Either area probably had a shredder operation. Where are the police?

Mike noticed the car only had a quarter of a tank of gasoline, if the gauge even worked. He called Ann, brought her up to date, and learned her brother's plane was on the ground. She expected him soon. Once they were on the road, she would call him to meet. His phone rang.

"Mr. Owen, this is Detective Larkin. Your office manager is insisting I need to call you. What's so urgent?"

"I'm following a roll-off truck with an old blue pickup in the roll-off box. I think it's the pickup. It needs stopped before it finds a shredder. He's on I-80 and may turn south on I-79 or continue on I-80 west in a few minutes."

"Stay on the line while I make a call." A few minutes passed, then, "I used up a lot of favors, but they will stop the truck and check. Which way did he go?"

"South on I-79."

Detective Larkin passed on the information along with Mike's vehicle and cell phone number. State police cars appeared like magic about two minutes after the phone call, one pulled the Volvo truck over and the other pulled Mike over. The driver was an older man in a cooperative mood, who loosened the box trap to allow the trooper to examine the cargo. The young trooper then walked the driver to the front of the truck. The older trooper cautioned Mike to

229

stay out of the driver's view, but for him to verify this was the missing Ford pickup. Mike walked to the roll-off box and looked inside. The shot-up pickup was as he expected and figured the odds of this not being the pickup were infinitesimal. Mike told the trooper the pickup was the one the Meadville police wanted.

The trooper had the driver drive to the Grove City rest area and park where they all waited for Detective Larkin. Mike called Ann, and she agreed to stop with her brother. He then called Steve and Frank and spoke with Katie, telling her the information appeared to be correct. He re-cautioned her to keep quiet about her tip.

Ann arrived while Detectives Larkin and Tan were examining the pickup under the curious stares of a dozen truck drivers parked in the lot. The beautiful white dress Ann wore made her look as Mike envisioned an angel. Her brother Jason was an imposing monster of a man in a US Army Capitan's uniform with a friendly smile, who as way of greeting, thanked Mike for saving his sister's life twice.

"Your sister is too modest. She shot the guy that was choking me to death."

"Sounds like you forgot a few details, Sis."

Detective Larkin returned for Mike while Detective Tan met Jason and talked to Ann.

"I agree that vehicle looks just as I would expect that Vine Street pickup to look. How did you know it was in the roll-off?"

Mike told him a good tip from a person he wasn't at liberty to identify because the homicidal principals behind this affair were still loose and might kill his informant. Besides, keeping the identity secret should not cause investigation problems. The old detective let the informant issue ride, but curious, asked who Mike thought were the homicidal principals.

"Lou Woodbrier, for sure, he had been talking to the truck driver. Possibly John Gambone, since the pickup was currently setting in his roll-off box."

The detective agreed Lou had some explaining to do, though maybe not John, since the driver they stopped worked for Sal Gambone out of Pittsburgh and the truck was Sal's, though the box did belong to John. Mike realized that might explain Katie's involvement. He couldn't picture her ratting out her father.

The detective thanked Mike for his help and suggested he leave before the Gambone driver connected him to the arrest. Ann talked Jason into driving the Escort, while Mike drove Ann in her pickup. He promised her brother to stop for gasoline at Grove City after they ran south to the first exit and turned around to head back north. They stopped, filled both vehicles, and bought sandwiches and drinks, before heading to Meadville.


Sal's driver had called the company dispatcher and advised him two State Police had pulled him over and impounded the truck. That, in turn, precipitated a call to Lou from Sal advising him of the stop, which released Lou's paranoia. He lashed out, accusing him and his driver since they were the only people aware of the move. Sal had actually felt sympathetic for Lou, but knew he wasn't the leak and didn't explode back as he would normally to such an allegation.

"I didn't rat you out, Lou. The driver, maybe? I'll check, though he didn't know what was in the box and you watched him load. Did he look?"

"No, at least he didn't where we loaded the box. He could have stopped and loo--Forget it, Sal. I have to go."

Lou wasn't feeling well before the call, his jaw and neck stiff, sore, and twitchy, but fear of arrest overrode health concerns as he packed a bag and included the two 9-mm automatics Paulie had with him. He then called Sam and told him the police had the pickup and his best option was to disappear for a while until he learned what the police had in evidence. Lou would take the old Pine Tree jeep parked at Ace's yard for a vehicle and grab ten thousand dollars in cash from Ace's safe. Sam needed to hide his car. If anyone asked where he was, he went fishing off the Jersey coast near Atlantic Beach. Sam could aid his story by having one of their Jersey friends use his Master Card for a room and for dinner at one of the casinos.

"I don't need to know where you are, but I may need to contact you, so when you get to where you're going, find a prepaid cell phone to call my prepaid. You still have that number?"

"Yes, and I have a new cell phone with me. Try to find out how the police knew."

Lou left for Jake's hunting cabin in a remote part of Venango County near the Allegheny River and Pearl, Pennsylvania. He stopped at the State Store in Franklin to purchase four large bottles of Dickel. Medication to treat his wounds and cold, he amusingly rationalized. The cabin, well stocked with canned goods, had the electric on and running water. Lou would be fine for a week or two.

## Chapter 13

The Shaffers had a full house that evening. Ann's boss appeared to enjoy providing a location for Ann's family to meet Mike. Her father, Harold Lane, was a strongly built man with a humorous demeanor that Mike instantly liked and figured that explained his daughter's ability with jokes. The Lane family didn't seem particularly alarmed or put out over the two attacks on their daughter and that amazed him. Mr. Lane, a poised person explained to Mike that where they were from, an occasional disaster--a tornado or a fire--strikes and destroys everything.

"You accept evil events happen. Do your best to survive and limit your losses and get on with life. Being alert, being prepared, and being lucky all help," her father said. "For sure you two were lucky. Ted drove me down to the police yard to see your Cherokee. Well that's yesterday's news. Her mother and I wanted to thank you for looking after her. Is it over?"

Mike realized the Lanes were just as apprehensive as he was.

"No one knows. We're not even sure of the reason or who is responsible. Last night was luck. At the apartment it was your daughter's decisive action that saved us."

The two men needed a moment to hide their emotions before Mike asked about the impact ethanol was having on the hog farmers, which started a wide-ranging discussion on markets and commodities and the foolish policies from Washington. Jason joined their group. Their talk effortlessly switched to how and when the Afghanistan war might end. They all had opinions, but none of them had solutions for there or Iraq. Their conversation drifted to fishing as they waited for dinner.

Ted served up a delicious standing beef rib roast for their dinner, and to tease the Lanes, their host offered the opinion that pork's fine for sausage and bacon, but beef was real meat. Harold looked at his wife with a questioning expression.

"Beef? What's that, Ted? Some part of a reptile from the swamps around Meadville?"

Later Harold inquired if Mike and Ted felt asphalt was superior to concrete for road pavements. So the meal went with everyone having a good time. Ann was happy her family had taken to her handsome man.

"Did Dad give you the be-prepared lecture?" she whispered in his ear.

Ann's wonderful fragrance enveloped him. Mike wondered if his beautiful love realized what her whispering in his ear was doing to him as he nodded yes, while wondering if his desire for the woman sitting beside him was visible to the room's occupants. Thankfully, the dinner party broke up soon after.

Harold and Ted Shaffer wanted Jason, a connoisseur of shot-up vehicles from his tour of duties in Iraq and Afghanistan, to see the Cherokee for his opinion on the intensity of the attack. Mike had no desire to see it and be reminded how lucky they had been. He asked Ann to drive him to the car rental lot to pick up his GMC Sierra rental and have some time alone.

"I've never been to your apartment. You have time to show me?" Ann asked.

"That fancy motel room, I don't know. There are dirty clothes lying around."

"Not a problem . . . as long as the dirty clothes are yours."
She gave him another kiss and ran her hand along his thigh. Thoughts
of rental vehicles vanished as he drove to the motel.


Helen wore a runner outfit that had Frank's focus on her fine
legs as she sat in his red Subaru. She was a hunter and loved fishing.
They had stopped at the south end of Tamarack Lake to scout out
future fishing sites. A shallow lake formed by dams at both ends of a
swampy area. Frank learned the lake was difficult to fish due the
weeds, but the prized crappy bass lurking under the lilies and weeds
made fishing worth the effort. The sun would soon be set, so they left
to find the farmhouse.

"Who's putting on the party?" Frank asked.

"One of the local rich boys, Jerry Woodbrier, has been a
student forever."

"No kidding? My boss got in a fight with him. He's a laborer
with Pine Tree working on the sewer plant project. Big guy, maybe
thirty," Frank said, "An asshole."

"That's the guy. His pal is Paul Taylor, looks like a troll."

"Why are we going to a party those creeps are having?"

"I'm curious to see how the other half lives. A lot of students
will be there," Helen said.

They found the farmhouse back a lane off the township
gravel road in the last of the twilight. Mostly open farm fields
surrounded the house though the neglected yard had many small trees
and berry bushes scattered across it. A small Cat dozer was at the end
of the lane. Two clean Ford pickups parked in front and lights in the
lower windows meant someone was there.

"Doesn't look like much of a party," Helen said.

Frank didn't like the place. It gave him a creepy feeling.

Jerry recognized Frank from the construction site. If they proceeded, there would be two bodies to handle. And he didn't want Mike Owens's involvement, which would occur if his summer's help vanished.

"Helen, what brings you out here? The party's next Saturday night," Jerry said, looking tense in the doorway.

"You're kidding. I know you told me tonight." Helen walked onto the porch and Jerry blocked her way.

"Can I see the place?"

"Not tonight, Paul and I have to leave. I'll give you the full tour next Saturday."

Paul was pissed about him chickening out. "I could handle that red-headed hillbilly with one hand tied behind my back." He said as they watch the two visitors leave.

"That wasn't the reason. Who knows whom they told about the party? The guy he works for has been asking questions about Jenny. We don't need the attention. He'll go back to school in a month and then we'll get her."

"Damn, we may not get the chance. Uncle Otto wants this demolished before that."

"Tell him I know a person that might buy the slate roof shingles. I need a few weeks to get his answer."

"No shit? You can sell that junk," Paul said.

"Hell, you can sell anything, but that I just made that up," Jerry said. "Keep your uncle happy and you'll get to play butcher in a few weeks."

They folded the blue sheet background and packed it with the floodlights, rope, handcuffs, knifes, and masks in a duffle bag. The video camera had its own case. The generator and five-gallon can of gasoline they placed back in Jerry's pickup. The hooks in the ceiling and plastic sheets they left.

Monday morning Mike was enjoying a final cup of coffee when he heard Sam Woodbrier barge into the RBO office and confronted Steve with the demand to speak with Mike Owen.

"He's in there. Hold down your racket," Steve said.

"Why did you send this letter? It threatens to throw Pine Tree off the site and take the bond," an angry Sam demanded of Mike while waving the letter.

Mike strongly suspected Sam was one of the persons responsible for the attacks on Ann. He also believed the man had deliberately planned to substitute substandard air-duct material and rip off the French Creek Sanitary Board and RBO.

"Your material did not meet the Norton and James specifications and was rejected. To date, Pine Tree has not exchanged the material for the proper stainless steel. That letter starts the ten-work-day period to correct the problem or forfeit your performance bond."

Sam hated this young man and Dennis Norton for having backed him into a no-win position. He realized threats were counterproductive and struggled to control his temper while explaining the mistake made on the air ducts required more than in a few days to correct. Stainless steel is in short supply and replacement air ducts would take months to fabricate. High-density polyethylene, aka HDPE, would work just as well for fabricating the air ducts, cost less, and was easy to obtain. He wanted Norton and James to change the specifications.

Mike's resolve hardened. He told the crimson-faced Sam that he was finished listening to his and Dennis Norton's whining. Start installing Type-316 stainless steel air duct next week or vacate the site and performance bond. Or offer the Board the option to install SDR-21 HDPE air duct in place of the stainless steel and reduce the bid price by the difference in cost between the two materials. RBO's price for the stainless steel had been two-and-half-million dollars. He doubted Pine Tree had found a better price, but if they had, be prepared to prove the price with documentation, because the difference between the cost of HDPE pipe and stainless pipe was the reduction RBO expected Pine Tree to cut their bid. If Sam didn't have any other matters to discuss, he was busy. Steve would show him out.

Sam's rage at this dismissive attitude from Owen threatened to explode in violence. He turned and marched out of the office to his Cadillac and left. On the way out of RBO's parking area an old black mutt waited along the edge of the parking lot to cross. Sam swerved to hit the dog. Too bad that wasn't Owen instead of a worthless mutt was Sam's only concern regarding his behavior. *If only Karl had been successful*, he thought. He dialed Dennis to discuss a solution to the air duct problem.

"I'm sorry to hear about Paulie's unfortunate accident. How is your daughter bearing up?"

"They were in the process of getting a divorce, so she's okay. Is Lou okay?"

"I assume so. He's fishing the Jersey coast this week. Listen you need to change the air duct to HDPE material," Sam instructed him.

They then discussed the best method to get a high price for the HDPE air duct material to minimize the difference between the costs of the two materials and the reduction of Pine Tree's bid price. They decided the HDPE pipe supplier needed to agree to a kickback after approval of the material. Timing was important. RBO had started the ten-day default period

Detective Larkin was waiting for Sam when he arrived at the Ace Ready-mix office between Saegertown and Meadville. Sam had recovered from his rage. He knew this interview was going to be difficult. He didn't need Larkin mad and wasted no time inviting the detective into his office and offering fresh coffee.

"Thank you for seeing me quickly. I need to find your brother, Lou. Can you help me?"

Sam explained his brother went to Atlantic City, supposedly to fish, but more likely to gamble, however when he returned or called, he would make sure Lou contacted him.

"Can you tell me why you need him?"

"Sure I'll tell you. A witness claims Lou was talking to the driver of the roll-off truck stopped on I-79 that contained the pickup from the Clinton Court shooting. The same pickup used to run over and kill Mr. Pelosi. I have a few questions and need a DNA sample to verify he's not a match for one of the bloods found in the pickup."

"Surely you don't suspect my brother was involved?" Sam asked.

"Actually I do, and if he doesn't turn himself in by tomorrow, an arrest warrant will be issued. If he's not involved, he will save a lot embarrassment by calling me. I believe we understand each other. Thanks for the coffee."

Remorse crept through Sam as he reflected on Lou and their failed plan to acquire Shaffer's gravel mine on the cheap. Atonement would be expensive for them. He wondered who the witness was and then realized the blood DNA trumped everything. His brother was doomed. Would Lou take the fall or talk and drag Sal, Dennis, and him into the mess? Sam needed to talk to Lou and grabbing a prepaid cell phone, went for a drive.

Lou sounded drunk and indifferent to the detective's threat. He had a bad cold. In response to Sam's question, Lou admitted he had a hangover, but wasn't turning himself in.

"You worried I'll rat everyone out?"

"You may not do it on purpose or intend to, but you can never be certain what information might provide the police with the opening that exposes one of us. Then everything unravels," Sam said. "Larkin knows we're close and worked together. The old bastard will never believe I didn't know your plans."

"Ah, don't worry. I'm not talking"

"What are your plans?" Sam said.

"Stay hidden for another week and then head south and establish a new ID. You will send money?"

"Yes, we can work that out. Don't get crazy drunk and attract attention. Your voice sounds slurred. How are your wounds healing?"

"The neck is red and hurts, the others are okay. My neck and face is stiff, and I don't feel so hot. Maybe I do need to cut back on the Dickel. I'll be okay. Find the rat. Goodbye."

Find the rat, sounds so easy. Sam mulled over his brother's request, perhaps Lou still thought eliminating witnesses would save him. Lou didn't grasp that events were no longer salvageable. He was one DNA test away from a murder conviction. Sam's limited conscience worried over his brother's health. He hadn't sounded fine. Hopefully, alcohol accounted for the slurred speech, not infection from the wounds Lou had treated with reckless disregard.

Sam understood his brother's death would protect him from the police investigation. He had remained at the Woodcock Reservoir parking area after talking with his brother and watched the fisherman out on the water. Lou and he used to fish the reservoir, would they ever again? He called Sal.

The black mutt's luck had run out. The front tire of Sam's Cadillac had crushed the dog's left front leg and paw. The old dog managed to crawl to the scale office where Steve rushed out to help.

Ann's father had brought the backpack as requested, and she had checked that the camera was still in the bag. It was and she had the bag behind her pickup seat to give to Mike. She passed Sam Woodbrier in his black Cadillac on the project's entrance road, neither acknowledging the other as they passed. She pulled up to RBO's scale office where Mike and Steve were looking down at Blackie lying on the ground.

"Someone just ran over Steve's dog. You pass anyone?" Mike asked.

"Yes, I passed Sam at the entrance. He looked mad. Is Blackie hurt?" Ann asked. Then she noticed the pool of blood under the dog.

"He's in bad shape. Steve, take him to that vet where you got his shots.'"

"It will be expensive."

"Don't worry about that," Mike said. "Sam must have been the one who hit him, he can pay the vet."

One of the Shaffer drivers walked over with his trip ticket to give Steve. The driver told Ann the black Cadillac had deliberately swerved to hit the dog. Her driver had been on top of the truck washing the concrete spillage off the mix drum, and from that vantage point, he had clearly seen the dog run over.

"The dog didn't have a chance. It wasn't even in the way."

The story made Ann sick as she wondered what was wrong with people. That dog had been friendly and harmless. She felt tears run down her face as Steve gathered the dog up and carried it to his car.


They went in his office and closed the office door for privacy. She emptied Jerry's dusty backpack on the drafting table. Two baseball-size wads of used duct tape were in the bag, a roll of duct tape, a box cutter, several pairs of latex gloves, a pack of condoms, and an older Olympus 3-megapixel digital camera. Mike got Ann a pair of vinyl gloves and he put a pair on before examining the camera.

Jerry's camera was an older version of the 5-megapixal digital Olympus that Mike still used. RBO had several of the cameras, mostly 8-megapixal units. The batteries were dead when he tried turning the camera on. Jerry's camera used an older-style Smart Media card. Mike had a reader for that type of memory card on his office computer.

Blackie's injury had upset Ann and now she looked appalled as he readied the camera card to read. They both understood, regardless of her desire for privacy, if the camera card had pictures of Jenny Lowell or other girls, she faced a stressful choice. Mike was confident in the end the woman he loved would do the right thing.

Mike inserted the camera card and the reader software asked what he wanted done. Copy, don't delete, to a new file on his computer named Jerry's Pictures and clicked his mouse. He was pleased the reader detected forty-two jpeg files and proceeded without a hitch to copy them into his file. When the computer completed that step, he removed the camera card from the reader and reinserted it into Jerry's camera, then opened the files. The first three pictures were of a naked Paul Taylor wearing a President Carter mask having sex with a girl in various positions. Two pictures were of a smiling Jerry in front of a new Ford pickup, then fifteen pictures of an old farmhouse and numerous people partying.

The next seventeen photos showed a naked girl, different from the one Paul had been raping. She was photographed laying in various poses, some of her spread-eagled naked on a blanket; others photos showed a masked man who looked like Paul raping her. She was on the floor of a bare room that Mike figured was a room in an old farmhouse based on the wallpaper with a faded pattern of large flowers seen in the background of the photos.

The next two pictures were too dark to see. Then two photos of Ann naked on her back in the bed of a pickup with her left hand and ankle tied to load tie downs. The last photo on Jerry's camera card showed him naked, blindfolded, and tied with duct tape, and standing at the edge of a gravel farm lane.

The exactness of Ann's description, the two photos of her, and the horror of what almost happened, stunned Mike. Ann had stood behind his chair and watched, crying quietly. He had heard her gasp when the last three pictures came on the screen. Mike got up and hugged her.

"The police need this Ann."

"I know. Maybe there's a way that keeps me out of the news, which will be dreadful."

"The wads of used tape, did you put those in the bag?"

"No."

Mike wanted Ann's cooperation before making Detective Larkin aware of the bag and camera. A few days to win her approval wouldn't matter to the police. He got her permission to put the backpack and its contents in his large brief case and lock it in the document vault in his office. He then printed a picture of each naked girl that best showed her face. He had a bad feeling that he already knew one of the other girls. He explained to Ann what he planned as he trimmed the photo to show a neck-up view and shredded the trimmings.

Ann hoped the discovery of the shot-up blue pickup meant the police would find the people responsible for the attacks against Mike and her. The photos on Jerry's damn camera card assured she would still have to live that horrifying night over in legal proceedings, but she was willing, if it shut down date rape operation. Her parents--how would they react when they learned? And her brother, he was quite capable of killing Jerry in a fit of rage, and that would ruin his future. If only she hadn't answered the job ad, but then she would never have met Mike.

The one bright development in the mess was Ann knew Mike really did understand her wish to forget that night. The lack of moralizing platitudes from him meant he had faith in her to do the right thing. That last photo of her in the pickup had driven home the realization that Mike had it right--she was alive today to worry about her privacy only because of Jerry Woodbrier's incompetence. Was that what happened to poor Jenny Lowell? Had she awakened and recognized her rapists? One item gnawed on Ann's conscience the most: had her silence on Jerry's attempted rape allowed more Jenny Lowells to occur?

One small comfort: Ann's brother had loaned her his FN 9-mm automatic pistol, until she got another replacement. Her left arm, though still in the cast with the bullet notch, now worked well enough to handle the pistol's action. Her brother and she had shot a hundred rounds earlier that morning, and Ann was comfortable with his pistol. Being a gentleman, he had cleaned the pistol and loaded two magazines for her. The FN was a large pistol not intended for concealment, so Ann resolved she would be carrying her camera case or large purses for several weeks in order to hide the pistol. She damn well intended to always have it handy. The only problem she encountered was the concrete crew wanting her to take their picture.

John Gambone had Ben and Katie sweating under a grilling over how his roll-off box ended up impounded by the Pennsylvania State Police near Grove City with the shot-up pickup involved in the Clinton Court murder attempt. Ben couldn't help him. He had worked that afternoon emptying the six roll-off boxes at the RBO site. Ben knew from the loads waiting on him that John's daughter had also, just as they always did. To Katie's relief, Ben told her father to find out who had ordered the box and ask them. John allowed that made sense and sent them on their way.

According to John's secretary's phone record, the Pine Tree foreman, Jake, had ordered the largest roll-off box Gambone had available and requested it be delivered to that West Mead address. He said it was for remodeling waste. John figured a visit would be more effective than a call and drove to the RBO construction site. Jake wasn't happy to see him.

"Look, bud, I meant for the box to be delivered here. I don't know where that address came from."

Jake was a lousy liar under the best of circumstances. Under the malevolent stare of an irritated John Gambone, Jake folded and admitted that Lou Woodbrier had ordered the box. John then drove to the Meadville City Building to visit Detective Larkin, who was in. The detective invited John back to his office. After the usual exchange of friendly greetings, John relayed Jake's information. John wanted the police to know that other than delivering the box to the West Mead address, his company had no involvement.

"I'll check your story to keep everything proper and legal, but I believe you. Have a seat. I want to ask a few questions, unless you want a lawyer?"

"I'm not wasting money on a lawyer. I don't like your questions I'll quit answering them, but this crazy behavior has to stop. Meadville will be as bad as Detroit if these attacks keep up."

"You like Ms. Lane?"

"Sure, everyone likes Ann, except who is ever trying to kill her and Mike Owen."

"How do you figure the State Police knew what roll-off truck to stop?"

"Obviously, someone in on their plans ratted on them."

"That's what occurred, but by whom? I know who called the tip in, but they were doing it for another party that they refused to name. Your driver was my original suspect. Maybe he saw something when the box was delivered."

"No, I talked with Ben and I'm confident he didn't see anything. They just dropped the box and spent the rest of the day at the RBO site doing the weekly cleanup."

"You said *they*. Who was the helper?"

John got very quiet as he looked away from Larkin for a moment, before telling the detective the other person was his daughter Katie.

"She's the one that won all those scholastic awards a couple of years ago in high school?" Detective Larkin said.

"Yes. Don't even think of dragging her into this cesspool." John was on his feet, pacing and looking furious.

He was well aware John had reason to be proud of his daughter. Katie had helped Larkin's computer expert, his granddaughter, with her calculus. He assured Katie's father that the police had no plans to involve his daughter in the investigation. However, the party that loaded the pickup will be wondering who had called the State Police.

"Could have been a neighbor out for an early walk and peeked in the garage. Maybe a neighbor saw the pickup during the delivery of the box. The weakness with that is how the neighbor knew the truck was on I-79 at Grove City. Kind of makes the roll-off truck driver my number one suspect for the tip."

"You're right. Otherwise, the police would have gone to the box's delivery address instead of stopping a truck on I-79. Damn, you had me going for a moment. Katie is so special. She got all the brains God withheld from the last couple of Gambone generations. She is going to be a doctor and the first Gambone to finish college."

"Well, you have every right to be proud of her. Thanks for the information on Jake and Lou Woodbrier, I'll keep you out of it if possible."

John left Detective Larkin typing the request to issue an arrest warrant for Louis Woodbrier and went to find his daughter. Just to be sure, he needed to know if his daughter might have discovered the pickup in the roll-off box, and she had told someone else who then followed the truck and called the police. Someone like that young surveyor she likes. John's relationship with his daughter was excellent, and he figured a direct question would get a direct answer.

John was worried sick about her safety. His brothers and the Woodbriers were big believers in vengeance. He feared one of them might attack Katie or Ben. His daughter was in the kitchen, and he asked her to come to the office. As they walked toward the garage, he could tell Katie was nervous. John stopped halfway across the parking lot and asked her to think before she answered him. Was she the one that reported the pickup in the roll-off box?

Katie looked tormented and in a barely audible voice said, "Yes."

He stamped the pavement while muttering, turned around a couple of times while getting red, kicked a golf ball-size piece of gravel clear across the lot that hit the garage wall with a resounding bang, and he turned back to his very worried daughter.

"You did the right thing . . . Now to keep you alive."

Katie burst into tears, explaining she didn't realize what she had seen until the surveyor had made a joke about hauling the pickup off in a roll-off box. She'd told Mike Owen, who told her absolutely to tell no one, that her life could be in grave danger until the arrest of the killers. The police needed the pickup. It was the critical piece of evidence, and Mr. Owen feared the killer had a plan to destroy the evidence, probably using a car shredder. Since the killers were already after him and Ann, he had offered to call the police for her.

John, beside himself with worry about Katie, felt the urge to beat someone surge through him. But everything Owen had said made sense, without the pickup, the police had nothing. This madness had to end. John hugged his daughter while wondering how to protect her without wrecking her life and schooling.

John called Detective Larkin and without a preamble informed him that he now knew, Mike Owen had told him. His daughter, Katie, had told Mike Owen. John had ended his call with a plea to wrap up this insanity. The detective assured John that the police hadn't known of his daughter's involvement. He would, as already promised, try to keep Katie out of the investigation.

"If it's any comfort, I issued Lou Woodbrier's arrest warrant an hour ago. I'll want your testimony on the sugar," Detective Larkin said.

"The sugar. . ." John asked.

"Please John, let's not be difficult--Shaffer's concrete trucks."

"I'll think about it. Goodbye." John was shocked that old detective knew about the sugar; maybe Larkin could solve this shooting.

A short while later John's brother, Sal, called and peremptorily asked if his driver had sold out Lou. If Sal had been present and asked that question, in that tone of voice, John would have decked him with a punch. However, the matter was too serious to allow tempers to influence his response. John remembered the detective's explanation.

"Brother, I had wondered the same thing. My driver, Ben, claimed he hadn't known about or reported any pickup." John said.

"Ben delivered the box? Yeah, I'd trust him. Did he have a helper?" Sal asked.

"Sure, it was Friday. But reflecting on the matter, if Ben or the helper had been the leak, well then, the police would have arrested them at the house, not on I-79. For that reason, I'm sure my people had nothing to do with the leak. Maybe your driver saw something and called for the reward. How else would the police have even known where he was with the box?"

"I questioned my driver . . . hard . . . and he still claims he did no such thing. I believe him, so how did they know?"

"Then I figure Lou messed up. Did you know there's an arrest warrant out for him?"

Concrete Girl

John could tell the news alarmed his brother. After promising to return John's box when the police released it, Sal ended the call. After his brother's call, he wondered if Detective Larkin had expected such a call might occur and had deliberately provided him with a rational explanation for why Gambone Disposal personnel were not involved.

Mike's call caught Katie hurrying to her one o'clock class, and she agreed to meet him in the library parking lot at two o'clock. He knew his answer as soon as Katie looked at the cutoff pictures.

"That's Jenny Lowell, the other one I've never seen. Where did you get the pictures?" Katie asked.

"I can't say, yet. Did you find who organized the party?"

Katie explained none of her friends knew, but the generator that powered the lights had Pine Tree Construction stenciled on it. The property owner was Paul Taylor's grandfather, as he already knew, so she figured Jerry and Paul were the main organizers, as much as these ad hoc affairs are ever organized.

Lou was maintaining a high blood alcohol level and watching the news about his arrest warrant. The news had shown his photo several times. He wasn't worried about being recognized. In another week, the beard he'd started would alter his appearance to where Sam might not know him. Lou wondered if Sal and Dennis were sweating over the possibility he'd decide to plea bargain for a reduced sentence. He chuckled at the thought and finished off his shot of bourbon.

Lou's problem was he felt terrible; in the past, he got his best ideas while drinking. Now it was just making him sick and confused. Maybe his brother was right, and he was drinking too much. In three nights, he had gone through two of those large bottles of George

Dickel. Lou resolved, after tonight, to cut back on the drinking. Get ready to travel, maybe hide in Key West for a few months.

More worrisome to Lou was his jaw and neck. It wasn't working right. Lou could hardy open his mouth. He laughed at the thought; *can't rat the boys out if my mouth won't work*. Lou managed to get another good swallow of whiskey down. He passed out shortly afterward on the bed.

An intense nausea woke a drunken Lou who proceeded to vomit, but his mouth would not open enough to allow him to clear his throat. During his violent struggle to unclench his jaw, Lou inhaled vomit.

## Chapter 14

Mike found Ann in her lab office. She smiled on seeing him, which he took as encouraging. He related Katie's information that the second girl was Jenny Lowell; the other girl was a stranger to her. Jerry was involved in organizing the ill-fated party, at least to the extent of supplying a generator and lights. Ann looked sad and resigned as she listened to him. He then explained his plan to stir the pot and find justice for Jenny Lowell.

That evening the Lanes and Mike invited the Shaffers out for dinner at Rocco's. Afterwards Ann wanted to visit his motel room. After a bout of delightful sex, Mike lay in bed beside Ann debating the best method to win her as his wife. His usually brazen side won.

"Sweetheart, marry me."

Ann sat up and smiled at him and then leaned over and kissed him while she whispered yes. Things got wild after that and Ann was late getting back to Shaffer's house.

The next morning the Shaffers fixed a large breakfast for the Lane family and invited Mike. They announced their engagement at breakfast. No one was surprised. Everyone expressed enthusiastic approval and joy over their engagement. Ann knew her family heartily approved of Mike, and as a result, she was thoroughly happy. The announcement delayed her family's departure to Indiana for several hours.

After the guests and Mike had left, Mr. Shaffer asked Ann to come in the kitchen, they needed to talk. Ann thought, *now the complications start*. The Shaffers were putting their concrete business on the market, and they wanted her to hear it from them first. Ann asked if they had decided on price. No, their plan was to put ads in the trade magazines and let the local concrete operator know the business was for sale. Let the market decide the price. They needed her help putting a fact sheet together on the plant and gravel mine.

"I'll do that. If I want to buy the company would you give terms?"

They looked surprised by her request. Mrs. Shaffer explained they had assumed her and Mike would be moving to Columbus after the marriage and RBO's project ended. Ann was perplexed as to how to explain that they were still resolving the issue of her ambition to buy Shaffer Concrete.

"That's a complication we're still resolving."

Based on the looks exchanged between the Shaffers, they agreed.

"Sure, I'll consider terms," Mr. Shaffer said. "Beat the best price offered and we'll talk terms if you're still interested."

They then headed to the office to compile an information package. The Shaffers assembled the equipment list and property deeds while Ann focused on the limited geological information available on the gravel deposit and mining permit. Mrs. Shaffer then formatted a four-page document to use as a sale pamphlet to mail to all the construction companies in western Pennsylvania. Ann whipped up a website for Shaffer Concrete to hold the sale information. Mr. Shaffer would inform their employees that the business was for sale in the morning.

Ann took a draft of the pamphlet with her and went to the RBO site. Mike was in his office with Frank and Larry. Next week was Frank's last week before heading back to Purdue University. Mike had him busy obtaining quotes on HDPE air manifolds. After Larry and Frank cleared out, Ann asked Mike to go for a ride.

Mike could tell his lovely fiancée had something on her mind and figured it involved Shaffer Concrete. To her truck they went.

Ann, an excellent driver, chose to swing out the old farm lane that Mike knew ended about a half mile south of the project at an old ford used by the farmer to cross French creek. The open windows allowed Mike to enjoy the sweet aroma of the fresh cut hay. Ann paused to allow a decent-sized black snake time to scurry off the track.

His fiancée appeared to be arranging her thoughts after parking at the edge of the creek. Then, sitting in the cab, Ann proceeded cheerfully to recount her falling in love with him and accepting his offer of marriage. The process of falling in love was a mystery, at least to her, it strikes with no warning or regard for a person's careful career planning.

Mike thought, *I know where she's heading.* Ann went on to explain that she still wanted her own business, specifically, Shaffer Concrete. She was confident the Shaffers would sell to her. Ann understood that Mike also had ambitions that would require him to move back to the Columbus area in order to run the family business. And children, she wanted a family. They needed to live together, not two hundred and fifty miles apart. What kind of marriage would that be? Mike figured he must have appeared alarmed.

"Relax, sweetheart. You're stuck me with for better or worse, forever. Have any suggestions on how to resolve my quandaries?"

"You sure know how to get a person's attention. I'm relieved to learn we're stuck with each other," Mike said.

They needed to live together, he told her. He also wanted children. The business issues required thought. He has known Ann long enough to realize her abilities in management, and her business sense ranked with the best. He respected her desire to own and run a business.

"What is your goal in buying Shaffer Concrete?"

"First, it's available and in my price range. My goal is to take that mediocre business, no disrespect to the Shaffers, and make it the best-run concrete business in the Crawford and Erie County area."

"Then you'll be tied to Meadville for a number of years."

"That's my predicament. I would hope to expand the business to a size that justifies a professional staff. I want to develop the gravel mine into a separate aggregate business in addition to the concrete operation."

"Why? I can support our family," Mike said.

"The best I can explain is that creating a viable successful business is like climbing a mountain. It's the challenge. If I don't do it now, then the rest of my life I'll always wonder if I had the ability. I have the financing."

Ann awaited his response with a concerned expression. He could relate to every point this wonderful woman had made.

"I understand. What you just said makes sense. My ambition is to do the same thing with RBO."

He had asked himself if he could live with her independence. Well, first, he viewed Ann Lane as an equal partner, not an acquisition. Mike could answer the converse of that question: whether he wanted to live without her. He did not. She was a woman with whom he had found a natural affinity, friendship, loves, and would do anything to help, his soul mate. Mike realized for her soul to flourish, she needed to satisfy this challenge. He didn't want Ann forced to choose between love and career. His response was easy.

"I can operate out of this area about as well as Columbus. The very nature of construction requires considerable travel, so I'll be fine while you build a first-class concrete business. Make them an offer."

"Thank you for understanding. Thank you for agreeing. I will never give you reason to regret . . . I'm so lucky . . ." She hugged Mike, soaking him in tears.

Paul had finally gotten a copy of the picture he'd heard about. The picture showed him screwing Judy Elverson, the college girl from Edinboro that Jerry and he had first tried roofies on with great success. She hadn't a clue the next day they had raped her. He remembered they had taken pictures, but where had this one come from? That party was even before the Lowell girl mess, nearly two years ago. They had used his new 5-megapixal digital Cannon camera and those pictures he had deleted. Did Jerry have a camera that night? He couldn't remember. Regardless they had better hope Judy doesn't find out her picture is floating around Allegheny. Fortunately, the photo did show their faces.

The following morning Mr. Norton arrived with Pine Tree's air duct proposal to replace the air duct material. The Pine Tree bid price for supplying the material and installation of the complete air duct system in Type-316 stainless steel was $3,200,000. The new bid was $2,600,000 using SDR-21 HDPE material, a strong noncorrosive polyethylene pipe. He enthusiastically explained that by switching material, the French Creek Sanitary Board would save over a half million dollars and the material was readily available. He wanted to take this change order to the Board meeting next Tuesday.

"What was their original quote for the stainless steel air duct material?" Mike asked.

"The cost was approximately $2,700,000 for Type-316."

"That's similar to RBO's quote for stainless, what was the price for the HDPE?"

"You understand the HDPE is more labor intense to install in the field?"

"What was the price for the HDPE?" Mike repeated.

Mr. Norton was looking concerned as he answered $2,100,000.

"How fortunate we compared prices," Mike said. "RBO has a quote for the HDPE air duct of $1,400,000."

"There are other factors. The pipe's harder to install than steel pipe," Dennis said.

"Get real. Pine Tree already has $500,000 in their bid for installation. Your change order needs to be $1,900,000."

"You're not serious?"

"A $1,300,000 savings should make the Board happy enough not to ask too many questions," Mike said.

"What do you mean?"

"Like why you didn't specify HDPE in the original bid."

Hatred radiated from Dennis Norton, who then tried another approach in an attempted to salvage some markup.

"I'll have to check your supplier's numbers to make sure they didn't overlook items that may account for the price differential."

Though Mike detested this corrupt engineer, he knew he had won and agreed to his request.

"I want a copy of the new change order by tomorrow," Mike said.


Sam Woodbrier received a frantic call from Dennis and agreed to meet at Ace Ready-Mix office. Dennis arrived in a huff and explained RBO's quote and Owen's request to use it instead of Pine Tree's supplier for the HDPE air duct.

"Dennis, what choice do we have?"

"Can't you and Lou arrange a hit or somehow run Owen off?"

"I'm not sure I'm following you. Are you suggesting something illegal?"

Dennis realized Sam no longer trusted him.

"No! I know you and your brother would never tolerate any illegal action, I meant for someone to reason with him on this issue."

Sam, unsympathetic, told Dennis that he couldn't help him. The sooner Pine Tree finished with RBO, the happier he'd be. The

Meadville project had been a curse for Woodbrier Construction. Dennis would just have to excuse Sam's total lack of interest in air duct material. However, he would approve the new change order, though his focus was on locating Lou. His brother not answering his phone had him worried. The police were even looking for Lou.

Dennis looked ill as he left with the approved change order. After the engineer left, Sam pondered his next move while wishing Lou was available. He would have had his brother take Dennis out of the picture. No, he needed to stop thinking that way. Where was Lou hiding? He hadn't asked for money or a vehicle so he can't be traveling. The police have checked all theirs and Paulie's properties, and probably tapped their phones.


Discovering Dennis Norton and Pine Tree's fraud to switch from costly stainless steel to low-grade noncorrosive resisting steel, and torpedoing it, gave Mike considerable satisfaction. Next week's French Creek Sanitary Board meeting should finally resolve the issue. He hoped it did not precipitate another attack, but figured Lou's troubles with the police would cool Woodbrier's ardor for another confrontation.

Katie had gotten Paul's picture circulating on campus, no response so far, but Mike figured the photo would find its way on to the internet and into the authority's hands. The hope was that a student would recognize the girl and her assailant, who Mike thought, was Paul Taylor. The new photo he had mailed out today should panic Jerry and Paul.

On a more pleasant note this evening, Ann and he were going house hunting. She wanted to show him an old brick farmhouse near Venango with some nice acreage. Friday they were going to Columbus to meet his family.

Apprehensive over her first meeting with Mike's mother, Ann tried to limit her questions and nervous chatter, finding comfort in her belief that Mr. Owen liked and approved of her. Still Ann wanted the mother's approval. The Owen residence in Dublin, Ohio, was on a street lined with majestic oak trees and multimillion-dollar homes set back on secluded, beautifully landscaped lots. The Owen residence consisted of a large two-story home of cut stone and white painted brick with a separate four-car garage.

"Your parents' home is beautiful, how are you able to tolerate that roach motel room after living in such splendor?" Ann teased as they drove up the driveway.

"Don't be too hard on my humble motel room. You seem to enjoy spending time there. Probably that black-and-white TV set. Are you ready to woo your future mother-in-law?"

Ann had wanted her original and now grimy cast removed for this visit, but the doctor insisted on another week. She knew its presence would remind everyone of the attacks. Unlike her family, who accepted life could throw violent events at you through no fault of yours, she worried Mike's mother might be one of those well-educated persons shielded from life's realities that thought all victims were somehow responsible for their misfortune. Could his mother be a vegan? What would she think of hog farmers, Ann worried, walking up to the imposing front door.

The quiet exploded as Mike opened the front door into a greeting frenzy from an old black lab and young kids swarming over their Uncle Mike. In a flash, he had two young girls, maybe four and five-years of age, in his hands hugging him. A beautiful boy of Hispanic appearance, she guessed to be about three, and a small girl, maybe two-years old, who had to be his sister, were intently inspecting her and the cast. The boy asked if she was Uncle Mike's girlfriend. Before she could answer, two trim women who had to be Mike's sisters and the children's mothers rushed up to rescue them.

The black lab sniffed her leg as the taller lady introduced herself as Mike's sister Linda and the two kids pestering Ann as her Carlos and Julia. The two hoodlums choking Mike were Abby's, Barb and Abigail.

Mike remade introductions all around again, including Linda's husband, Jose Sims, and Abby's husband, Ben Walker. The lab left Ann's leg to sniff Mike, who the Walker girls had abandoned in order better to examine her cast. The bold one, Abigail, asked while pointing at the notch in her cast if that was where the bullet missed her. All eight sets of eyes focused on Ann. *So much for a dignified gracious entrance*, she thought, as the old black lab returned to join the four kids staring at her cast. She told Abigail that a bullet had come close, but thanks to her Uncle Mike, they had not been hurt.

The commotion brought an attractive woman with a patrician appearance into the hallway. She paused for a moment taking in the scene and then walked directly to Ann, with kids and adults clearing out of her path. She held out her hand and welcomed Ann to the Owen family, while introducing herself as Nancy. She asked Ann to please excuse the commotion, the whole family was thrilled her son had met her. Her husband was out back trying to get a charcoal grill going, and she suggested the rest of them help him while she showed Ann her room.

Ann wasn't sure how to take this formidable woman, but being intimidated wasn't in Ann's genetic code as she followed Nancy Owen through the imposing home.

"Those kids get on your nerves?" Nancy asked.

"The kids, no they're akin to sunshine, always welcome. You have nice looking grandchildren."

"Thank you. Have you picked a wedding date?" Nancy asked as she opened a door in a large elegant bedroom.

"Not yet, but it will be this year and in Indiana. We both have business items that need resolved over the next two months." She noticed the room had a bathroom with a nice full bath, which she looked forward to soaking in later.

"What is your business, Ann?"

"I work for a small ready-mix concrete company. The owner is retiring and putting his company on the market. The extra work from the big RBO contract made him financially secure. I hope to buy the company when it goes on sale in September."

"Is my son going to finance the purchase?" Nancy asked, just a bit sarcastic, as she sat down in one of the comfortable chairs. Ann realized she was in for an interrogation of sorts, and she following her lead, sitting in the chair facing Nancy.

"No, I'll be handling that on my own. I understand Mike will be buying RBO from his father. He hopes to accomplish that transfer at the end of the Meadville project, if he meets his father's condition of a ten percent net profit."

"I own half the stock in RBO, and your understanding is correct. Will my son manage a ten percent net profit?" responded her gimlet-eyed future mother-in-law.

"You'll have to ask him that, though if anyone can, Mike will. My impression is he expects to. Have you lived here long?"

"My father built this house in the early fifties when the area was first developed. I have lived here all my life. Operating a business requires a major commitment of effort and time. Will you put off or even have children?"

Ann figured at the rate this interrogation was progressing Nancy will want to know if she liked oral sex. She explained that being a farm girl at heart, she considered children a blessing, not a burden. She was comfortable having them underfoot and around. The nice thing about being boss was that she didn't need other people's permission to have her kids at work. Ann intended to raise any children fortune blessed them with, not pawn them off on a nanny.

As for living here all her life, Nancy was fortunate, not many people in this day and age have lived in the same house all their life.

"My father and his father have lived in the same house all their life, but they're farmers. Was your father an architect?"

"No, he was an attorney. My two daughters and I are all attorneys, a result of my father's influence. Linda and Abby work for law firms in Columbus. Mike and his father are the engineers of the family. What is your family background?"

Ann thought, *I should of brought a copy of my résumé,* and decided meek wasn't the way with this woman.

"You said my daughters, are they from a previous marriage?"

Startled, Mrs. Owen colored slightly.

"We've been married forty years. Forgive me, I been acting as if I was doing a due diligence on some legal agreement instead of visiting with my son's fiancée."

"That's okay, Mrs. Owen. If I have a son someday, and he brings home a woman, I'll probably be asking her plenty of questions myself. As to my background, I'm a civil engineer. My two older and one younger brother are all Purdue graduates and my younger sister is a sophomore at Indiana University. Mom's a math teacher and my Dad is a farmer. He is a Purdue graduate and Mom's a Ball State graduate."

Mike's mother wanted to understand the reason for the violence in Meadville. Ann explained there were two issues. The concrete bid and gravel mine permit that directly involved her, and the Pine Tree air duct swindle that involved her son. She talked of their suspicions that the Woodbrier brothers were behind both attacks, and that an arrest warrant was out for Lou Woodbrier. Ann felt that arrest threat should help crimp Lou's enthusiasm for violence. As to the attacks being over, no one knew, she told a decidedly pale future mother-in-law.

Mike realized Ann had been gone for a while, and he asked the grill crowd where Ann and his Mom were. Linda, smiling, answered that their mother was showing Ann the guest room and probably giving her the family interrogation. Concerned, he told his sister and father that his fiancée had a mercurial streak best left alone. He should go check on them. His father told his son to quit worrying about Ann. She could handle his mother.

"Be useful," his father said. "Bring out the steaks, and let Linda know, so she can tell the gang that I'm putting the steaks on the grill."

The evening in the Owen's backyard reminded Ann of her home on a typical warm August evening. The day was turning from purple twilight to full darkness. The lightning bugs were starting to appear around the shrubs that formed the yard border. Looking up, Ann saw several bats and a nighthawk pursuing insects, while a multitude of insects created a soft background murmur occasionally punctuated by traffic noise, laughs and shouts from the children playing and chasing each other. Ann was content and happy. She told Mike the visit with his mother went well.

After the delicious rib steak dinner, Linda's little girl Julia, clenching a *Curious George* book, snuggled into Ann's lap and asked her to read a story. Afterward the nieces and nephew talked Mike and Ann into playing hide-and-go-seek around the property. The older Walker girls thought her arm-cast was cool, and they scrawled their names on the plaster with a felt tip marker.

Mike's parents discussed their son's fiancée as they lay in bed.

"Mike found himself an exceptional young lady. She has a first-rate mind and a low tolerance for nonsense. Our future daughter-in-law is a formidable woman," Mrs. Owen said.

"And she's friendly."

"Yes, sweetheart, that she is. Mike chose well. He was fortunate to have won her love."

Paul Taylor's reflexive nihilism had suffered a serious blow. He now realized his cherished contention to friends and freshmen girls that social mores were clever restraints to prevent them from enjoyment of life was an absurdity. He had lost count of the times he had argued that virtue was meaningless, that truth had no objective basis. Worse, he had actually deceived himself by believing his foolish prattle that nothing was worthwhile or meaningful other than satisfying your cravings and needs. Tonight he knew otherwise. Paul's past sexual cravings threatened to cost him his freedom for the rest of his life.

Paul sat in Jerry's pickup truck in the Allegheny library lot sharing a six-pack of Bud. He was waiting for Jerry, his stunned partner in the crime, to explain the photos that Paul's grandfather had received in the mail today. Photos of Jenny Lowell just before she had awakened with the message "Otto Taylor beware; Jenny Lowell demands justice." The return address was to Justice for Jenny with Jerry's apartment address.

Paul understood that someone was playing mind games with them, but who. The picture along with the other one of Paul and Judy Elverson could have only come from Jerry's old Olympus camera. Paul wanted to know how a stranger had ended up with the photos. Jerry's excuse had been the theft of his digital camera over a year ago relieved him of any responsibility.

"You idiot, I can't believe you didn't delete the pictures after what happened," Paul said.

"I did. I'm not stupid, there must be some way to recover deleted files from the memory card or someone hacked your computer. That's where all our pictures are."

"There're no pictures like these on my computer. I don't remember downloading your camera. We used the Cannon that night. Judy was the only time we used your Olympus. Anything with Jenny, I deleted. Did you take some pictures of Jenny?" Paul said.

Paul's beer tasted like dishwater. He now feared that there was much more to Jerry's robbery.

"How'd you get robbed? Why were you left naked along the road?"

Jerry launched into his tale of stopping to help a couple who then attacked and robbed him.

"What'd they want your clothes for?"

"I don't know. Maybe they needed clothes."

"Were they the ones that stole your camera?"

"Yes. I'm lucky they didn't murder me, but no one seems to give a damn."

"The police might have believed your BS. I don't. Sounds to me like you messed with the wrong girl and her boyfriend caught you. Who was he?" Paul demanded. "Is he the one with the camera and blackmailing you?"

Jerry swore his story was true and admitted he hadn't thought of the blackmail angle. Maybe the thieves sold his camera to some computer nerd that had recovered the pictures and the nerd was setting him up for blackmail. As soon as the blackmailer contacted him, they would have a name and could recover the pictures and pay the creep back.

"Sure, and maybe frogs can fly," Paul said.

"I'll find the guy. You'll be happy to hear the hillbilly is leaving end of next week. We can do Helen the following Saturday. Make some money. Have some fun."

Paul liked the Helen news, but was skeptical of his partner's explanation.

"We have a more pressing problem. I have to tell my grandfather something so he won't follow through on sending the photos to the police."

"We can't admit to knowing about the photos. Our only choice is to deny all knowledge, while trying to find who has the camera. We sure don't need other pictures showing up," Jerry said.

"My grandfather is not kidding. He'll send the photos to the police. Then Jenny Lowell's disappearance will be back in the news."


Monday several of the Shaffer Concrete employees stopped by the lab to ask Ann if she was going to bid for the company. They wanted her to buy the company. She told them it would depend on the price and thanked them for their support.

The cute neighbor girl, Helen Smith, knocked on the lab's open door, and asked if Ann had a moment.

"My dad's red sow had ten piglets. He wanted your father to know. Your dad had expressed an interest in buying one or two on his last visit," Helen said.

"That Tamworth hog your brothers had to wrestle out of our lower pond?" Ann said.

"Yes, she's the independent type. Dad said she's been a good mother. He's ready to wean her brood. Be a good time to buy a couple of the piglets, if your father is still interested."

"I know he is. I'll tell him. He wants a couple of those old English bacon hogs. So what have you been up to this summer?"

"Mostly making hay for dad. Alfalfa is bringing top dollar."

"Any new boyfriends, wild parties," Ann ask. Helen had picked up a piece of a broken concrete cylinder to examine.

"Don't have much time for that between chores and college. I did meet a neat guy from Purdue. Surveyor on the new treatment plant project," Helen said. "Is this good concrete?"

"Yes, you can tell when the gravel pieces break along with the cement matrix. Frank Arthur, I've meet him. How'd you two meet?"

"I ran into him at Allegheny's library. We went to the Goat Barn and were going to one of Jerry's parties, but I had the date wrong."

"Jerry Woodbrier?"

"Yes, he and that Taylor guy, they're fixing up one of those abandon farm houses out by Frenchtown. He invited me to a party, but when Frank and I got there last Saturday, no one was there, only Jerry and his pal. He told me that I had the wrong weekend," Helen said. "I didn't, but why argue? It's a creepy place, be a great location for a Halloween party."

"Oh man, you're so lucky. Don't ever be alone with him or drink anything he hands you. Same for that troll he runs around with, Paul Taylor," Ann said.

Ann told Helen what Mike Owens had learned and suspected on Jenny Lowell, Lucy Kerbert, and Betty Deere. Ann had not mentioned her own experience with Jerry Woodbrier. An unnerved and shaken Helen Smith left for home.

## Chapter 15

Mike knew the French Creek Sanitary Board followed the practice of dealing with local residents and their requests or complaints before addressing consultant and contract issues. An elderly and tiny black woman demanded the Board honor the pledge made two meetings ago to correct the odor problem at the Poplar and Liberty intersection. The Engineer explained he had thought the crew had corrected the problem. Obviously, they hadn't and the engineer promised to meet her the next day at the intersection, at 10 A.M. Another resident complained of a noisy manhole lid that banged every time a vehicle drove over it at the North and Market Street intersection. After several similar problems, the Board was ready for RBO and Mr. Norton's proposal.

The Board was both amazed by and suspicious of RBO's proposal to substitute HDPE pipe for the air ducts in place of Type 316 stainless steel, and to reduce the air duct cost by over a million dollars. Two members of the Board, the Engineer and the County Commissioner member, wanted an explanation as to why Norton and James specified stainless steel in the original bid. Mike had the pleasure of watching Dennis Norton suffer through a desperate prevarication to explain his original stainless steel design. The Board members were not satisfied with his explanation, but choose to let the issue ride for the moment as they questioned him on how, without a bid, did he know this was a fair price. Dennis asked Mike to explain.

Mike started by relating his original query to Norton and James regarding their rationale for specifying stainless steel air ducts. He thought the choice overly conservative, but since RBO wasn't the

267

design engineer, he had to bid the requested material. RBO's best quote from suppliers for the stainless steel was approximately $2,700,000, which would have resulted in a bid price of four million dollars. Pine Tree Construction submitted a bid to supply and install the air ducts for $3,200,000, which RBO accepted as part of their subcontract package.

RBO's tests discovered that Pine Tree's air duct material was chromoly steel, and not the Type 316 stainless steel specified. Chromoly was not suitable for air ducts. Pine Tree had messed up and RBO was prepared to throw them off the project, and order stainless steel using their performance bond to cover the extra expense. However, before taking that drastic action Mr. Norton wanted to explore alternate solutions. The one he presented was a fair and reasonable solution.

The Engineer wanted to know why Mike Owen believed that.

Mike explained he knew the cost for the stainless steel air ducts from the initial bid information RBO had obtained, and the price for HDPE air ducts from bids RBO had received last week. The best quote for HDPE air ducts was $1,400,000. Pine Tree's price was considerably more, but they agreed to use RBO's supplier for the HDPE and the difference between RBO's original stainless steel price and Pine Tree's original bid price to determine the cost for installation. That difference was a half million dollars, which when added to the HDPE material cost, made the quote for air ducts total $1,900,000. RBO in turn had offered to cut the Board's cost by the difference or $1,300,000, which was a fair and good deal for the Board.

At Mike's conclusion, the Board members proceeded to ask the Engineer his opinion. Mr. Norton handed out samples of the heavy HDPE material along with a sample of the stainless steel material, so members could compare the two air duct materials. The HDPE was over inch thick verses a tenth-inch for the stainless air duct material. The Engineer agreed with Mike that stainless steel was an expensive option, and he expressed his satisfaction with using the new HDPE material. After several more questions about delivery and blower flanges, the Board approved the change order.

Mr. Norton thanked the members for their vote to approve the change order, gave Mike a disgusted look, and left. Ann sighed and offered that Mr. Norton did not appear very happy.

"You think it was the return of the $1,300,000, or the loss of his kickback from Pine Tree?" Mike said.

"Poor man, he must not believe it's better to give than to receive. I'm a bit surprised Sam Woodbrier wasn't here protesting. Then again, with his brother's troubles, Sam is probably keeping a low public profile," Ann said.

"You ready for a beer, sweetheart?"

"I'm not in the mood for a beer. Let's find a bench in the park. I need your opinion and suggestion on my pitch."

"Good, I'd like to hear what your offer to the Shaffers will consist of." Mike got comfortable on the bench while she paced back and forth on the sidewalk.

Ann started spewing out numbers on how she had determined the value of Shaffer Concrete's core business. She explained about the property and buildings and the gravel mine and land. The 400 acres of land was worth one million dollars and the garage and lab building another three hundred thousand dollars. The value of Shaffer's equipment, property and improvements ranged between a low of $1,800,000 and a high of $3,500,000 with the lower value being most realistic due to the age of the garage and equipment. Then there the value of the current Shaffer concrete customers and future gravel sales.

"Any idea what Shaffer's profit is for a year?"

David C. Brown

"Yes, by my estimate, not from anything Mr. Shaffer told me. I figure his net is $200,000 a year."

Mike realized she's on top of the business and there would be no stopping her on this venture.

They watched a city police car drive by and then she continued with her assessment. Shaffer's gravel mine was potentially worth a million dollars a year to Ace. Normally, someone like her wouldn't have a chance of buying Shaffer for a reasonable price, because the best she could hope to earn starting out was two to three hundred thousand dollars from Shaffer's current volume of concrete sales. Ace on the other hand starts with a million-dollar-a-year savings before even considering the additional business from being the sole supplier in the Meadville area. Her only chance was Sam Woodbrier's greed would make him lowball his bid for Shaffer Concrete.

She planned to offer Mr. Shaffer the appraised value of the land and buildings that she estimated to be $1,300,000. Then offer to pay him five percent of Shaffer Concrete's gross sales for ten years, or did Mike think just offer a five-year period and let him haggle the pay period to ten years. Mike smiled at her question.

"Generally, not initially offering your final price is the best approach, but in this case, unless Ace is unusually foolish, your final offer will be half of Ace's, so put your best offer up front and count on his friendship."

"That's what I'll do."

Mike was curious about where Ann's money would come from.

"You have that kind of money to invest?"

"Sure, a million dollars is no big deal."

She had to laugh at his surprised expression, and Ann clarified that Putnam International Investors would loan one hundred percent appraised value on commercial land and industrial buildings.

270

Putnam charged three percent over the LIBOR interest rate or offered a fixed rate, fifteen-year mortgage, at seven percent, which was around one hundred and fifty thousand dollars per year. Ann was confident the company's earnings could easily cover that size mortgage payment.

He felt the deal needed to sweeten with a buyout of the royalty after ten years, say a onetime payment of five times the highest yearly royalty payment.

"If your efforts and inflation increase Shaffer's gross sales to four million dollars in ten years, that's an extra million dollars for Mr. Shaffer."

"That's a good suggestion. I'm thinking to wait until Ace bids before submitting my proposal. What your thoughts on that?"

"I wouldn't wait more than a week, Ace may not even bid. Are you hungry?"

"Yes. Also I'm going to give Jerry's bag to Larkin."

They walked to the Pizza Villa and had several slices of pizza.


Ann's decision the previous night to take Jerry's bag and camera to Detective Larkin affirmed his faith in his fiancée's moral integrity. However, before she went to the police Mike wanted to check out a hunch. He needed to visit the abandon farmhouse where Jenny Lowell vanished. To avoid a parked vehicle that might attract unwanted attention, Mike had Frank drop him off at the farm's driveway and then drive around until called to return.

Mike walked back the gravel lane and passed numerous NO TRESPASSING signs. Strangers were not welcome. The house was a wood siding farmhouse with a second floor. The house's yellow paint had mostly peeled off the wood siding from years of weathering, resulting in a dreary gray appearance to the house. The windows were the old-fashioned multi-pane wood frame. None of the window glass was broken, and that was unusual for an abandoned house in the country. The roof had a noticeable sag in the ridgeline that suggested structural problems; a half dozen bricks were missing from the sole chimney. The missing bricks had imparted a precarious tilt to the chimney.

Several fruit trees still struggled for survival in the overgrown front yard. One of the apple trees had a considerable number of apples hanging on the branches. Mike detoured over to the tree with the idea of grabbing an apple for a snack, but he discovered the apples were scab and rot infested. The sway back look of the house along with the peeling paint, diseased apple trees and uncut weeds conveyed a sense of an unloved and melancholy place decaying into oblivion.

If Mike's conjecture was correct that Jenny Lowell died during the party in this house, then her body wasn't far away. Jerry and Paul had struck him as lazy and short sighted. Those two would want to dispose of her body with minimum effort. That Jenny Lowell's car was found at a motel near the Pittsburgh International Airport meant their goal for explaining her disappearance was that she had run off. Even those morons were smart enough to know that story depended on her body not showing up.

Both the front and rear doors had padlocks. The rear doorframe had deteriorated from rot and Mike easily pried the hasp loose with the machete, leaving the padlock dangling intact from the hasp still attached to the rear door. Most of the wallpaper in the first floor rooms was missing. The upper rooms had most of their wallpaper remaining. Mike found the room with the large flower pattern wallpaper, a back bedroom. The room looked empty, but Mike stayed in the hallway. It had to be the same room in the photo and he was confident her grave was nearby as he reattached the back door hasp.

Mowed early in the summer, the back yard grass and weeds only came to the top of his boots. Mike could clearly see the ground surface as he worked his way around the old fence line that separated the yard from a cornfield. Along the way, he surprised a large woodchuck in the grass. The rodent made a frantic run for its burrow in the fence line. *Are woodchucks any good to eat*? Mike wondered as he examined the backyard. He'd have to remember to ask his wildlife expert, Ann.

The backyard area was a rectangle of approximately half an acre. His search turned up no suspicious depressions or mounds. The mowed area ended by the old garage and a wild tangle of elderberry bushes loaded with dark purple berries that filled the corner area directly behind the garage. The berry patch area extended from the end of the garage to the fence line and cornfield, a distance of forty feet and the width of the garage. The fence and field then made a sharp turn and ran back along the far side of the garage to the township road.

Mike wondered for a moment if they buried her in the cornfield and the farming activity had destroyed any evidence of the grave. He was confident they wouldn't have used the basement area to bury the body, because if the police ever decided to search for the missing girl, they would surely start at her last known location, the farmhouse. Mike walked over and looked in the garage behind the house.

The front doors of the old garage had broken hinges and were leaning against the side of the garage. The dirt garage floor almost looked like asphalt from seventy-five years of farm equipment leakage of oil. The floor surface was undisturbed by any sign of digging. He noticed a rear door and a wooden workbench along the garage wall. The bench still had bits and pieces of rusted parts from past equipment repairs littering its surface. Mike picked from the bench an old vacuum tube radio to examine. It had to be a radio from the 1930s. He put it back and walked through the garage to the rear door while brushing away several large spider webs.

Mike forced the rear garage door open. A dense growth of elderberry bushes partly blocked the door from opening completely. The nice feature of elderberry bushes was the lack of thorns, which allowed him to bull his way into the patch without being jabbed and scratched. Near the center of the patch, he found a small recent-looking depression that might contain a body. Now he was ready to visit Detective Larkin and called Frank. He picked and sampled the elderberries as he waited for his ride.

In his heart, Sam knew the letter was no joke and that his son, Jerry, had a serious problem. The letter had come in the mail, addressed to him. It had a photo of a naked girl lying spread eagle on a blanket in a bare room. The message was "Jenny Lowell wants her murderers, Jerry Woodbrier and Paul Taylor, to face justice." Did those two fools have anything to do with that missing college girl from a couple of years ago? Then he remembered Betty Deere's allegations against his son.

Sam found his son working with Jake's crew. He passed several workmen while walking from the parking lot to where Pine Tree's crew was installing sewers. The men were cold, no greetings in return to his greetings. What ailed the jerks? Even Jake was cool. He found Jerry and curtly told him to follow him to the car.

"This photo came in the mail today. You know a Jenny Lowell?"

Sam knew the letter's petition had some basis from his son's reaction. Jerry opened the car door and vomited.

"I'm not feeling well. I need fresh air. . ." Jerry said. He got out of the car.

"Son, walk away and this letter is going to the police. Is it true?"

"It was an accident," Jerry said.

His son started crying, and Sam told him to get back in the car. The office manager, Steve, stepped out of the RBO office onto the deck as Sam drove by. Sam reflectively gave RBO's office manager a brief wave. Steve startled him by giving him the finger in return. He would deal with RBO's office manager later. His son, sobbing, told an astonishing tale of date rape and a porn picture business with sales to foreigners.

Sam drove aimlessly around Crawford County back roads as his only child told about Jenny Lowell waking up unexpectedly from the drug and realizing Paul and him had drugged and raped her. Worse, she knew Jerry from class. Jenny had started screaming for help when he hit her. She wouldn't quit screaming. Finally, he had managed to smother her with his hand. Paul had helped him by holding her legs down. The blaring party music covered her few screams for help. They buried her on Otto's farm after everyone cleared out.

Horrifying as it was, Sam was pleasantly surprised and pleased to learn his son had the toughness to do what was required, though in truth his son probably just panicked.

"Son, sometimes you have to be hard. Do what needs done," Sam said. "But where'd that picture come from?"

Jerry haltingly told his father about his failed attempt to rape Ann and her overpowering him and stealing the camera. Sam knew his son wasn't much of a thinker, but surely even an idiot would know to secure the person before proceeding with such a plan. Why did his son leave such incriminating photos in his camera? That defied understanding. Jerry was crying again. Sam figured screaming at his inept son would only make things worse.

*What was wrong with this younger generation*, Sam wondered. Could he save his son? Maybe he had better focus on that question. He knew Ann Lane was a formidable opponent from Lou's troubles. Now she was engaged to Mike Owen. If they were behind the photos, then his son was in deep trouble. Sam wasn't sure even he could handle that pair.

"What did you fools do with the body? Where's the body?"

"Behind the garage," Jerry said. "We dug a hole."

"Is it deep enough that dogs can't find it?"

"I think so--the top six inches had been frozen. It was hard to dig."

"How deep? Six feet?"

"Maybe three feet. . ."

"Knowing your lazy ass, it's more like two feet and the animals have dug it up," Sam said.

"It was hard digging, and cold. We were tired. Besides everyone thinks she ran away. No one has found it. What's the problem?"

"No one has found it because they never looked."

Sam wondered which party was more incompetent, the police or his son. Had the police early on suspected foul play and inspected the property, they would have discovered the grave. That the police had never searched Otto's farm was surprising, but if whoever sent him the letter had sent the police a copy, Sam was confident the police would soon correct that oversight.

Her body needed to disappear. It was his son's only chance of avoiding a murder conviction. Sam couldn't comprehend why Ann hadn't gone to the police if she was the source of the pictures. Regardless the letter Sam had received was proof something was stirring. If his son didn't hear from the police soon, then he figured a blackmail scheme would follow. *That* Sam knew how to deal with.

The game warden's favorite turkey area was State Games Land No. 39. The public hunting area encompassed five thousand acres of hills and deep valleys along Sandy Creek to the west of the

Allegheny River and Kennerdell. Numerous hunters had constructed hunting camps-lodges along the township roads within the game land. The camps-lodges ranged from fifty-year-old trailers setting like woebegone relics on cinder blocks at the end of a dirt track, to half-million-dollar log structures on landscaped lots and with paved driveways. Most of the hunting camps were unoccupied that late August weekday evening as the game warden slowly drove the various back-roads searching for signs of illegal turkey and deer hunting activities.

A person had occupied one of the older log cabins early last week. He hadn't seen the person and the person's vehicle hadn't moved since that first night. The game warden figured some guy was on a drunken bender and no threat to the turkeys and deer. The lights were on and the game warden, by stopping and turning off his vehicle engine, could faintly hear the TV on the Fox news channel, which meant a window was open or the TV's volume was turned up. The fact that nothing had changed over a week--same lights on, Jeep hadn't moved and same TV channel--was making the game warden curious. He had decided last night if nothing has changed by tomorrow, he would knock on the cabin door.

The game warden stopped by the cabin with the old Jeep and could detect no change in lights or TV from the previous several evenings. He pulled into the driveway and parked. As soon as he walked onto the porch, the smell hit him and he knew. Instead of breaking in and possibly disturbing a crime scene to satisfy his curiosity, the game warden called the state police.

Detective Larkin called Sam Woodbrier early the following morning to inform him the state police had found his brother Lou dead. Sam, surprised, and then worriedly asked where and how.

"He choked from vomit in a Venango County hunting camp owned by Jake Cooke, though to be sure, the coroner's report will be needed. Foul play doesn't appear to have been involved. Will you be in town tomorrow?"

"Yes."

"Good, I have several questions about your brother's activities. I'll call in the morning to set a time. Goodbye."

He was the last of the family--his father and mother died years ago, cancer killed his only sister--and now Lou was gone. His ex-wife hated him and their only child was a fool or worse. He should have been sad. Instead, he felt relief. Sam wandered to the coffee pot, poured an unwanted cup and meandered back to his seat in front of the window, lost in thought.

The crime trail should end with Lou. Sam had no direct involvement with the Russian or Paulie. His only exposure was if Dennis taped their meeting in the Pittsburgh office or the meeting in this office with him and Lou concerning the air duct material. Sal Gambone only dealt with Lou. Sam realized the rarest of opportunities was available to him because of his brother's death: a chance to mend his ways. He just needed to avoid entanglement in his son's troubles. Sam, turning off the lights in his garage office, looked out the window at the mirror-smooth Conneaut Lake brightly illuminated by a full moon. The sight was beautiful.

Sam sat in the detective's office waiting for the interview to start and thought Larkin looked unusually fossilized this morning. He thought Lou's escapades must have been wearing Larkin out as he waited on the detective's first question.

"Lou's last phone call came from a prepaid cell phone that used the cell tower near Woodcock Dam. Who do you figure called him?"

"I have no idea."

"He had several pellet wounds and may have had tetanus. His blood was in the pickup truck that ran over Paulie Pelosi. When was the last time you saw your brother Lou?"

"Two weeks ago on a Monday at the office."

"What did you discuss with Lou?"

Sam figured Larkin had talked to Dennis about Paulie before this meeting. He explained that Dennis Norton had asked the meeting to inform Lou and him that Pine Tree had ordered the wrong material for the air ducts. Dennis had suggested changes to correct the problem, which they had agreed to.

"Was this the change order that the Board approved Tuesday evening?"

"Yes."

"I heard the mistake cost Pine Tree over a million dollars, is that correct?"

"That's the difference in the material cost for the two types of air ducts and not directly a loss. The loss will be the difference in the price Pine Tree paid for the wrong material and the price they receive for selling the material to a recycler. Regardless it was an expensive mistake on Pine Tree's part."

"Do you have any idea why your brother and Mr. Pelosi felt the need to shoot eighty times at Ms. Lane and Mr. Owen and endanger several residents of Grove Street and Clinton Court?"

"I have no knowledge of my brother shooting at anyone. Paulie I've never had any dealings with," Sam said. The old scofflaw was getting annoyed.

"There exists a school of thought that your brother believed RBO would be less interested in the air duct material if Mike Owen wasn't involved. Did you discuss with your brother the murder of Mike Owen?"

Sam's cool composure was fraying under Detective Larkin's pointed questions. Does he know or was this just an educated guess

279

by the detective to stir the pot? Sam decided from the general nature of Larkin's questions that the police had nothing connecting him to Lou's activities. He also decided the detective hadn't received the girl's photo. He needed to be cautious and not inadvertently provide the detective an opening. Sam told Detective Larkin if these outrageous questions continued, he would be talking to Sam's lawyer, however to answer the detective's last question, no, he did not discuss murdering anyone with his brother.

"Did you discuss with your brother having John Gambone place sugar in two of the Shaffer Concrete trucks to make the concrete fail certain tests at the RBO site?"

Sam could feel sweat beading on his forehead as fear returned. The detective could only know about the sugar if John was talking. Did Lou say anything else to John? That dreadful thought riled his composure.

"I have no idea what you're talking about or why anyone would even bother to do it."

"Mr. Woodbrier, you and your brother Lou were business partners. You expect me to believe you were unaware of his efforts to sabotage Shaffer Concrete, or involvement with Pelosi's attempt to kill Ms. Lane and Mr. Owen, and the murder of Karl Karadzic. Your brother was involved in several illegal activities. I can prove it. The depth of your and Mr. Norton's involvement remain to be determined. That's all for now."

Sam figured the police had tapped his phones. The allegations the detective had just made concerning Lou, Sam believed were to spook him into making a mistake. Sam left Detective Larkin's office, drove to the RBO site to find Jake, and had him call Dennis for a meeting on the site that afternoon. He told Jake to clear the Pine Tree construction office trailer for the meeting. Three hours later Sam returned to the site and found Dennis waiting, who after greetings and a moment to express condolences over Lou, asked Sam what the problem was.

"Has Detective Larkin contacted you?"

"Yes, last week about my son-in-law Paulie Pelosi. He wanted to know why he was shooting up the neighborhood. I told him I had no idea."

Sam had a device that Sal Gambone had loaned Lou several months ago that could detect transmitters, aka bugs. It hadn't moved and he wondered if Dennis was clean. A couple of more items required inspection before the real discussion could start. Sam asked Dennis to take off his shirt. The consultant offered a comment on being paranoid, as he removed his shirt and pants. No wires or odd devices, although with today's miniaturization Sam realized that didn't necessarily mean a recording device wasn't present. He then asked for Dennis's brief case. He found a small tape recorder in the brief case. It was off. Sam rewound the tape and then pushed the play button. The tape had a series of reminders by Dennis for himself on various issues that required a written response. None of their meetings were on the thirty some minutes of taped messages spanning the last several weeks.

"Are you satisfied Sam?"

Sam ignored Dennis's question and explained that with Lou dead, the only connection tying them to Lou's craziness were those two meetings between the three of them, unless Dennis had been careless with Paulie. He asked Dennis if there was any problem regarding Paulie that had the potential to involve them.

"No. All I ever did was pass on Lou's requests for meetings or a call. Paulie always had side deals of which I wanted no part. I agree with your assessment that nothing existed to connect us with Lou and Paulie. I intend to keep it that way. I'll be happy when this project is finished, and RBO and that sanctimonious jerk Mike Owen are out of my life."

"We're in agreement on that. That was all I wanted to discuss on Lou's past business. Anything you need to add?"

"No."

"Good, now I'll get Jake back in here and the three of us can figure how quickly we can finish this project and quit losing money."

Jerry met Paul in the Green Lizard to give him a highly edited version of the talk Jerry had with his father. His father's concern was that the police, on receiving a copy of the Jenny Lowell letter, would reactivate the dormant investigation into her disappearance. If the police then decided to search Paul's grandfather farm for a body, the chances are they would find her grave. At that point, it would no longer be a disappearance, but a murder investigation. They didn't need that. Who knows what evidence they had inadvertently left on her body?

"So what do you suggest? Paul asked.

"We dig the body up and rebury it someplace not associated with us."

"You kidding, it will be a stinking mess, maybe give us some disease," Paul said.

"You want to spend the rest of your life in jail."

Paul wasn't interested in going to jail and the discussion turned to where they could dispose of her body. Jerry's father had suggested sinking the body in Conneaut Lake at night using his boat. Paul liked that idea. Their talk turned to the details and tools required.

Detective Larkin acted like a man that thought after forty-eight years of police work that he had heard every possible combination of foolish and evil behavior people were capable of doing. He was wrong. Ann's story of Jerry Woodbrier's attempted rape and her response had clearly amazed him. After Mike explained his reason for sending those letters, the old detective couldn't decide if he was mad at Mike for interfering in a police matter or welcomed the action.

"My concern was its Ann's word against his. That he would deny the bag and camera was his," Mike said. "Or say Ann and him were just playing. Deny he planned to rape her."

"All you did was put them on guard and maybe endanger Ann. You two like getting attacked?"

"The real issue is Jenny Lowell, not me. She didn't runoff. She was murdered over a date rape gone wrong," Ann said. "I should have reported Jerry that night. Finding her body is the key and Mike's purpose. He has to be stopped."

Mike explained his reason for sending the letters. His opinion was Jerry and Paul didn't plan on killing Jenny, but something went wrong, either a fatal drug reaction or she woke up ahead of time and realized they had raped her. They panicked and murdered her. Regardless, they were responsible for her death and had her body to hide. He has met both of them and figured they would take the easiest path to disposal of the body, burying it on the Otto farm.

Mike figured Sam was unaware of his son's activities. The letter would motivate Sam to learn the real story from his son. He would realize Lowell's body needed to disappear. Mike's goal was to scare the murderers into moving her body and have the police catch them in the act.

The previous day he had visited the Otto farm for a quick check and found a likely location for the body behind the garage. The police need to verify Jenny's body was there and then monitor the site for a few days to catch Jerry in the act of digging up her body. Or if he's wrong and that's not the burial site, then follow them. Sam Woodbrier would make them dispose of Jenny's body in a fashion that ensures the destruction of the body as evidence. One way or the other Jerry will lead them to Jenny Lowell in the next few days, Mike confidently predicted to a skeptical Detective Larkin.

"Unless they done a thorough job of eliminating the body. You should have let the police handle this. Now they will make damn sure it is never found," Detective Larkin said.

"Might, should, may, spare me the excuses, if you want justice for Jenny Lowell, get with the sheriff and catch those bastards before they murder and rape another girl. Remember Sam just got my letter."

## Chapter 16

Sam Woodbrier reread the form letter requesting proposals to buy Shaffer Concrete. The irony of that letter depressed Sam. They had schemed, spent thousands of dollars, and murdered to force Shaffer's sale. Lou had crushed Shaffer's son to death, Paulie had killed Karl, Lou had killed him and now Lou was dead. The whole purpose of their failed deadly efforts had been to precipitate the sale of Shaffer's business. Now suddenly the company was for sale. Was the request for an offer to purchase Shaffer Concrete a trap, some clever method to link him to all the mayhem?

The police had conclusively linked his brother to the Ford pickup involved in Paulie's death and the attack on Ann Lane and Mike Owen at Vine Street. Evidence found with Lou in the hunting cabin linked him and Paulie to the earlier attack by the Serbian Karl Karadzic on Ann Lane at Henry Street. Lou had the pistol that fired the bullets that killed Karl. What had his brother been thinking to keep that incriminating pistol?

The Shaffer's son's death wasn't being mentioned, and Lou's death ended that trail. Thankfully, Paulie and--though he felt shame for thinking so--Lou were dead, or he might be setting in jail today. Sam couldn't help thinking about the travesty. In a twisted sense, he was free because that Lane girl and Owen had caused the death of everyone who could have testified to his involvement. However, Sam wasn't free of those two yet. She had his son's camera and that contained sufficient evidence to put Jerry and Paul away for life.

Sam accepted that Detective Larkin was convinced of his involvement with Lou and Paulie. He knew the detective was not sure of the motive for the attacks, and the detective had nothing to connect Sam with his brother's activities. The detective was talking to the Lane girl, who was smart enough to explain that Shaffer's old equipment and meager sales meant nothing to Sam and Ace. He figured she understood the gravel mine was the valuable Shaffer asset and had told Detective Larkin. The detective probably believed the goal of obtaining Shaffer's gravel mine and mining permit on the cheap had motivated Sam and Lou to commit capital crimes. If Sam put out the word that Ace was not interested in bidding for Shaffer Concrete, what's that going to do to the detective's effort to find a motive for Sam's involvement in his brother's crimes? If asked why, he could give some nonsense explanation that Ace was worried about possible environmental problems related to Shaffer's gravel mine permit.

Detective Larkin might very well think Sam was scared off, but the detective will have no reasonable explanation as to why Sam would have been involved in Lou and Paulie's fiasco. What about offering Ann a deal? Ace would bid low for Shaffer in return for the camera and pictures. He had heard she was interested in buying Shaffer's company. She had to know she could never beat his bid. Still, the woman was a dangerous adversary and might try to set him up, but he had experience in avoiding law enforcement stings.

Ann wasn't sure what to make of Sam Woodbrier's visit. Her boss obviously believed he wanted the inspection because of the letter. Her boss had asked earlier that she give him a tour of the facility. The gangster had been the perfect gentleman in Mr. Shaffer's office and during the tour, until they were alone by the gravel pit area.

They were standing on the mined area edge looking down at the loader carrying gravel to the screen conveyor when he got to the purpose of his visit.

"Ann, you have something my son needs back, and I have a bid offer for Shaffer to decide on. Would you be interested in an understanding, a deal?"

His question didn't surprise her. She knew about Mike sending him the photo of Jenny Lowell. The good news was that Sam was now involved with Jerry and Paul's problem.

"Mr. Woodbrier, your son was not very nice to me, but I might be interested."

"I want the bag, camera, and original memory card and in turn Ace will put in a one-million-dollar bid for Shaffer."

"How do I know you won't submit a new bid after I give up the card?"

"I don't want this junk. Ace has better equipment in the scrap pile. The only reason to bid is to stop you. You surely know I can match any offer you tender."

"And you know I don't trust you. I'm surprised you haven't tried to kill me again. I know you sent Karl. I know Lou drove the pickup. I know you were in the thick of it for the gravel, and then there's Shaffer's son, so let's not kid each other."

"I never did any such thing. That's all wild conjecture on your part, but I don't want to argue. Are you interested? Want the company?" Sam asked.

"I'll call you tomorrow. I need to think on this."

After Sam left, she called Detective Larkin and Mike to advise them that Sam was considering the bait. She would drop off Detective Larkin's recorder after lunch.

The sun had just set when Jerry parked his pickup in the old garage on the abandon farm. Paul and he unloaded the shovels and large plastic trash bags and carried them through the rear garage door. Paul noticed the broken elderberry brushes.

"Someone has been walking around here recently. You think the police have been looking?" Paul said.

"Berry pickers have been here. You didn't notice some of the berries are missing," Jerry told his partner.

The first foot of soil was clean, then the musty odor started and the soil started showing dark gray patches. The body was an intact skeleton coated with black slime and pieces of more solid material and hair around the skull. The whole area reeked with an offensive musty odor. Worms were in abundance in the soil around the body.

They dragged the skeleton out of the excavation and wrestled it into the extra-large trash bag. Paul threw up in the process of hauling the body out of the grave. The sun had set and Jerry worried their light might attract attention. It had attracted a swarm of mosquitoes that added to the misery of the job. The two of them had the slimy matter smeared on their clothes, hands, and boots with no way to clean up except for dry paper towels. Jerry wished he had thought to bring hand cleaner and coveralls.

After bagging the stinking bones, they picked up the bits and pieces of rotten material, hair, clothing, and stained soil in the excavation. That material went in two more trash bags. Paul finished filling in the excavation the best they could; they didn't have sufficient soil and the mat of elderberry roots made raking more soil from the area around the grave impossible. If the police showed up now, Jerry couldn't imagine any explanation that would explain their presence and conditions, other than they were busy excavating a body. He realized more than a few months would be required for the weather and vegetation to obscure the evidence of the excavated grave. They both policed the area for any litter from them before leaving.

Jerry was happy to leave Otto's spooky farm and head to Ace Concrete to meet his father. Sam had been busy. He had cut the top off a fifty-five gallon drum and had a yard of concrete in the test mixer ready for the water and mixing. Sam told them to dump the skeleton in the wash bay and hose off the slime before placing the bones in the drum with fresh concrete. He had to tell Paul not to waste time trying to wash the attached hair from the skull. Just concentrate on hosing off the worst of the slimy material so the concrete would bond to the bones. The dirt would go in another drum after mixing some cement with it.

"What are you doing with that skull?" Sam said. Paul had a pair of pliers.

"There's a gold crown I'm going to get. I'll bet it's worth fifty bucks," Paul said.

"Your stupidity is amazing. That evidence links you to her," Jerry said.

"You're the dumbass. After I melt it no one will know where the gold came from," Paul said. He wrenched the gold tooth out and dropped the skull. The piece of gold went in his pants pocket.

Shaking his head in disbelief, Sam told Paul to add the water and start the concrete mixer. After they had the body parts properly packed, they would haul the drums to Sam's boat, then drop the drums in the deepest part of Conneaut Lake around three o'clock in the morning.

Sam had gotten involved to be certain the body was disposed of with no more screw-ups. After seeing the two morons in action, Sam hated to think what they would have done without him. Once the body was gone for good, he didn't much care if Ann returned the camera or not. In the end, it would be one person's word against another without a body. They had just finished packing the skeleton in the drum and waiting for the concrete to finish mixing when Paul noticed the blue lights.

289

Ted Shaffer was disappointed with the response to his offer to sell his concrete business. He had one reasonable offer from Grove City Ready Mix and two low-ball offers from an outfit in Erie and one from Pittsburgh. Sam Woodbrier and Ace had not submitted a bid. The arrest of Sam, his son, and Paul Taylor with Jenny Lowell's body had stunned the community.

RBO had another large pour today. Ann spent an hour checking that everything was ready to have the first truck on site at 7 A.M. to start the final clarifier foundation. Only delivery of two thousand cubic yards of concrete remained under the original fifteen thousand cubic yards of concrete order. The project's concrete demand would wind down over the next month. Shaffer's business would revert to the prior five-hundred-cubic-yards-per-week average sales of concrete. She would miss the activity at RBO's site. Ann, after one more set of instructions to Tim, headed to the garage to find Mr. Shaffer. He was at his desk looking lost and smiled at Ann's request for a bit of his time. She put her proposal on his desk.

"This is my offer. Briefly, it's $1,300,000 up front for the real estate and buildings, and five percent of the gross sales for the next ten years. As you'll read, I plan to develop an aggregate business along with the concrete operation."

"You have sufficient money to pay me and cover payrolls if business suddenly weakens or Ace cuts their prices?"
"I wouldn't have made the offer if I didn't think I could make it work. I would appreciate an answer by next week on my offer."

Ann got up to leave and Mr. Shaffer motioned for her to stay.

"Can you believe Sam Woodbrier and his son were involved in that girl's murder? He seemed so normal the other day."

"Yeah, I can. He tried enough times to kill Mike and me. So what did Grove City offer?"

"The offer was two million dollars, half on signing and balance over two years. Your offer is the best one, but you need to convince me you can pull it off."

"Fair enough, first are your properties free and clear fee simple deeds?"

"Yes, everything is paid off, there is no mortgage."

"Thanks to the new demand for sand, Putnam International Investors will loan me 100% of the property's appraised value. I need to call them and request they send their approved appraiser here and evaluate the value of the land and buildings."

Mr. Shaffer was skeptical the gas drilling would amount to much and commented that reputable banks didn't lend hundred percent-appraised values on land. Ann responded that perhaps they shouldn't, but today Putnam would and it was the one with the best interest rates on fixed terms.

"Do we have a deal?"

"I'll read your proposal tonight and give you an answer in the morning. Go ahead and set up the appraiser's visit and decide on who you will use for a lawyer."

Ann left Mr. Shaffer in his office, busy unwrapping a cigar and studying her proposal. She called Putnam International Investors to schedule the appraisal. She next called Mike for his opinion on who would be a good lawyer. Her call caught him finishing the inspection of the first HDPE air ducts. The Board's engineer had just left the site very satisfied with the material.

After listening to her excited news that Mr. Shaffer had received only one bid and none from Ace, he congratulated her and offered that, she would have her company before he had his.

"I hope he doesn't change his mind. I'll need a lawyer to draw up the sale agreement. Any suggestions?"

"If you don't mind, call RBO's law firm or try Linda. My sister is licensed, or whatever lawyers call it, to practice law in Ohio and Pennsylvania and she's into corporate contracts."

Ann thought that a fine idea and proceeded to track Linda Sims down in her Columbus office and explained her needs. She was very friendly and receptive to representing her. The Putnam International Investors appraiser returned her call. He was in Cleveland and could meet her and Mr. Shaffer tomorrow. She cautioned the appraiser Mr. Shaffer hadn't agreed to the terms, but the appraiser was still willing to meet and told her to expect him tomorrow morning around eleven o'clock.

Ann's deal with Mr. Shaffer closed several weeks later.

## Epilogue

Mike and Ann married that December and bought a beautiful old brick farmhouse north of Venango built in 1903 by a retired machinist, Frank Osborne, from the oil fields around Centerville and Titusville. Several generations of machinists working for the oil, rail, and zipper industries in the area had lived and owned the farm. Osborne's grandson had died in the late eighties and left the farm to his daughter who resided in Pittsburgh. She had recently put the property on the market.

Ann, on touring the large house, advised Mike that Osborne's great granddaughter had told her that wives living in that house seemed blessed with fertility. She had counted eighteen children between the three Osborne wives who had lived there. She teased her husband they wouldn't need to worry where to put children. The house had five possible bedrooms. The three leg black dog claimed the porch. Ann tossed her birth control pills in the trash that night.

The Woodbriers never recovered from the arrest with Jenny Lowell's remains. A jury found Jerry Woodbrier and Paul Taylor guilty of murder and gave them long prison sentences. Found guilty of a conspiracy charge, Sam Woodbrier ended up serving a four-year sentence. The legal defense cost bankrupted Sam and forced him to sell Woodbrier Construction. Ann, through her company, Shaffer Concrete, bought Ace Concrete.

Dennis Norton's engineering firm won an award for the innovative use of HDPE material in advance wastewater treatment plant aeration systems.

Mike completed the French Creek Waste Water Treatment Plant on schedule and on budget, and his father transferred control of RBO to him. Mike learned ambition was the desire to achieve an end or goal. The goal determined whether the ambition was healthy and beneficial or led to misery. Ann and his ambitions, Mike concluded, were of the healthy and beneficial nature.

The novel, The Trashman's Daughter tells the story of the baby Lou Westfield abandoned along the interstate. .

David C. Brown is a retired environmental engineer who lives in Scott Depot, West Virginia. After military service, he worked in highway construction and then coal mining. In the mid 1980's he was city engineer for Charleston, West Virginia. He left city employment to work in the waste disposal industry where he specialized in water and air pollution control. He is a member of the American Association for the Advancement of Science and West Virginia Writers.

# THE TRASHMAN'S DAUGHTER

At his wealthy uncle's urging, Jerry Ray, a young engineer, accepts the job of managing Ridge Landfill in Tyler County. His cousin, the uncle's only daughter, recently died in mysterious circumstances at the nearby Burgess Goat farm-cheese operation. Jerry's new job will connect him into the area's ethos and with its leaders. The uncle's hope is that interaction will allow Jerry to form an opinion on whether the police report is correct that his cousin's death was the result of an accident or if it was murder.

The discovery of a dead infant in the trash involves Jerry with the beautiful driver of the truck that delivered the murdered infant and a mysterious recluse. Illegal dumping of hazardous chemicals and a plot to install bombs in fourteen propane railcar tankers by the man Jerry suspects murdered his cousin add to the story's explosive climax.

He never imagined managing a rural West Virginia landfill would be so interesting.

## SERENDIPITY HOLLOW

The first story of a fiction trilogy set in Boone County, West Virginia. The story follows the adventures of two people on opposite sides of a contentious Appalachian issue, surface mining of coal. Mark Hopkins is a 27-year-old wealthy landowner and coal mine operator whose business is under attack from environmentalists. He considers lawyers in general a plague and thinks the environmental activists should be addressing Appalachia's other problems and social issues instead of trying to wreck one of the region's few viable industries.

Sarah Austen is a 23-year-old public defender and part time environmental lawyer working to preserve the Appalachian Mountains' beauty and environment from the devastation of surface mining coal. Her goal is to close the Hopkins' mine. She is not above trespassing to find permit violations to use as the basis for legal action that will revoke the company's permit.

Mark's effort to save a poor neighborhood boy, Frank Arthur, from jail soon entangles him with Sarah, the public defender.

# GAP HOLLOW

A fishing trip to Gap Run explodes into a confrontation between Frank Arthur, a young instructor at the local science college, and a methamphetamine operation in Boone County West Virginia. Frank views the encounter as bad luck, a distraction from his quest to discover his father's identity, but quickly realizes after joining the effort to save an ancient grove of trees on the college property that a festering morass of corruption exists in the Appalachian hollows. A septuagenarian coal baron, an alumnus of the college, offers to help save the grove. Frank knows the man has leveled many a forest across Appalachia amassing his wealth, and he worries it's a Faustian bargain, unaware the elderly alumnus has a secret buried in the college's grove.

The plot is tense, complex, and gripping as Frank must decide how far he is willing to go to protect the people and land he cares about from development and the vengeance of the drug dealers and unscrupulous DEA agents.

David C. Brown

## SANDLICK HOLLOW

The novel is the sequel to the book <u>Gap Hollow</u>. An intense rivalry develops between Frank Arthur, a young physics instructor, and Roger Doddson, a financial planner and broker, for control of a thirty million dollar endowment. Roger, swindlers, lethal racists, and fools are soon hatching schemes to murder Frank, seize control of the private scholarship endowment, and then steal the funds. The discovery of crimes committed decades ago in Boone County, West Virginia by Frank's father further complicate his determined efforts to assure the safety of the scholarship fund entrusted to his stewardship.

Murder may be his only option to save the endowment.

David C. Brown

## DONNELLY'S WAR

**The adventures of a modern man plunged into an alternate-history world of nineteenth century technology, slavery, drugs, and competing human and nonhuman empires.**

Rex Knight, an Afghan War vet, is mysteriously teleported from a peaceful surveying job to the semi-lawless frontier of an alternate Appalachia. Slavery and bootleg cocaine from the blue winter-sloe nut finance the murderous warlords. Rex witnesses the oppression and murder inflicted on the indigenous Wapitis by Warlord Donnelly and the not quite human Ichneumons.

The Wapitis, locked in a deadly struggle to avoid slavery and extinction, appeal to Rex, who looks like a Prussian, to help them obtain rifles and ammunition. The world straddling Prussian Empire bans the sale of firearms to all indigenous people and hangs anyone caught selling firearms to them. Rex agrees to help the Wapiti and a ferocious war engulfs the frontier.

"A notable kickoff to an intriguing alternate-history series." – *Kirkus Reviews*

David C. Brown

## BOILERMAKER

Rex Knight is a survivor and intends to make a life for himself in the quasi-civilized Erden where he was mysteriously teleported. Opportunities and hazards exist for a modern man in a nineteenth century world of Civil War era technology, slavery, drugs, cotton, and competing colonial empires. With Rex's help, the indigenous Wapitis have prevailed in their confrontation with warlord James Donnelly. Unfortunately, that success has earned him the odium of the not-quite-human Ichneumon emperor who has much gold and a predilection for hiring bounty hunters to collect his enemies' heads.

Rex figured an alien emperor couldn't be any worse than the Afghanistan Taliban and focused on making a living in an alien world. He believed the new river steamboats and hauling cargos offered an opportunity to build a business, if their boilers would stop exploding. A young female slave claims to have solutions to that problem and Rex's Ichneumon predicament. She's willing to barter. He's not sure either of them can afford her price for helping him.

## CAROOM'S RAID

Rex Knight has a contract to deliver the Wapiti's cargo of prized winter-sloe nuts to Port Delta, a risky voyage of 1000 kilometers down the pirate infested Erie River. East from the port, along the Gulf coast, is Orleans where Rex's partner, Amy Caroom, an escaped slave, wants to go. She intends to collect a debt owed her by Herr Purnell, her former owner and father. Rex thinks Amy's idea is reckless since her father has posted a large reward for her capture, dead or alive. Then the Ichneumons arrest Rex while he's collecting the gold payment for the cargo. He escapes the merciless humanoids' dungeon, only to have his alluring partner drug him, and find himself, the gold, and his boat in Orleans. Then there's the matter of the Ichneumon navy waiting on the Erie River to confiscate the gold and his steamboat, the Mischief.

The adventures of a modern man plunged into an alternate-history world of nineteenth century technology, slavery, drugs, and competing human and nonhuman empires.

David C. Brown

# NITRO WILD

Nitro Wild is the chronicle of a modern man endeavoring to survive on an alternate earth of 19$^{th}$ century technology, slavery, and completing colonial empires. Rex Knight, an Afghan War veteran, has been mysteriously teleported from a peaceful surveying project in West Virginia to the semi-lawless Appalachia on Erden where

The Prussian and Ichneumon Empires are vying for dominance. Endangered by the clashing empires are Rex's friends, the indigenous Wapiti and an escaped slave, Amy Caroom who is, among other things, his partner in a river steamboat and a machine shop.

The Ichneumon army is poised to ravage the Wapiti homeland when the winter ends. The Prussians are willing to help the Wapiti, but lack to means to stop the Ichneumon armored riverboats with their new exploding shells. Complicating matters for the Prussian army is the threat of rebellion by the slave owners in their territories over the emperor's edict outlawing slavery. Rumors of a coup d'état in Berlin are rampant. The Mongol Empire of Prussia's eastern border is mad over the stopping of the slave trade and threaten invasion. The Ichneumons sense opportunity to deal their rival a knockout blow. Their army will help the rebellious plantation owners seize control of the Prussian territories along with the Wapiti homeland.

Rex will need all his wits, shrewdness, audacity, and even duplicity to survive.

www.ingramcontent.com/pod-product-compliance
Lightning Source LLC
Chambersburg PA
CBHW020341180626
46812CB00001B/288